My Name,
A Living Memory

My Name, A Living Memory

Giorgio van Straten

TRANSLATED BY MARTHA KING

STEERFORTH ITALIA

AN IMPRINT OF STEERFORTH PRESS · SOUTH ROYALTON, VERMONT

English translation copyright © Steerforth Press 2003
ALL RIGHTS RESERVED
First published in Italian as *Il mio nome a memoria*
by Mondadori, Milano, 2000

My Name, A Living Memory is winner of the 2000 Zerilli-Marimò
Prize for Italian Ficition, sponsored by New York University and the
Fondazione Maria and Goffredo Belonci. Funding is made possible by
Baroness Zerilli-Marimò, as well as through contributions from Casa
delle Letterature in Italy. The publishers would like to thank Baroness
Zerilli-Marimò for her support of this publication.

For information about permission to reproduce
selections from this book, write to:
Steerforth Press L.C., P.O. Box 70,
South Royalton, Vermont 05068

Library of Congress Cataloging-in-Publication Data

Straten, Giorgio van.
[Mio nome a memoria. English]
My name, a living memory : Giorgio van Straten ;
translated by Martha King.
p. cm.
ISBN 1-58642-071-2 (alk. paper)
I. King, Martha, 1928- II. Title.
PQ4882.A56 M5613 2003
853'.92–dc22

2003015639

FIRST EDITION

CONTENTS

I. The Time of Legends

1. *Rotterdam 1811*, Hartog's Choice / 3
2. *Florence 1996*, Of Memories and Restorations / 15
3. *San Francisco 1854*, Benjamin's Arrival / 18
4. *San Francisco 1855*, Benjamin's Departure / 27
5. *Rotterdam 1879*, The Reward / 33
6. *Florence 1997*, More on the Concept of Restoration / 42
7. *Libau (Latvia)–London 1874*, Henry Goldstück, Third-Class Passenger / 45
8. *Rouen 1878*, Regarding a Great Idea / 56
9. *Geneva 1996*, Cause and Effect / 61
10. *Monte Carlo 1928*, The Arrival of the Rally / 64

II. The Time of Family Life

11. *Rotterdam 1901*, The Shame / 75
12. *Odessa 1903*, The Frozen Port / 88
13. *Winschoten 1906*, The Wedding / 98
14. *Florence 1997*, A Second-Rate Restorer / 108
15. *Genoa 1913*, Childhood / 111
16. *Rotterdam 1919*, Rites of Passage / 119
17. *Scheveningen 1924*, The Vacation / 132
18. *São Paolo (Brazil) 1995*, Chocolate Letters from Oom Emanuel / 142
19. *Pegli 1927*, A Common Experience / 147
20. *Naples 1928*, In a Hotel Bathroom / 154

III. The Time of History

21. *Stettin 1928,* The Substitution / 165
22. *London 1932,* George Fles Departs for the Orient / 175
23. *Florence 1998,* Exhumation and Delicacy / 184
24. *Livorno 1934,* A Love Story / 187
25. *Tbilisi (Georgia) 1936,* The End of the Revolution / 196
26. *Rome–Genoa 1939,* The Arrest / 209
27. *Amsterdam 1940,* A Night in May / 219
28. *Atlantic Ocean 1940,* The Flight / 229
29. *Amsterdam 1942–1943,* Saul's Dream / 237
30. *Castellina in Chianti (Siena) 1943,* The Telegram / 247

IV. Epilogue

31. *Europe 1945,* These Are the Names / 261
32. *Holland 1946,* In the Flooded Anthill / 265
33. *Atlantic Ocean 1948,* The Last Voyage / 274
34. *Florence 1999,* All the Stories I Have Told / 284

Acknowledgments / 287

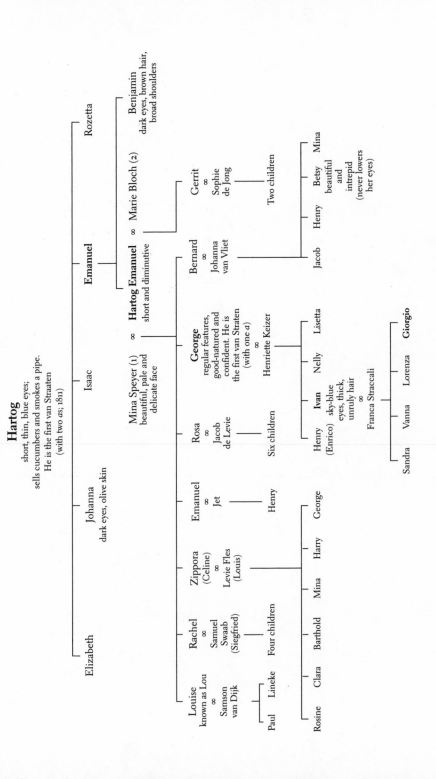

PART I

The Time of Legends

Rotterdam 1811

Hartog's Choice

A NAME, IT WAS only a name.

He woke up while it was still night, the room altered by a suffocating anxiety and emptiness. For a second he did not even recognize the pitch-black room, or the smell of his family. Only fear. And there was nothing to justify it: the same house and the same life. So why was it so difficult to breathe the air in that cold room?

A name, nothing but a name. And names cannot change men's lives. So he believed, so he had always thought. Except that he had never actually thought about it before that moment; for him, Hartog, son of Alexander, this had never been a problem, and he did not understand why it had to be one now.

It was still night and would not even be light when it was time to get up. But it wasn't the dark that frightened him.

He took a deep breath and blew into the icy air. He felt Elizabeth's small body pressed against his. With an arm he sought the back of his wife, who turned in her sleep at his touch. It was December 16, the canals were frozen like the windowpane. But it wasn't the cold that frightened him. It was the emptiness.

‿ဝ

Why was it up to him? Why not his father or one of his children? Why was it his responsibility? And yet in the beginning he had laughed at that French edict. "We, Louis Bonaparte, King of Holland . . . ." A name, only a name, in exchange for his rights as a citizen. In order to be equal with other men, as the French said as soon as they arrived with their armies and functionaries, when they granted the Jews emancipation. "In the year of grace 1811 . . . ," as if those years numbered from a false Messiah's birth made sense.

He had laughed about it. Look at all the attention given a little Jew who sells cucumbers. An edict from the king, no less. It had seemed like a joke to him, a game. But this had been earlier, many months earlier.

It was when he saw the ice on the window barely begin to shine, a mere glimmer, as if it had managed to absorb a hint of the sun still below the horizon, it was then that he decided to get up.

He touched his wife's back again and whispered her name.

"Mietje."

Then again.

"Mietje."

She moved. Opened her eyes.

"Hartog, it's still night."

"It's almost time," he said, "and anyway I can't sleep."

"At least don't wake the little ones," Mietje said as she got up.

Hartog looked, almost without seeing, at her body bundled up in the dress she had kept on as protection from the cold. He imagined, or he saw, her heavy breasts, her graying hair gathered in an untidy bun.

He followed her in the dark, closely, silently, as he had done thousands of times before. He went to the kitchen fireplace and started a fire. She, in the meantime, had already gone to fill the water pitcher.

Hartog Alexander was a small man, with small dreams. Thin, with grayish blue eyes. A Jew like many, who would have been satisfied with his cucumbers, his pipe, and a tranquil life, more tranquil than those endless years of war and interrupted trade had allowed him. He expected nothing more than days like those that had come before, and he never imagined living anywhere other than Rotterdam. Then the French edict had arrived. For many it was a joke: What name will you choose? Some invented names of animals, others of colors. Anyway, what could it matter? But for Hartog, as the winter grew dark and cold, everything had become complicated.

Mietje came back into the room.

"I had to break the ice to fill it," she said, placing the pitcher next to the fireplace.

He made a vague gesture.

"And the fog's so thick I couldn't even see the gate."

The gate, the Schiedamsche Poort, was at the end of their street on the right, and the wide river ran on the left.

"Maybe the Meuse is frozen over, too," Hartog said, but he said it softly, almost in a whisper, because actually the Meuse wasn't at all important to him that day.

A name, it was only a name. Or, to be exact, a surname. Like almost all the Rotterdam Jews, they had never had one. But this did not go down well with the French functionaries. They filled huge books with information about all the inhabitants: birth dates, addresses, professions. And they wanted a first and last name for everyone. It wasn't enough anymore to say *Hartog, son of Alexander.* It wasn't sufficient.

A French fixation, they said in the synagogue, this mania to put everything in order. A great empire needs a great bureaucracy: so said the government officials. In the beginning Hartog hadn't understood or, simply, hadn't cared.

It had happened gradually, like a slow tide that rises above the dike, beyond all defense. A slow mulling over, smoking his pipe. And in the end it seemed even to him that something was lacking. As though a last name were an arm or a leg. Those who do not have them are not citizens.

"We, Louis Bonaparte, King of Holland . . . ." It was up to him, to Hartog, to choose it. Whatever he wanted: an animal, a color. But a choice had to be made. And then he would have arms and legs like everyone else.

The fog was suffused with an attenuated brightness, an imperceptible film of light. Hartog took the pitcher and poured water into a basin, dipped in his hands, and rinsed his face. Taking a thin strip of velvet from his pocket, he tied his hair back in a short tail. Had it been up to his father he would have worn a wig, as had been done until a few years ago. But it was up to him, as he knew, with his ponytail and curly hair.

"Why are you so preoccupied?" Mietje asked.

He didn't have time to answer. He heard the children in the next room. A stifled laugh. Then Johanna appeared at the door.

"Good morning, Papa."

This was why he was worried: for Johanna, who was already fourteen years old; for Isaac, who was seven; for Emanuel, age five; for Rozetta, age three, and for Elizabeth, who was only one. For the weariness that came over him thinking that he was already forty years old, that perhaps they had waited too long after Johanna to have other children. He had decided to have more when the war ended, but now the conditions of the world were frightening him again.

A name. As if his salvation depended on it; as if not having one were a way of hiding, of escaping destiny, while having one made a man stronger and at the same time created much more danger. If he remained a cripple, without that leg of a name, would he feel less tired, less frightened?

He was afraid of the world's inexorable pace, and of breaking out of the daily rut of repeated existence. That name was tantamount to an army on horseback, of cannon and infantrymen. That name meant to choose, to find oneself in an open field without protection or cover. But the emptiness, how would he and his children fill it?

Johanna put a plate on the table in front of him: smoked herring and black bread.

Hartog looked at her dark eyes, her olive complexion. Jews came from all over the world; her blood was mixed with families from the East and those escaping from Spain. And so in the same house there were light colors and dark, and that daughter bore no resemblance to him. Yet she was his favorite. He loved her even more than the boys. And she returned his love with affection, smoked herring, and black bread.

But Johanna was already fourteen and her thoughts were beginning to veer away — incomprehensible to Hartog and perhaps at times even to her. Her father was embarrassed and almost frightened by it.

Now, for example, she was looking at him, uncertain. Her eyes seemed to hound him with unspoken questions.

"What's the matter?" Hartog asked.

"Have you chosen a name, Papa?"

He looked at her, surprised. They hadn't talked about it yet, about the business of a name. He didn't answer.

"I like *Hert*," she said — deer.

"It isn't up to you to decide. Or even to make suggestions," Hartog said, almost angrily.

Johanna lowered her eyes and was silent.

"Anyway, you will only bear it for a few short years," Hartog whispered.

"What did you say, Papa?"

"Take the plate away," he said, getting up.

He put on his best suit, which was becoming a little snug around the waist. A brown suit of heavy cloth. Then he wrapped himself in his dark cloak.

"I'm going," he told Mietje, while the children scampered around him. His wife held the smallest child in her arms, ready to nurse her.

"Whatever you decide will be fine," Mietje said.

Hartog drew her to him and kissed her forehead. Then he turned to Johanna.

"Not *Hert*, for sure."

And he ran down the steep stairs, so steep that he risked falling.

On the street he smelled the strong odor of the country dung that the wind spread over the city. It didn't bother Hartog, it was a natural odor, like the heavy smell of the canals or the house in the winter after the windows had been shut for months. They were the odors of his world, odors of security.

Schiedamsche dyk rose out of a gray fog that smelled of the sea. He greeted the shadowy figures standing in their darkened doorways. The cold gripped his head, brought tears to his eyes.

A faint, pale light began to spread through the fog, almost making it thicker. The city noises intensified, bounced off the street walls, reverberated in the doorways. Rotterdam was waking up, doubtful, like him.

He had almost reached the end of the street when he saw Saul in the doorway of his workshop. He looked at Hartog and smiled. "Today's a holiday?" he asked.

"I have to go to the burgomaster's."

"We've become important, we Jews! Emancipated citizens, received by the *Maire*, as our masters call him. Because we are emancipated, but, like everyone, we're still French servants."

"Just hush."

Saul laughed.

"Business doing well, Mr. Shopkeeper? Are you thinking of buying yourself a decoration? You must have done quite well yesterday if you can't even put up with your friends' jokes anymore."

Hartog had a hard life and he knew it wouldn't change. But he also knew that no one had it easy. That every day he had to press on with determination and pride, in silence, without presumptions. That it wasn't up to a little merchant to ask too many questions. This was why Saul's words sometimes frightened him. Too pointed for a cobbler. He, on the other hand, had few of them, cautious and clear.

"I'm late," he said and started to go.

Saul took him by his arm. "Have you decided on a name? I suggest *Komkommer*," cucumber.

This time Hartog laughed.

"It's an idea," he said, and started to walk away, leaving his friend in his shop doorway.

At the bottom of the street he turned right, crossed the bridge, and entered the lanes that went to the main market. From the wide canals rose a cold and salty sea breeze. The fog rolled overhead like foam and fell earthward without subsiding.

Hartog also rose, with the wind pushing at his back, until he came into the large square, with the enormous Church of Saint Lawrence in the middle.

It was the only thing for which he envied the Christians. As large as his synagogue was, next to the building of the Dutch East India Company, there, on the last bit of land before the Meuse, he felt that the grandeur, that bell tower, those gray stones represented the symbolic supremacy of the Gentiles.

He stopped in front of it, as though seeking inspiration. He felt that all the warmth he had absorbed in his house had been dispersed by now, leaving him alone. He thought of turning back; but then he reminded himself it was not the cold he was feeling, but fear. And from that there was no escape possible.

He had to find a solution on his own, an answer, a simple way out. He looked again at the church. In those gray stones, smoothed by water and wind, he tried to read the history of future generations, those for whom he was choosing. A name is not a destiny, and yet . . .

Bent by the wind that was rising, and which perhaps would clear away the fog on that morning of December 16, 1811, Hartog Alexander for the first and last time in his life tried to rise above his pipe and cucumbers, tried to read the future of his race, of the generations that would follow, and which he, like God, was about to give a name.

Perhaps he did see something of the future: He saw the sea and war, migrations and destroyed houses. He saw the quiet countryside season after season, and snow-covered expanses. He saw dense and heavy smoke penetrating the sky. He heard voices, made out the expressions of unfamiliar faces, perceived cries of fear and songs of liberty. He understood there would not always be cucumbers, but greater joys and greater tragedies. Then he forgot everything. Because that future was not made for him; he could not hold it inside.

After all, no man could.

Then he left the square and walked toward the town hall. He stopped at the foot of the steps leading up to the entrance. Now he had to find a name; he had run out of time.

Maybe, for a moment, he would have liked to make Johanna happy and choose what she had suggested. But what did a deer have to do with their life, what would it ever have to do with it?

He wanted that arm, which he had never had, and of which he now suddenly felt the lack, to resemble him. It should not be strange: Rather it should remind everyone, even those distant descendants he had glimpsed on the facade of Saint Lawrence and then forgotten, where they came from, how they had begun.

This he decided, and once his decision was made, he felt free from the fear and cold. He was happy to have made a choice, and at the same time he felt exhausted by all the years behind him, as if that name had also become an overdue child.

It was only then, with pride and weariness, that he could climb the town hall steps.

The hall was large, longer than it was wide, the ceiling high. Against the far end, opposite the entrance, a low platform ran from wall to wall. On it was a table, and behind the table was Monsieur Suermondt, sitting in a high-backed chair, wearing the tight uniform of the *Maire*, with gold buttons and a stiff collar. Behind his back were two high windows overlooking the square.

Monsieur Suermondt was very self-contained and satisfied with his responsibility, but also annoyed, deeply annoyed, by the bureaucratic tasks involved. That procession of Jews in search of a name, for example, he found most tiresome. But unavoidable, absolutely unavoidable.

Monsieur Suermondt also felt cold, in spite of the heavy underwear he was wearing under his uniform, and he hoped to be able to leave that large, frigid room soon.

With this in mind, he beckoned to the little Jew who was standing uncertainly in the doorway and encouraged him to come in quickly. He did not speak, because that was not within the province and dignity of his role, except when provided by protocol, but he raised his arm and waved his hand toward himself to let the man understand that it was his turn.

The little Jew, who until that moment had kept his eyes down, moved forward, removed his cloak, and stopped in the middle of the room. He looked around for a moment and turned his eyes back to the floor.

Monsieur Suermondt turned to the clerk and let out a long sigh. The clerk reciprocated with a comprehending look. He, too, understood how the *Maire* had more important things to do than this.

"Let us proceed," said Monsieur Suermondt to the clerk, who opened the book in front of him. It contained printed forms bound in a large volume, which were to be filled in with the appropriate information. The first particulars were the same for everyone:

> *Before us MAIRE of the community of*
> Rotterdam, the clerk wrote.
> *Canton of*
> Rotterdam
> *Territory of*
> Rotterdam
> *Department*
> Delta of the Meuse
> *has appeared*

Here ended the automatism and the clerk looked up from the sheet of paper, reread what he had written so far, and looked at the little Jew.

"Has appeared . . . ," he repeated in response to the silence.

Then the man, almost startled, looked at him, turned to the *Maire*, and said:

"Hartog Alexander."

"Residing at . . ."

"Schiedamsche dyk, number eighty-six."

"Who has declared he takes the name of . . ."

Hartog ran a hand over his mouth, turned to look at the *Maire*, and remained silent.

Monsieur Suermondt was a patient man and he was also numb with cold, but just the same he allowed himself a show of impatience. It was a barely perceptible gesture even for a man of his girth and impassive, open face: His right hand rose slightly and then fell back upon the table. But the motion did not go unnoticed by the clerk, who knew Monsieur Suermondt well.

"The name of . . . ," the clerk repeated in order to alleviate the *Maire*'s discomfort.

"Van Straaten," the little Jew said.

"As family name, and that of . . ."

"Hartog."

"As first name, and who has . . . how many children?"

"Five."

The clerk struck out the entry for *grandchildren*. Then he read:

"And specifically . . ."

"A son Isaac, seven years old; a son Emanuel, five; a daughter Johanna, fourteen." He paused before continuing. "A daughter Rozetta, three; and a daughter Elizabeth, one year old."

In his own handwriting, the clerk added: "who all live here, and who are named as listed." He rose, taking the large notebook in both hands, and then approached Monsieur Suermondt, stepped onto the platform, and propped the book on the table.

The *Maire* got up, took the pen he kept before him, and signed his name next to the date. He then turned to the Jew.

"Step forward, please."

The man came forward, stepped onto the platform almost wearily, and asked, "What name should I sign?"

"Hartog Alexander," the clerk replied.

Hartog bent over the page, took the pen in his fingers, and with a slight shiver, signed his name.

"Fine," Monsieur Suermondt said. "Now you may go."

Hartog found himself back in the square. Above him a very pale sun was drowning in the fog. He felt empty, devoid of energy, and he thought maybe he would not even open his shop that day.

But he was happy about his choice. Straaten, like the little Flemish town of his ancestors. So no one would forget his origins, down to the last of his descendants.

And Straaten — street — because they were Jews, and therefore wanderers through the world. And even this was a sign, though he knew only the canals of Rotterdam and was certain he would never move from them.

There he was, little Hartog; now he had everything he needed to face the world, and even to lose himself in it. The fear, come so recently into his life, was destined never to leave. But he finally had a real history, with names and dates: a complete life. He felt like a young boy on his bar mitzvah day, grown up and lost.

"Papa!"

The voice surprised him, there, in the middle of the square, his breath oppressed by an indelible melancholy. He recognized it at once, felt it inside himself, just as he had in that moment when he briefly paused while listing the names of his children.

He turned toward her and opened his arms in an automatic gesture, but he could not manage a smile. Johanna ran to him with her look of faith and anticipation, as though she expected everything in the world from him. And Hartog felt inadequate, was afraid of disappointing her. For that reason he remained somber, with a melancholy that showed on his half-open mouth. He hugged her to him.

She saw him wrapped in his cloak, still as a post. She looked at his sharp profile, his half-open mouth, the white vapor of his breath. Hartog, her father. She felt the love and admiration she had for him.

She came closer. He was looking in the direction of the canals, lost and vacant. It made her sad and ashamed to surprise him this way, when he thought no one was watching him. That was why she had called out *Papa*, and waited for him to turn.

He turned toward her and opened his arms. But his face did not change its expression. Johanna thought he wanted to scold her for being there, for not waiting at home, for following him to suggest some other fanciful name.

Oh, Papa, she thought. *Whatever you decide is what I want.* Then she ran to him and tried to justify her presence. "Mama sent me. To see if you needed anything."

But already Hartog's features had returned to their usual expression, which to Johanna meant serenity and strength. His family was his constant concern; he protected them and made decisions for everyone. Even now.

"It's all right, *schatzi*. You now have a last name."

She didn't ask him what it was. She didn't care. What was important was that he was smiling again, that he was the same father as always. Hers. She walked proudly by his side along the canals of Rotterdam.

The sun had not dissipated the fog. The air was as cold as it had been at dawn. But Johanna van Straaten did not notice.

Florence 1996

Of Memories and Restorations

*W*HAT HAPPENED afterward? After that cold December morning in 1811?

I hold in my hands the creased photocopy of an old document,
written during the Napoleonic occupation of Holland, which
someone, with my same last name but a different ancestry, sent to
one of my distant relatives. Beyond this I have nothing, a void of
some decades. An entire generation missing.

I could certainly invent everything: Johanna's marriage,
Hartog's and Mietje's old age, and a life, some kind of life, for
Isaac and his younger sisters. I could do what I have already done,
starting with a photocopy: reconstruct the faces and a story.

But in this case there is nothing, no crumpled sheets of paper,
and the real people, those who really lived, once they disappear,
dissolve into thin air, cannot be revived on command. Their
memory vanishes, nothing remains to signal their existence; they
are dead forever.

My father left nothing in writing, either. I don't mean a will; that
is not what is lacking. I mean he left no letter, no record of himself, much less a diary.

There is nothing that he made with his own hands or that he particularly loved or that was like him. This means he will not endure beyond the memory of one who knew and loved him and preserved his words and gestures in his mind. In the end he will disappear. Like the greater part of humanity.

But he was my father. Consequently I miss talking with him, and have questions I would like to ask that cannot be answered now, and so I am still hoping to discover, in some forgotten drawer, a message he left to future memory.

While waiting I can look for little signs, some traces. Delve back in time.

That is how this journey began. And it continued until it reached his grandfather's grandfather. As far as covering some lacunae, bringing people and stories to life. As far as discovering the path that the forest had invaded and, to all appearances, destroyed.

The most dreaded Jewish curse says: May your name and even your memory be forgotten. Therefore, to save a man you must repeat his name, as in a liturgy. But the memory? That, as I said, dies with the people who preserve it. Unless someone decides to transform it — to write it down, for instance.

As a restorer I can revive colors that have faded with the passing of centuries, colors that second-rate painters have painted over. Give back life, breath. But there is an insuperable limit for me: Just as with modern restorations, in places where the painting has completely disappeared, something totally lost cannot be reconstructed. Between one restored area and another a coat of white plaster is laid down. It is a declaration of both surrender and respect; I cannot re-create what someone before me has already painted. I cannot reinvent a life that someone has already lived.

Therefore, when I do not have even a piece of paper so creased as to be on the verge of flaking away, a sheaf of files, a yellowed photograph, an object saved by chance . . . when nothing remains, I will give it, lovingly, a coat of white paint. With the respect every man must feel for every other person who has actually existed.

I imagine that Hartog's life went on the same, without surprises or changes, in a Rotterdam that has since disappeared. His pipe, his small commercial dealings, his fat wife. So I can leave him there without regret.

But I will miss Johanna, with her hopes, her passions barely touched on. I cannot know what she did with her life: where she lived it, or with whom. I do not know where her light, heedless step took her.

Her sisters were so young I did not have time to become fond of them. They remain names, nothing more. But Johanna I followed on that walk along the canals, and I cannot forget her.

I know nothing about Isaac, either. About Emanuel, however, I know this: that he continued the family tradition and gave a son his father's name. Emanuel Hartog and Hartog Emanuel. In spite of the surname, he followed the Jewish tradition. Besides, the French had been gone for some time. The House of Orange was in power and the United Provinces had become the Netherlands.

Perhaps Isaac also named a son Hartog; perhaps he also passed down the family name. Or he may have died young and had no children. It is a fact that Emanuel waited a long time — until 1840, when he was already thirty-four years old — before giving his descendant his father's name. And the one he called Hartog was not the first son; but that is another story, one in which a veil of color remains, something that can be recovered.

Emanuel's youth, on the other hand, is only a fog, painted white. An unobserved passage in the world. Not a trace remains. Therefore, from 1811 we go to 1854, and from Rotterdam we move to San Francisco.

San Francisco 1854

Benjamin's Arrival

*H*E WAS SITTING there on the wharf, with the bay at his back and his eyes turned to the hills. He didn't want to see the ocean any longer, he didn't even want to hear about it.

Benjamin was little more than twenty years old, and already he was in another part of the world. He had known two oceans; now he had had enough of water, and he wanted land.

He had arrived only a few days earlier, and had already been told that beyond those hills, toward the northeast, were mountains and forests; that to the south one found endless, unexplored deserts. And most of all, if one knew how to find it, there was gold. Gold on the ground.

This was why he remained turned toward the city, toward the streets that climbed up the steep sides of what in his country would be called mountains; he knew that before him lay an entire continent, a world of strangers, immense and empty expanses. This gave him hope.

In the bay behind him was anchored the sailing vessel that had brought him into port: three-masted, awkward, solid. And behind him also were the long weeks he had spent in and out of ports along the continent from New York to San Francisco. The calm and the storms, but most of all the boredom, the wish to disembark, the dream of what lay beyond the strip of land that he could see at times from the bridge, or beyond the wharves in the ports where they had stopped. And the fear stretched over the days that it had taken to round Cape Horn; a short time that did not diminish the terror. Those enormous buoys of ice that slid over the surface of the sea, the waves nearly as high as the ship's masts. No, he wanted no more water, he wanted land.

The *Sea Lion* was anchored in the bay behind him. It would leave in a few days, taking up its voyage again. Benjamin's journey ended here. Once he felt completely separated from the ship he would be able to look at the sea again as a landscape, as the background of his life, as he had looked at the Meuse from Rotterdam bridges. He would look at the ocean until he didn't see it anymore.

Benjamin was not tall, but for generations everyone in his family had been shorter than he was. He had broad shoulders and strong arms, dark eyes and brown hair, a sharp nose, not aquiline. If he had been uglier or thinner, he might have had a different life. Instead that face and chest had made him bold, decisive.

In Rotterdam he often went to the sailors' haunts looking for an excuse for action in their hard, weather-beaten faces. He could not stay still, could not be satisfied with Saturdays in the synagogue or the Jewish girls. He spurned his father's stiff collar, his absent and formal look. The wind and the sea were before him. He hated the smell of dung in the countryside around the city, and was looking for a way to escape.

There was an energy inside him that could be exhausted only by constant motion. And the farther he was from his father, who did not understand him, the more detached from him he became, the more his energy expanded, made him tremble. He saw the colorless lives of his mother and small siblings, and knew that he could not adapt, that being like them would kill him. Yet he felt more annoyance than pity for them; they offended him.

Only in his aunt Johanna's eyes had he seen a reflection of

what he felt. But he had never found the courage to talk to her about it.

He left the house in his customary frenzy, with the exaggerated energy that kept him from exploding. What he did during those evenings along the Rotterdam piers no one in his family knew, and it was better that way; they would not have understood. His companions were like additional arms, useful on many occasions. He had the ideas. And the ideas often turned into money.

That night was no different from any other, except for its outcome. As he returned home he did not look up at the windows. He imagined they were dark as usual. He ascended the stairs, trying not to make noise. He almost always managed to be quiet because the night was movement, it was life, and Benjamin returned from it calm.

A light was on in the house. He stopped, surprised by that light, almost blinded, like a nocturnal animal. He was already defensive, angry, when his father appeared on the landing at the top of the stairs. Emanuel had red eyes; he must have been dozing while he waited. In his right hand he held a sheet of paper. A letter.

"Benjamin," he said. "Benjamin, you will be the death of me."

Benjamin did not reply. He looked at the letter and wondered what it could be about. About some business, some woman? He could not imagine what it was. And this was one of his weaknesses.

"You are the disgrace of this family," Emanuel said in his sharp, nasal voice. "Now stop it. Stop it."

"What do you mean, *stop it?*" shouted Benjamin. "What right do you have to give me orders?"

"You are my son and you must obey me, the same as every generation owes its elders. But you don't want to understand. You seem the opposite of every decent thing we believe in. You ignore the responsibilities of the eldest son, you shirk your duties, you even hide from your father. All this is intolerable."

Benjamin looked at him but did not recognize him. He saw only the empty face of a stranger whom he hated. He came closer.

He heard footsteps in the hall; their shouts must have awakened his mother.

"You pretend not to hear?" his father continued. "But I'll make you do what you don't want to do, beginning with an honest job. I've already talked to Polak . . ."

"You can't speak for me!"

Emanuel's lips were tight and livid. He raised the hand that held the letter.

"Do you want to read it, you miserable idiot?"

At that moment Benjamin forgot everything: home, family, the night itself. He felt only a knot of energy, hurled without impediment toward the world. And that energy was concentrated in the fingers that he squeezed into a fist.

The sheet of paper floated in the air. His father fell to his knees, his arms clutching his stomach.

"Papa! What happened!" Benjamin turned. It wasn't his mother who was awake, but Hartog, his fourteen-year-old brother. And now he was standing in the doorway watching the scene.

"Go away," Benjamin said unsteadily. In his brother's eyes he saw horror and passivity. Benjamin wanted to rip them out, but his energy was spent.

Hartog moved to help his father. Emanuel, however, was already getting up by himself. Bracing one hand against the wall, he found his breath again. For a moment all three stood motionless, crowded on that little landing, as though what had happened did not concern them. The next moment Emanuel turned to Benjamin.

"Get out of here!" he shouted. "Anyone who raises his hand against his own father cannot be part of the family. You have no respect for anything, not for our laws, not for the name you bear and should pass on. Everything important to me, to us, you have dirtied with your godless behavior. Damn you! I would like every sign of your presence in the world erased forever! Get out of here, you good-for-nothing, and don't come back as long as I live."

Benjamin left two days later without returning home. He met only his mother for a few moments, but her dark dress, the threadbare shawl on her shoulders, left him distant and cold. His mother cried and kept her arms around Hartog at her side; his brother's eyes were still the same. Benjamin paid no attention to her, he barely listened. In fact, he immediately forgot her words. He only remembered the sound when she blew her nose amid her tears. Without a word he took the money she handed him.

He left two days later on a cargo ship heading for New York, along with the sailors he had met in his nights in Rotterdam. He vomited, laughed, won money gambling. Weeks of sea and nothing else. After a time they sighted land on the horizon. Thus Benjamin arrived in America.

There were three types of men in San Francisco: those who had not found gold, those who had found it, and those who profited from the situation. Three kinds of men and very few women. One to every six men.

But what counted for Benjamin was that the city had his same energy, a sense of continual movement, unstoppable. Almost all the houses were new, the streets full of lively people, young men, almost all with beards, looking arrogant and resolute. It seemed that life was there, nowhere else in the world but there, and it expressed itself with guttural shouts, like the seals in the bay.

It took determination and courage. Whoever lacked these attributes was left lying by the wayside, wasted by desperation and alcohol, broken by a light that resembled no other: clear, sharp, and at the same time coarse-grained, suffused. This was the city for Benjamin, he was sure of it now, so different from New York, which had been no surprise because that city was too much like Europe, even like Rotterdam, with its life at the mouth of a river.

Benjamin did nothing but walk up and down the steep slopes with his caracole prance, with his uncontainable energy. He couldn't decide how to begin, how to choose a direction and move without hesitation. But he had time now, he felt it, he had all the time he needed.

No one in San Francisco reminded him of his father, and sometimes that diluted his hate, deflated it. He dreamed less about fists and knives, and he rarely imagined vendettas. He thought about writing his mother, but didn't do it. He was even able to think about Hartog's eyes, how he had seen them before that evening: like the innocent eyes of a younger brother. And yet a gesture or a word that reminded him of the past was enough to stir up his resentment. At such times, wherever he was, he had to go out, he had to start walking until his energy was exhausted in the clear city light and he could rest again, without the nightmare of that sheet of paper hovering in the air, rising and falling to the floor.

"I'm a practical man." He put it that way. "I'm down-to-earth." And he was right.

Zbignew Korciak belonged to the third category of San Franciscans. Those who didn't look for gold, but waited for it to come to them.

"It's the final link in the chain that counts," he said. "The first one does all the work."

He still remembered the men who had returned from Sutter's Creek when there was gold for the taking. He saw their faces and knew that the desperation driving them so far, pushing them to the extreme, would not abandon them simply because the nuggets were in their hands. Lucky strikes do not exist. Or at least you have to know how to deserve them.

Korciak knew that the gold was destined to leave those hands quickly. He began to buy and sell it, to buy when the price was low and sell when it was high. How he had found the money to start that business no one knew, and no one asked anymore; people admired that rich Pole with his curly mustache, with his brown three-piece suit, starched shirt, soft tie, and a cigar in his mouth.

Korciak had grown fat, as happens to satisfied and sedentary men, because by then he spent most of his time sitting behind his desk, waiting for customers. Others could do the legwork for him, those whom he had hired to follow his expeditions, protecting them from bandits and the natives.

It was one of his men, an Irish lad escaping famine, who had first spoken to him about the Dutchman. He had put it this way: *I met a strong, clean-cut, broad-shouldered Dutchman;* and Korciak inquired no further. Because that city was full of men of all nationalities: American, Spanish, French, Italian, German, even Chinese and Australian. But no one had ever mentioned a Dutchman. Even Poles like him were few, and he liked the idea of the two of them, alone together.

"Bring him here," he said. "I want to talk to him."

Benjamin was getting ready. San Francisco was still permeated by that dusty, thin light, the *Sea Lion* had sailed away, and he kept on walking. But now he was listening more, and the news he heard was not good: Gold wasn't right on the doorstep anymore. Expeditions were returning without finding so much as an ounce. And those who had enjoyed some success — and they were fewer and fewer — were keeping mum. Rumors kept circulating, and the Sierra Nevada was mentioned most often.

Parched ground and forests, deserts and mountains. Benjamin dreamed of going to these mysterious places, but he hadn't made up his mind yet. He was content with occasional work, slept in an inn near the port, frequented saloons. It was in one of these that he was stopped by an Irishman, a man with whom he had conversed and shared drinks on a few occasions.

"The boss wants to see you."

"I don't have bosses," Benjamin said.

The Irishman smiled. "Mr. Korciak would like to talk to you. He needs men like you, and you need work."

Benjamin wanted to say that he was getting himself ready, and that was his work. But what such preparation was good for, he truthfully did not know. And besides, Benjamin was not a man who could stay still for long.

"All right," he replied. "Let's go see Mr. Korciak."

He was a Jew, he knew at once, like every clever Pole. But that wasn't important to Korciak anymore. Poland was far away, a part of his life he wanted to forget.

Korciak observed Benjamin sitting on the other side of the

desk. He liked his restlessness, his inability to sit still, the nervous way his fingers drummed on the arm of the chair. He asked him his name.

"Benjamin," the boy answered.

"Benjamin who?"

"Just Benjamin," he said.

For Zbigniew, he immediately became Benjamin the Dutchman, and he dropped the subject. He thought he must have a good reason for not giving his last name. He explained the work and asked Benjamin if he had a weapon. The boy pulled out a knife, a nice one with a bone handle. That wasn't enough.

"Sean," Korciak said to the Irishman, "give him a pistol."

He looked Benjamin in the eye. It was the best way he knew to figure a man out, to decide if he could be trusted. That boy had cold eyes, as if hate resided deep inside him. But it was something in the past, and Korciak didn't think it had anything to do with him. So he considered the boy manageable, and therefore useful; not because of his hate, but because of the coldness he interpreted as determination.

"You'll start tomorrow," he said.

The boy nodded.

At times there were long trips. He came to know the mountains and the endless prairies, unimaginable expanses, even for someone born in a flat country. He met prospectors, caravans marching toward the west, railroad workers proceeding slowly toward them. He even returned to New York, saw New Orleans for the first time, but he never again boarded a ship.

Other weeks he spent in Korciak's outer office checking those who came and went. When he was forced to be still, he thought. Often his thoughts were about the reason he hadn't wanted to tell Korciak his surname, but he didn't find the answer. Of one thing he was certain: He could no longer say that name. He had a feeling it contained something that was agitating him inside, something best not let out, because even he was afraid of it.

His boss paid him well, and he spent almost all his money with his companions, but without finding the intimacy of his nights in Rotterdam. He didn't tell his friends his name, either. So everyone called him Dutch, as Sean had done the first time they met, and that was just fine with him. No one really knew him, and this gave him strength. He preferred to pay for women as well, and forgot them immediately afterward.

He felt he was still in a temporary situation, that secretly he was preparing himself for something much greater. Only once did he talk about it — to a prostitute who had let him kiss her on the mouth and had then asked him what he was thinking about.

"I have great hopes," he said. "And great plans for revenge."

She believed he was looking for nuggets like everyone else, and shook her head. "Even you, chasing after that gold . . ."

Benjamin laughed heartily, got up and dressed, and went away without another word. Outside, San Francisco was lost in the fog; even the bay had disappeared, along with the islands and the ships in the port. Benjamin ran through the streets without stopping, shouting with life and vigor.

—◦ IV ◦—

San Francisco 1855

Benjamin's Departure

—

*H*E WAS LYING flat on the ground and couldn't have
stood up even had he wanted to. His head was resting on
his horse's saddle, he had a blanket under him, his arms were
stretched out alongside his body, and he was looking at the fire in
front of him. The other men were in the same position; they were
in a circle around the campfire and a bottle of whiskey was
passing from hand to hand, from mouth to mouth.

There had been many bottles, and consequently Benjamin
could not move. At any rate he had no intention of doing so. He
felt warm and had a pleasant sense of vertigo. Finally he could
forget time; not its passing, which pulsed in his temples with a
regular beat, but its order, the terrible chain of events that now,
for the first time, appeared to be separated from each other, inde-
pendent, and not lined up in that continual series he had tried to
escape. Every fact was now an island, a bubble that floated in the
void and went its own way; therefore, it was less frightening.

They stayed there, together around the fire. Other men had gone
off in search of gold, as they had already done, and would continue
to do. Benjamin, however, wanted only to escape. But now the

tiredness, the whiskey, that unknown, dark expanse surrounding them had done the job, and the fragments of his anguish had separated from each other until they became innocuous.

"Hey, Dutch, a penny for your thoughts," the man beside him said.

"Don't call me Dutch," he replied. "My name is Benjamin."

"Whatever you say, Dutch," the other man said.

He did not reply. In the tongues of flame a spark reminded him of his gleaming watch. The goldsmith had turned it over, looked at it attentively, and given his assessment: nice, heavy, well made. It must have cost a lot of money. Benjamin had only nodded.

It was a watch for a pocket or vest, of engraved gold with a double lid. One lid covered the dial; the other covered the case and the winding mechanism. The case, under the lid, was smooth. This was what had given Benjamin the idea. Now, while he took another sip of whiskey, he couldn't remember how it had come to him, or what meaning he had given it. That was not important. As usual, his decisions seemed dictated by strength and instinct, not by reflection. His life had always been that way.

The goldsmith had wiped the surface with a cloth and asked him what he wanted inscribed on it. GIVEN TO E. H. VAN STRAATEN BY HIS SON BENJAMIN (SAN FRANCISCO 10.18.1855). The goldsmith wrote it on a piece of paper and told him to come back that afternoon. Benjamin shook his head. He was in a hurry and had no intention of leaving the watch. The goldsmith frowned at that lack of faith, but made no comment.

"Right now? If you have the patience to wait . . ."

Then he took a burin and began to engrave. Benjamin sat on a bench for an hour, almost hypnotized, watching the goldsmith work.

"You were one of Korciak's men," the one lying by his side continued. "That devil who swindles everyone. I remember you. They called you Dutch."

Benjamin knew he should react, but he didn't have the strength. And he didn't have the time, either.

"Leave him alone, Malone."

The voice came from another part of the circle, from a large, bearded man with blue eyes. He had brought Benjamin to that fire; he was one of the reasons the boy was trying to break away from that frightening chain.

It had happened outside, in front of Korciak's office building. The man was standing, pompous, his mouth twisted and mocking, leaning against a fence. Benjamin remembered Korciak shouting.

"Shoot him, Dutch. Shoot him, damn it!"

He had held his arm out stiffly, the pistol aimed, his finger on the trigger. But he didn't squeeze it because he had never killed anyone; and at that moment he realized it was a very hard thing to do. The more time passed, the more he looked at the man's face, the more impossible it became.

But Korciak did not give up.

"Shoot him, you dirty Jew."

So finally the real Pole had come out. Korciak's rage, his purple lips pressed tight. Benjamin's hand on the pistol and the bearded man's face challenging him. Did the watch have something to do with all this?

Benjamin didn't know anymore; and that was fine with him.

"Who did anything to him?" the man stretched out beside Benjamin said. "Tell me something, O'Brian, can't anyone ask a question without your permission?"

The bullet broke the bottle that Malone held in his hand, scattering glass and whiskey. Frightened, he jumped to his feet, still holding the neck of the bottle in his fist, while the others started laughing at his fear.

"Not even a question, if I don't want," O'Brian said.

Benjamin was under his protection because he had saved his life. Or at least from one point of view it had undoubtedly happened that way. But Benjamin knew, just as the bearded man knew, that it had been more complicated. That the expression on O'Brian's face had something to do with it, as well as the nervous way he tapped the toe of his boot on the ground; a mannerism that reminded Benjamin of his own excessive energy.

Whatever the reason, Benjamin had lowered his arm and let the pistol fall to the ground. After that he had turned to Korciak. The boss was yelling, even though Benjamin couldn't remember a word after that *dirty Jew*. Maybe he hadn't listened, or maybe the whiskey was doing its work accurately and precisely, erasing what there was to erase.

Certainly he had hit him. He didn't know exactly when, whether right after he turned, or after an interval of hours or days. It was one of those bubbles floating freely now. A physical sensation remained: his fist sinking into Korciak's fat paunch. And in the time it took him to reflect that Korciak's belly was softer than he'd expected, the man was already lying on the ground. Perhaps the watch came out of his pocket at that instant and Benjamin had taken it. Perhaps. But it was only a hypothesis. Because the watch was an island, and the punch he gave Korciak another island, and both barely emerged from the ocean of prairie and whiskey.

Now the man next to him was silent, rolled up in a blanket. Someone sang softly, almost absentmindedly. Benjamin closed his eyes and couldn't find the strength to open them again. But he still didn't think he was sleeping, because behind his eyelids he saw other islands.

For example, Korciak who had said to him: "Bravo, you did a good job."

And he had patted him on the back, with a smile he reserved for special occasions.

He had also put something in his hand. A gift, a reward. Maybe that very watch. So perhaps Benjamin came by it honestly, as a bonus for following his boss's orders, and for that reason he had decided to give it to his father.

But when had that scene taken place? And did it really happen?

Benjamin remembered now. He remembered other words, other days. Little mosaic tiles floating on the whiskey.

O'Brian, who said to him, "Whoso will come after me, let him deny himself, and take up his cross, and follow me." And he began to laugh.

"No," he had added when he saw Benjamin's puzzled look, "you can't understand why I'm laughing, it's not your religion. But I'm serious: If they find you here they'll kill you."

When? Hours earlier? Or weeks?

And at last there was the ship anchored in the bay, when the sea had finally gone back to being just a landscape, a background, and he could look at it again. A Dutch ship, a ship from Rotterdam. It stayed there, quietly, like a tired warrior, and as soon as Benjamin saw it, he went to the port.

"Benjamin, my boy."

He opened his eyes. On the horizon the sky was barely brighter than when he had closed them, and its color was between gray and blue. Dawn was approaching. The fire had gone out. O'Brian's face was almost touching his.

"You went on one fine drinking spree, boy," he said.

Benjamin closed his eyes again. He didn't feel like he had slept at all. But hours had passed. The whiskey brought on a feeling of nausea, and the islands were reconfiguring to form a solid piece of land.

"Let's go in half an hour," O'Brian concluded. "And never come back here again. Look, over there, you can already see the mountains: It's the Sierra Nevada. We'll follow it south, to a place no one has ever been except some savage tribes. We'll go as far as the desert if we have to. That way we'll find gold." He scooped up a fistful of dirt and let it sift through his fingers. "Get up now, boy. You only have half an hour to get ready."

He had half an hour at his disposal. Really, half an hour? He had needed much less time to change his life. And only a little more to explain everything to the captain of the ship, a man with a Dutch face who smoked a pipe like his grandfather's.

And the half hour that Benjamin took to open his eyes, gather his belongings together, and begin his journey was the same amount of time it had taken the captain to decide.

"You trust me and I'll trust you," he said in the end. "You didn't ask me questions, and I won't ask you. We're both Dutchmen, that's enough for me. I'll take your package and address, and I'll follow your instructions. You know I won't be in Rotterdam for another two or three months, so I can't guarantee how long it will take to deliver the package to its destination. But I swear on my honor that I'll do it."

That was it. Benjamin no longer knew how he got the watch, but now he remembered how it had left him, and for where.

On the edge of the faraway hills appeared the greenish flush of day. The last bubble was about to burst, about to restore its contents to the chain constricting Benjamin's life. But now he was no longer afraid. He would be protected by the mountains, by their blue peaks, or by the desert, by the empty space that was before them and would soon be behind them. And the ocean on which the ship sailed would protect him, because the message would be delivered.

Benjamin stood up and stamped on the ground with the toe of his boots, right where the fire had been. He felt the life inside himself expand like the light in the sky. Unstoppable.

He was ready to go.

_ɔ v ɔ_

Rotterdam 1879

The Reward

O N HIS OFFICE desk Hartog found a small bound book.
On the cover was a little metal plate: SOUVENIR 1854–1879.
Hartog sat down and placed his briefcase on the desk, on the left
side, as usual. Then he opened the little book. The first page was
inscribed in embellished letters and a variety of colored inks:
green, black, gold, blue, and red.

On the occasion of his twenty-fifth anniversary with the firm of
Polak and Sons, H. E. van Straaten was presented with a *canapé
met stoelen:* a divan and armchairs. And then the date: December
10, 1879. The subsequent pages listed the thirty-eight colleagues
who had contributed to the gift, from A. Abrahams to S. P. Zoest.

Hartog Emanuel closed the book and looked up at Roodschild, who was sitting across from him.

"I am really touched by this thought," he said.

"And who knows what you will say when you go home and see
the present!" Roodschild replied.

"I expected something, but nothing like this . . ."

"Come," Roodschild said, addressing him with the familiar *du*
because they saw each other every Saturday in the synagogue, and
because for more than fifteen years their desks had faced one other.

All his colleagues were waiting for him in Polak's office, and they applauded while an embarrassed Hartog tried to hide his feelings.

"It has been twenty-five years," Polak began, "since young Hartog Emanuel van Straaten joined our family. We were actually expecting his older brother. A husky man, as I remember, whom we thought destined to work in the warehouse. But his father arrived with Hartog, who at that time was fourteen years old, and short and slender." He paused. "Just as he is today at almost forty." Polak laughed at what he considered a witticism, and then went on: "Few clerks have been as painstaking and efficient as our Hartog. His devotion to the firm is an example for us all, even for me, and I believe that every colleague has shared willingly in the cost of the present we want to give him. Come over here, Hartog, I want to shake your hand."

Again everyone applauded, while that slender, short man with thinning hair walked uncertainly toward the owner of the firm. Someone loudly suggested that Hartog also make a speech, but he refused, cheeks flushed with embarrassment, and limited himself to shaking Polak's hand. Polak, taller by a foot and much fatter, squeezed Hartog's hand between his, making it almost disappear, and then drew him close, kissing him on both cheeks.

Polak and Sons was a wholesale fabric business, a solid and steady company that had operated in Rotterdam for many years. Hartog dealt with the orders, writing all the necessary details in a ledger: who requested fabrics, of what kind, in what quantity; then he sent the requests to the other clerks to be dispatched. When he received confirmation of the delivery he made a mark in red ink next to the order.

Hartog, wearing the black sleeves of a clerk, carried out his work quickly and precisely, devoting all the time necessary, and when business was heavy he often returned home late in the evening. He had never considered how much this might please the owner; everything he had done over the years he had considered his duty.

Consequently he had been surprised by the gift and festivities, even though he had seen similar celebrations for others. He considered himself less important than many other employees in the firm, and did not think his colleagues would pay any particular attention to him, even though he often saw them outside the office, since Jews were in the majority.

Now into his routine and therefore unremarkable flow of days had come this fracture, as affecting as the birth of one of his children, in fact even more so for being unexpected. No, it was not only embarrassment that kept him silent; it was also the feeling that now, on the threshold of his fortieth year, there was an accounting to be made of figures that did not appear in any ledger. Operations of which he knew nothing, numbers that he would never manage to read.

At home he found a great commotion, excited children running from the kitchen to the parlor, then to the kitchen again, and back to the parlor. Emanuel, the oldest, who had already celebrated his ninth birthday, welcomed Hartog along with his two sisters, six-year-old Zippora, and four-year-old Rosa, who stood at his side like two attendants.

"Papa," Emanuel began, "something came . . ."

"I know," Hartog said, caressing the boy's head, but he did not go to the parlor. Instead he went to the kitchen where he was sure of finding Mina. And in fact his wife was there with George, who was almost two years old, attached to her skirts, and Bernard, recently born, in her arms.

Mina smiled her rather sad smile, wan as her skin, diaphanous as her eyes. She had a tired aspect; those five children born to her made her seem older than her twenty-nine years.

"Oh, Hartog," she said. "That was so nice of the company. The divan and armchairs are very beautiful!"

Hartog felt an impulse to draw Mina close, but was afraid it would only be an awkward gesture, impeded by the baby in her arms. So he stayed where he was, in the middle of the room, overcome by a tenderness he could not express.

It was his wife who moved, as if Hartog needed a guide to find his way in their small apartment. They entered what they optimistically called their parlor, which finally contained something appropriate to that definition.

Emanuel and his sisters came fast behind their parents, shouting about this novelty that their modest life had not previously allowed them. Hartog looked at the pieces of furniture, which certainly did not cancel the fatigue and discomfort of the years; in fact, they almost underscored them, but also redeemed them, and offered a closure of sorts.

Soon he would be forty years old, and nothing was different from what he had sought; from what could emerge from the narrow horizons of his existence. A life well woven and of good quality, like the fabrics of Polak and Sons.

He put an arm around his wife's shoulder, uttered a half-hearted objection to the continual whoops of Emanuel, Zippora, and Rosa, and he felt moved. Twenty-five years of work. Ten years of matrimony.

"Have you tried them yet?" he asked Mina.

She shook her head. "I was waiting for you."

"And the children?"

"Not even them. I wouldn't let them."

The divan was made of dark wood, with a carved frame and two armrests with slightly raised volutes, also of wood. The padded back and seat were covered with a blue-and-white floral pattern. The legs were fairly thin, curved in front and straight in back. The two armchairs were made like the divan and covered with the same material.

It was a bourgeois parlor, and Hartog was looking at it with a certain emotion, while his children pushed him toward the divan. And even though he knew that his weariness was not likely to end, that his work as a clerk would never allow the affluence and serenity he would have desired, he felt at that moment that something concrete, something hard and resistant, had defined the course of his life.

He sat on the divan and gestured to Mina. "Come here beside me."

She sat down beside him, but stiffly, with Bernard still in her arms, worrying about the damage George could do to that light-colored material. Hartog, in contrast, had let himself go, legs stretched out, head resting against the back of the divan. Perhaps he didn't even notice Mina's discomfort, since the tenderness and love he felt for her was intermittent, frequently turned off along with his attention. She was his wife, forever, the mother of their children, and of any still to come, but the times, worries, thoughts sometimes made him distant, made him take her presence for granted, made him assume she would do what was expected, without the need for words or gestures.

And Mina Speyer, now Mina van Straaten, perhaps did not even notice the distance that on occasion created something like a curtain between them; or at least she accepted it, considered it natural, a thing that came between all men and women as they carried out their daily lives. Hartog worked hard for his family, and he worried about his wife and children; surely it was inevitable that he often seemed distant and detached.

So when she heard his regular breathing, when she realized that Hartog was asleep on that divan, symbol of twenty-five years of work, Mina motioned to the children to leave the room, that room where they, too, after the first enthusiasm, seemed to feel a little uncomfortable. One by one she had them file through the doorway, and then she left the room, too, with Bernard resting his head on her shoulder, fast asleep as well, and with George still clinging tightly to her skirt. She looked at her husband once more on the divan and closed the door behind her.

A familiar voice awakened him, a voice that in the passage from sleep to wakefulness transported him to a familiar and distant place, full of anguish and fear, to another awakening, one that usually drowsed in the depth of thoughts, or rather even deeper, where thoughts were extinguished, crushed by the weight of routine days.

Hartog's father had become bent with age, but at that moment he seemed to his son to be once again a foot taller than him, as if enlarged by Hartog's drowsiness and his seated position, ensconced in the new divan. The fabric, in fact, was the first thing Hartog recognized, and it saved him from fear and anxiety.

Outside it was already dark, and the oil lamp in the entryway provided the only light in the room, outlining his father's figure in the doorway.

"Are you sleeping? I thought you were still at work."

Hartog sat up but didn't even try to rise.

"I have the afternoon free. It was Polak . . ."

"Mina told me all about it, and now I can see this marvel for myself. Everyone is talking about it."

His father sat in one of the armchairs, and now that Hartog was fully awake, he saw the man as he had known him for some time: older than his years, and tired, even if he never would admit it.

"It's cold," Emanuel said, "and every time the temperature drops I feel more aches and pains. But you're still young; you can't know about such things."

"How can anyone be young after working for twenty-five years? Of course I haven't broken rocks or built dikes, but there are many kinds of work . . . never mind, I'm happy today, everyone was very nice to me, including Polak . . ."

His father made a vague gesture with his hand.

"You've done your duty conscientiously for years. At work and at home. I'm proud of you, because when I took you there, to the elder Polak, I had no idea how it would turn out, and I wasn't thinking of you. But you have repaid me by your outstanding dedication, and you have been a son like all sons should be."

But you are not Benjamin; that is what Emanuel did not have the courage to say. Not that evening, not ever. Hartog vaguely intuited it to be so, though afterward, fortunately, he would forget. He had always tried to do his best, by whatever means he had, giving everything he had. His mother understood this; his father only accepted it.

"I've just done my duty."

Emanuel nodded.

"But if Polak can give you a present, I don't know why I shouldn't give you one too."

"I don't think that would be right, your finances — "

"My present costs nothing, at least not in money."

Emanuel rummaged in his pocket, as though checking to see if what he had put in it was still there. Then he put his hand back on the arm of the chair, testing its solidity with his fingertips.

"Not only have you worked for twenty-five years, but it has also been twenty-five years since Benjamin left, and the two things are connected, as you know."

Hartog did not want to hear that story again, not only because of the pain it caused him, but also because of the boredom. He had been sixteen when the captain with the thick beard came to their house with news of Benjamin: a few words, dry as his fingers. Nothing more after that until the news became mere conjecture, vague hypothesis, and in the end absurd hope. *The one who runs away is always in the wrong,* was what Hartog thought, even though the absent often garner more attention than those who, like himself, never abandon their post.

And then there was that special tone people affected when talking about America. For others that country was a dream, a fantasy of freedom; for him it was an empty and meaningless word.

No, he did not want to hear his father repeat the story he had already told a thousand times in order to convince himself that Benjamin was not dead. For Hartog, one of man's greatest defects was his imagination.

Perhaps Emanuel had continued speaking and Hartog had not been listening, or perhaps his father had paused while waiting for him to return his gaze. Certainly it was only after their eyes met that Hartog started hearing his father's words again.

"But there is something I've never told you. Out of pride, I think, in order not to admit I accepted a gift from Benjamin, from that son I swore never to see again; and I have been granted that much. Or perhaps I did it to have a secret that gave me hope. It is hard to admit failure, even when it's not yours, but your son's."

Emanuel put his hand in his pocket again, and this time he took out a little velvet bag, which he put on the coffee table in front of him.

"This is my gift."

Hartog took the little bag and opened the drawstring. He searched with his fingers and drew out a gold watch. He held it in his hand, looking at it.

"Open the lid," his father said.

Delicately, with extreme care, Hartog opened it, pressing in a notch with his fingernail. He read the dedication. Then he closed it again and put the watch on the table.

"You are the future of this family," Emanuel said. "You are my only descendant. You have my father's name and will continue our history. That is why I want to give you this watch. So that someone remembers."

Hartog was surprised, happy, and wounded. He had never heard his father talk like this; it seemed too emotional to be natural. But old people often let themselves be carried away by emotion, by a fragility they would have disdained in earlier years. He was also happy that his role as head of the family had been recognized, that he had been entrusted with passing on a name, the name his sons had already guaranteed continuity. But why the memento? So that everything regarding Benjamin would not be erased, so he would not disappear along with his father? It was a wound best allowed to heal in silence, best abandoned to the flow of years it had taken for his own eyes and ears to eradicate the images and words of the most horrendous night of his life. *Papa*, he thought, *haven't you had enough yet?*

"I am grateful for this gift," Hartog said in a calm voice, while his head spun, "and I will keep it as a part of myself."

Neither of the two moved, neither found the courage nor had the heart to touch the other. They remained like that, waiting for nothing, until Mina appeared at the door.

"Supper's ready," she said in her thin voice.

Hartog got up and walked toward the kitchen, so that his father's words were spoken to his back. "And you, too," Emanuel said, "when the moment comes, don't give it to the oldest son, but to the one who deserves it."

It was truly a strange day for an employee like Hartog, and he felt proud of everything he had received: the divan, the armchairs, the gold watch. Just the same, he hoped he would not have many other days like it, because he wasn't prepared to face them.

"The stove must not be working right," he said to his wife as he entered the kitchen, nonchalantly wiping his eyes.

VI

Florence 1997

More on the Concept of Restoration

THERE ARE MANY ways to tell a story, many ways to lie while doing it; all equally legitimate, because lying is inevitable. Every story is a betrayal, an arbitrary reconstruction, and as such it requires choices, deletions, adjustments.

Still, I don't believe there are many ways to restore a fresco well, because that kind of restoration is a more precise undertaking, with a greater scientific basis, and consequently fewer alternatives. But there is always a way.

For example, I know that sometimes when there is an area where the fresco has disappeared but the undamaged parts allow us to discern what was painted in the lost areas, a different system can be followed from the one I have already mentioned, that of laying down a coat of white plaster. One can proceed by way of the so-called chromatic selection.

That is, by using an extremely fine brush and watercolor paints, one can apply small dabs of the color that the fresco is presumed to have had in that place. An image is not reproduced, but only some suggestions: not a shoe, if a shoe is missing in that area, but many tiny brushstrokes in brown.

Viewed from a certain distance, the wholeness and significance of the fresco seem to be recovered. Only upon close examination does one note the difference between the original and the restored. I saw this system used in Arezzo in the restoration of Piero della Francesca's *Legend of the True Cross*, but I imagine it is a technique followed in other cases as well.

There are two objects on my table: a dark notebook with a hard cover, and a gold watch. My grandfather gave me the watch when I was born in 1955, and I believe I can guess the reason: because that watch was exactly one century older than I was. I no longer remember how the notebook came into my possession — perhaps a cousin sent it to me — but it is a more recent acquisition. These items are useful in defining the areas where the color was salvaged. For the rest, I have not wanted to limit myself to applying a layer of plaster; I have enough evidence to reconstruct the colors, even to invent them. In short, to warrant lying, but with an awareness of what I am doing.

I am not abandoning the respect for others that I promised myself to maintain; it is just that every world needs color, even pale colors, delicate colors like watercolors. Colors to restore a flavor of truth to my involuntary lies.

On the table I actually have a third object: a framed photograph. On the bottom right, on the white passe-partout, a signature is stamped in red: WILLIAM, AMSTERDAM. A name and a city.

We are in 1886. Hartog's family is now complete, even if it will not remain so for long. In the photograph are the seven van Straaten children. All of them elegantly dressed for the occasion.

Standing, already dressed like a man, with a high-necked jacket, white shirt, and dark tie, is Emanuel. His fair hair is parted in the middle and he keeps his left hand in his pocket, almost as though to give himself an adult stance. He is sixteen and seems to want to assume his role of older brother, but the expression he projects to the camera is timid and lost.

Next to him, also standing, is Rosa in a black dress with decorative braided button closures. Thin, her emaciated face framed with fine, wavy hair, she leans her small, bony hand on the shoulder of one of her younger sisters sitting in front of her. Rosa is much shorter than Emanuel, so short that her head does not reach his shoulder.

Seated, from right to left, are the other four siblings: first George, dressed in a sailor suit, bearing a sly look and a vague, ironic smile. In spite of his eight years, and unlike his older brother, he appears totally at ease. Then Louise, five years old, with her round face and an odd dress that seems made of heavy material, although it leaves her plump arms bare. Next to her, Rachel, barely two years old, with a light-colored tunic and blond hair, is in the arms of Zippora, her oldest sister, already thirteen. Zippora has smooth, black hair, a pointed face, wide deep-set eyes, a slightly aquiline nose. She looks toward the lens with great seriousness and a hint of sadness, or at least of remoteness.

In front of them, half reclining, his elbow propped on a low bench, is Bernard, with an open mouth and a look of surprise, wearing a sailor suit similar to George's.

The children do not look much alike. Only Emanuel and Zippora, whose faces have the same shape, and perhaps George and little Rachel, whose nose and mouth are similar. In the others I find no common features, perhaps because I have only one very faded photograph in sepia that may not be faithful to the reality of those times.

The children's parents do not appear in the portrait. It is, as I mentioned, 1886; the next year Mina, too, will pass silently out of their lives. Convinced she had done her duty, tired from those numerous deliveries so close together, frightened by the idea of having to abandon her children.

I cannot follow her. I do not have a brush with a point fine enough to trace the light lines of her death.

Besides, I must turn back a few years to tell the beginning of another story that appears to have nothing to do with what has happened up to now. But appearances very often deceive, and stories have imperceptible ties that only time, with its slow pace, can illuminate.

VII

Libau (Latvia)–London 1874

Henry Goldstück, Third-Class Passenger

*T*HERE WERE ONLY two possibilities: either he had not noticed him when he passed by, or he had not passed by at all.

Seaman Martin Abbott, of Her Britannic Majesty Queen Victoria's navy, in service on a steamship en route from Saint Petersburg to London, had stood beside the ramp as passengers embarked at the Libau port. So he had seen them all, he had carefully observed their faces, and imagined, as he often did, what kind of lives they led. But he could not remember seeing that small, slender young man who seemed both bold and frightened.

He had found him in the third-class corridor and had stopped in front of him.

"Do you need something?" the sailor asked in English with a gentleness he never used with passengers in the lower classes. But the boy shook his head.

Martin had stepped aside to let him pass, tracking the boy with his eyes until he went up the steps to the deck. Then he had followed behind him.

Outside, the sun was still high. Summer was just beginning to wane, but it still stayed light until late into the evening. The boy was leaning on the railing, watching the Baltic Sea flow by. The

coast was far away by now and land was nowhere to be seen. A
light breeze blew and the water around them was barely ruffled,
as though it were a lake.

The boy had not noticed the sailor, and when Martin came up
beside him, he jumped as though he had been caught doing
something wrong.

"What's your name?" the sailor asked.

"Henry Goldstück," the boy replied. "Third-class passenger."

He was wearing a frock coat with cloth-covered buttons, as was
the fashion in bourgeois circles, but his polished ankle boots betrayed his origins.

"Where are you from?"

"From Grobin, in Courland."

No, Martin thought, *I did not see that face come on board. I
would have remembered those sharp features, those lively green eyes
and full lips. Even when he's standing still, that boy seems nervous
and jittery. Someone must have let him on at another time,
someone who was paid to do so.*

Perhaps he should take this Goldstück to the captain; let him
question the boy and clear up the situation. But Seaman Abbott
was more curious than loyal and did not do it. Besides, Abbott was
of a certain age, and that boy could have been his son. He felt ob-
ligated to protect him. So he told Goldstück to go back inside; it
was growing cold, and his suit was too lightweight. He said it
kindly, with a hand on the boy's shoulder.

The boy nodded, but stayed where he was, his gaze fixed on the
horizon. Abbott shook his head and started walking toward the
prow. When he turned for the last time the boy had not moved.

Goldstück did not venture out often, and when he did, he tried
not to draw attention, his small body slipping among the passengers like a shadow. Even his words were limited to the essentials,
inane enough to be soon forgotten. Abbott put these utterances
together, patiently and attentively, from shreds of conversation or
travelers' jokes in third class, without questioning, only listening.
And he was able to assemble a story.

Young Goldstück was nineteen, the son of a small landowner. He worked for a wheat merchant and was on his way to France, where he would represent the sellers of a large grain concern, avoiding disputes and fraud once the cargo reached Rouen. The business involved oats for the General Omnibus Company of Paris, a corporation so large it owned more than ten thousand horses.

Those were the words Abbott overheard; but he had to keep his questions, and there were many, to himself. If that was the reason for Goldstück's trip, why didn't he travel with the cargo? Why did he come on a British navy ship and not on a Russian boat? And why, for such an important mission, had the grain merchants picked a youth, doubtless a very intelligent youth, but surely little versed in life and confidence games?

He asked no questions so as not to draw attention to his interest in the boy. More precisely, in order to prevent others from watching Goldstück and discovering his secrets. Because Abbott was now certain Goldstück had secrets.

No: He was not good looking, no doubt about that. Short, thin, with narrow shoulders. Lips too large, and a Jewish nose. But his eyes could bewitch anyone: They laughed, capable of slicing through you and making you blush if they suddenly concentrated on you. Green eyes, like a cat's, but deep as a snake's, wrapping around you until it enclosed you in its jaws. And his laughter: rare, but sincere and hearty.

Anja was sixteen years old and had never spoken to a man in private. And many years would pass before she would again. But on shipboard everyone is freer, conventions relax, contacts seem easier and more innocuous.

No one knew how Goldstück got into the first-class ballroom. Perhaps no one was paying any attention, aside from Anja and a sailor who observed in silence. Some people were dancing; Anja's mother was talking with the captain at a separate table. Anja, meanwhile, was standing by the door that led to an outside passageway, looking through the windows into a profound darkness that had swallowed the sea and sky. She was imagining the cold and damp of the night outside, dreaming of adventure and escape. She saw eyes reflected in the glass; only the eyes, and the dark, indistinguishable shape of a face.

The boy spoke in Russian. "You can't see anything," he said.

Anja replied in French, "What I see and don't see doesn't concern you."

Then the boy opened the door and the darkness entered with a cold breath that made Anja shiver.

"Even outside you can't see anything, but at least you can smell the sea."

This time Anja said nothing, but did not move. He gestured with his hand for her to follow him. And she followed, after hesitating a moment, stooping to collect the shawl she had left on an armchair. She bent over nonchalantly and turned her head quickly, like a bird in self-defense, to see if her mother had noticed anything. But her mother was talking and the captain was laughing. So she wrapped her shawl around her shoulders and went out.

It was already cold, and they kept to the wall to shelter themselves from the wind. But what pleased Anja was that the darkness outside was not total. There was a silvery gleam, a glow from the absent moon that guided their glances.

"What's your name?"

"Henry."

"I'm Anja."

Again she saw those eyes like magnets, like snares. She also saw the clothes unsuitable for evening wear, the too-large collar, the poorly tied cravat.

"What are you doing on this ship?" she asked.

He told her of an adventure and an escape such as she had dreamed of in the glass reflection, in the darkness of the world. But different from hers, as it was a true story, or at least it seemed to be.

He had arrived at the wharf at night, in the same darkness that was now enveloping them on the bridge. He had had only a few hours to flee to safety; his pockets held what little his parents had been able to scrape together in a couple of days. Loans, help, promises. The czar of all Russia had made a decision: His subjects had to join the armed services for sixteen years. Henry had pretended to accept this regulation, which the terrible emperor had also imposed on Latvians. He had a uniform made, chose his boots, and prepared to leave.

This during the daytime. But the czar sleeps at night, too, doesn't he? Anja was Russian, but she must have understood how wrong her emperor's decision was. A life ruined, lost. A youth spent in war.

Thus Henry had managed to persuade a sailor to let him board before the other passengers. The man had hidden him in the hold, next to the engine room, and in that infernal racket he was told to keep quiet, under cover, until the ship set sail. "After that, you'll be safe," the sailor told him. "No one will send you back."

"I'm cold," Anja said.

Goldstück took a blanket that had been left on one of the chairs outside, under the overhang, and wrapped it gently around the girl's shoulders.

The glimmer of moon had grown larger, and the wind made the light dance on the water, scattering it toward the horizon.

"You are a deserter, then!" Anja said — though without a hint of disapproval in her voice, much less condemnation, but a kind of dreamy admiration and envy.

Henry said he didn't know if, from the military point of view, he was a deserter yet; he didn't even know if anyone was looking for him, if a dispatch had already been sent from the barracks at Riga where he should have presented himself.

In the beginning, in that engine room, it had seemed to him, too, like an adventure, and he had felt proud. But then, Henry said, he remembered his flight was without return, that he would not see his home again, or his parents. For years, perhaps forever.

"I even cried when the ship began to move," the boy said, looking at her with dry, quick eyes.

Anja had blond hair, blue, almond-shaped eyes, high cheekbones. Henry made out her features when their faces came close, almost touching, and the girl's eyes were bright, almost feverish. He was only nineteen and far from home. At that moment he heard the sound of the ballroom door opening behind them. Then he turned.

The girl ran back in, letting the blanket fall to the floor. Henry picked it up as if it were a glass slipper. He looked at the sailor and put the blanket on a chair.

"What are you doing here?" Abbott asked. "Aren't you a third-class passenger?"

He would not let that boy get away from him again. Abbott was aware of his presence in spite of his slick way of moving among people. And so he had immediately noticed him in the ballroom, but he hadn't moved, waiting to see what he would do. And when he saw the girl go out, he had strained to see through the salt-encrusted porthole, trying to understand what that Latvian boy had to do with an aristocratic Russian. Wondering what might be waiting for them in the darkness.

But he could not hear what they were saying, and when he guessed the distance between the two was becoming too close, then, and only then, did he remember his sailor's duty and interfere, knowing that his action had forfeited a piece of the story.

He escorted the boy to the belly of the ship, amid the strong odors of sweat, food, unwashed clothes. Third-class smells. And just as he was about to leave, Abbott bent toward him, wanting somehow to cover him with his strength. "Now tell me, Goldstück, what are you doing on this ship?" he asked.

He looked hard at the boy and thought he had him in his grasp.

"I'm traveling because of work. And because I'm angry," Goldstück said.

Abbott was a man of experience, but the boy had intelligence and speed. The sailor had only curiosity. That word *angry* was all it took to divert him.

"What do you mean?" he asked.

"My boss," Goldstück said, "thinks I'm swindling him because the wheat weighs more when it leaves than when it arrives, and so the buyers pay less. He thinks I'm scheming with the shippers to rob him. But I know that's not true. So I told him to send me to Rouen. I told him I would find out what happens down here. For God's sake, I don't want anyone to call me a thief."

The boy's eyes were narrow, strong. Abbott's were wide, almost cowlike.

"You've got courage," the sailor said.

"Actually, I'm afraid. It's the first time I've ever left Latvia."

The sailor saw him as he had been that first afternoon on the bridge; he felt the need to protect him. Putting a hand on his shoulder, he said, "In any case, you can depend on me as far as London."

He said it and forgot about the secrets he was so certain the boy was harboring. And he also forgot about their day of departure, didn't think to ask him why he hadn't seen him then. But had he asked him, Goldstück probably would have had a good answer.

At last, one could imagine a thin streak of land on the horizon. It could not be distinguished with certainty, yet at the same time it could not be ignored. It was England.

Goldstück stood on the bridge, the collar of his jacket turned up as protection from the hard wind that blew from the south, pushing the ship sideways, making it slip off course. But he barely noticed.

His eyes at the moment, like that distant land, were a thin stripe; they didn't have to impress anyone. Instead he used them to scan the horizon, as if some answer were there. His stories, those true and those false, had no meaning now. He could not fill the future with fantasy as he could the past. It no longer had anything to do with Anja or the sailor Abbott; they both ended there, at the approach of that coast. They would both get off the ship and be lost in the big city, both belonging to worlds unknown to him.

And there, at the mooring of the steamship, Henry Goldstück's first objective had been accomplished: to escape from Latvia. Then what would happen?

The other travelers seemed to have definite objectives, a destination. He only had a letter addressed to someone who had already escaped, and who might not even be in any position to help
him. Perhaps his father had been right to try to stop him, to try to
convince him to stay. But he knew one could always turn back;
the important thing was to be able to leave.

Certainly, if all men were like Martin Abbott, even big like
him, protective, and easily deceived, Goldstück's future would be
auspicious. If the women all had something, even one feature
fleetingly glimpsed, of Anja and her youth, he would be happy.
And with the freedom and strength he felt inside himself he
would be able to bewitch them as he had her.

But the boy knew that the world — what waited for him beyond
the thin stretch of land that was expanding and was now as clean as
a strip of velvet — was much less hospitable than an English ship.

That was what Henry Goldstück was thinking, lost in his nineteen years, leaning on the railing of that steamship of Her Britannic Majesty Queen Victoria. And yet in spite of his worry and
uncertainty, he felt what all her life Anja had only dreamed of becoming: He felt free.

Abbott stood near the ramp, arms folded, closely watching the
passengers as they left the ship. Even those from first class who
had the right to disembark immediately, with their elegant
clothes, followed by porters carrying their leather suitcases and
trunks. Because by now he knew that Goldstück was capable of
passing unobserved with those boots of his, even in the middle of
that luxury.

He saw Anja pass by, with her mother and the servants; he
looked at the girl's Oriental eyes, which she kept lowered, almost
as though searching for something on the ground. Abbott straightened his sailor's cap and made a slight bow.

All first-class passengers had disembarked, but Goldstück was
not there.

He observed the second-class passengers: merchants, small
bourgeois who tried to assume a dignity that in reality they never

possessed. Men like Abbott, with lives like his, but without a uniform. Even among them he did not see the boy.

He waited for the people in third class to leave, with their shabby clothes, awkward packages, heavy smells. He watched them come up from the ship's belly, like rats scurrying away from a fire. Confused, uncertain, ignorant of their destiny, devoid of the strength even to question themselves.

Toward the back of one group he saw an arm, a sleeve, the flash of a profile that might have been Goldstück's. He waited for that compact mass to come closer. But the passengers crowded toward the ramp, pushing each other to descend quickly. And then the group dispersed, mixing with the others. Abbott tried to find the jacket, the profile, again. He thought he saw him, but was mistaken. Perhaps he had lost him and would never find him again.

In a few minutes they were passengers no longer, but people leaving the wharf in all directions, like a handful of sand flung to the ground.

Abbott, however, was still there, near the ramp, futilely searching below. He had lost the boy, and this time he had no hope of finding him. He leaned on the ship's railing and for the first time in years didn't feel like going home.

But he had no alternative, so he headed below to pack his duffel bag.

She kept her eyes lowered for the entire time it took to walk down the corridor, cross the ballroom, descend the ramp, and reach dry land. Always beside her mother, imitating her formal and cautious gestures, reproducing her grace and detachment. Proud of her elegant dress of striped silk, with the bodice of black velvet, the cashmere shawl on her shoulders, the bonnet tied under her chin.

She hoped somewhere, for just a moment, Henry might see her, try to approach her with a wave of his hand and comprehend the distance that now separated them, that separates an aristocrat from a young Jew. Angrily she thought back over the intimacy he had extorted from her, of the closeness of their faces, and she felt her cheeks flush with shame.

The sea, in its vastness, gave the world a breath of adventure that she now rejected because of the fear it stirred up in her, and also for its vulgarity.

When she reached the ramp and raised her skirt slightly with one hand to make the descent easier, she saw her mother salute the commander with a light nod of her head. Then she looked up for an instant, and at the officer's side she saw the sailor who had caught her with the boy. She felt even more anger and embarrassment. But fortunately the man was looking over his shoulder and did not see her.

Anja cautiously descended the ramp, hurt by not being able to show Goldstück her superiority. She left the ship without seeing his eyes again, without being able to challenge them. She felt like crying, but with the frivolity of a young girl's hate. With few tears.

Her mother noticed and touched her arm.

"Oh, darling," she said, "it has really been a wonderful trip, and I'm sorry it had to end, too. But to cry . . . doesn't that seem a little excessive?"

In the distance, beyond the wharf, some carriages were filling up with first-class passengers. The other travelers were filing out of the port. Except for the boy who stood still, with his nervous energy concentrated in his hands and neck: He was searching. He didn't look at the ship; the sailor wasn't important. He had already won that contest, because he had avoided his look, his questions, his suspicious patronage.

Instead he wanted a confirmation from the girl, some sign of her lingering embarrassment. He wanted to rob her of the assurance that money gives, the superiority of wealth. But when he managed amid the crowd of passengers to spot her Asian features, Anja was already far from him, and near, too near, the line of carriages.

Henry moved anyway, hoping to reach her. He slithered around people with the agility he had learned on shipboard, but without proceeding too quickly, because he didn't want anyone from above to have the satisfaction of catching sight of him. Only the click of his heels on the stones of the wharf could have betrayed him, but there were too many other noisy footsteps for the sound of his own boots to be recognized.

He went toward that tired and unsteady group; he came closer, certain he was nearing his goal. The entire time he didn't give a thought as to what good it would do, what gestures or words he might muster once he was beside her.

He was a slender man, Henry Goldstück; just the same, sweat began to run down his temples while he dragged his suitcase, leaning to one side, almost running with his short, quick steps, his eyes searching for a bonnet, breathing hard through his mouth. Lost in that physical effort, how could he have thought of words?

Finally he saw her, one hand on the carriage window, the other lifting her skirt in order to place her foot securely on the footboard. The trunks had been loaded, her mother had already climbed up. With a stillness that betrayed her impatience, Anja was waiting for her mother to get settled before she climbed aboard beside her. Then the girl turned, and for a few seconds she looked around indifferently at the people behind her. Henry was immersed in that crowd, was a part of it; no one could have picked him out. Perhaps if he had thought of a gesture, or an action, or a shout, she might have noticed him, but the boy did nothing. In fact, he stopped short, aware by then that he had lost her. And he thought the very act of running after her was a sign of weakness, for in any case it wouldn't have been a surprise; it was better not to have reached her.

The window closed and the carriage started off, forcing a man to step out of the way to let it pass. Goldstück set his suitcase on the ground and wiped his forehead with a handkerchief. A cold wind suddenly chilled his back. The first part of his journey had ended.

Rouen 1878

Regarding a Great Idea

*A*NOTHER PORT. Men shouting, moving about, goods being unloaded. An enormous mechanism without rest. The whistles of the sirens, like the breaths of giants, dictating the rhythm.

A port like any other. But now no one with the time or the desire to busy himself with Henry Goldstück, no one to notice his presence, to wring his secrets from him. He, however, could observe the others at his leisure.

For some hours he had been standing there on the wharf watching the ships, casually, without any objective. Then his eyes narrowed, curious. It wasn't the men who attracted his attention, not their frantic activity that struck him, but a thin cascade of wheat falling into the water between the side of a ship and the wharf. The unloading operations proceeded slowly: The grain was brought up from the ship's hold and turned into a loading chute that carried it to the wharf's weighing station; but the chute moved, wavered, maybe even had cracks in it, and a substantial part of the load was lost in the water. No one seemed concerned about it, because the buyers would pay according to the weight verified at the port of arrival and not on the basis of what was declared at departure. So the loss did not hurt them. The only one who lost out was the seller, who wasn't there — nor was anyone else who could protect his interests.

That sailing ship had come from Latvia, which was the reason Goldstück had stopped to watch it, and he had noticed the trickle of grain falling overboard. It seemed wasteful to him, and it bothered him that no one tried to stop it.

Henry had just arrived from England. In an attempt to forget his country, he had become a watch salesman in London, something he considered more modern than the expanse of fields, lakes, and forests from which he had come, more up-to-date than the buying and selling of grain that had occupied him up until then. But perhaps even he was too dated for that business and he soon gave it up. Furthermore, he knew no one who could help him in a country so different from his own, in a city so crowded, its character so gray.

Goldstück realized that his roots still had a hold on him. Even though torn from the earth, uprooted by flight, they continued to inhibit his actions. Separation is a slow process, in which there is always room for nostalgia and regret.

Maybe the French coast, he had thought, where so many ships from his country went. Perhaps it would seem more familiar. Even that city of Rouen, which he had never visited, but which he had heard mentioned at least twice during the voyage to London, would greet him more warmly. So he left by sea again, this time on a short trip to that river port.

That was why he was watching the Latvian ship. It was why he considered that grain to be his, too, and watching it sink in the port waters was intolerable.

So he went on board and asked to speak to the captain. A sailor led him to the command deck along the little bridge crammed with objects and people; there was even a rope stretched from one mast to another for drying the crew's shirts and jackets.

The captain, a bald, courteous man, replied to his questions with the readiness due a fellow countryman. He spoke of the voyage and the cargo, the sailors' weariness and the merchants' indifference.

"That loss of grain?" he said. "Certainly I have seen it, but that's not unusual. It happens all the time. And no one has ever objected."

He rummaged through the papers for the information Goldstück requested. Yes, the load of grain belonged to a cultivator from Courland, his name . . . his name . . .

He held the paper out to the boy, his finger pointing to the name. Goldstück broke into a smile. Not one of his hearty, sincere laughs, but a sort of sneer that came from the observation of how the world was sometimes both unpredictable and small, for that cultivator from Courland happened to be Goldstück's distant relative.

The captain looked at the boy without understanding the reason for his reaction, the meaning of that expression on his face, and he asked him, "What are you doing in Rouen?"

His voice contained a hint of suspicion, a reflection of doubt.

"I intend to defend the interests of the landowners of Courland," was Goldstück's answer.

The captain looked down at his papers again.

Henry wrote to that uncle of sorts, an old man whose face he could hardly remember, offering to represent him at the Rouen port: He would keep a close watch so that neither chance nor men could go on cheating him.

"The small percentage that I ask," he wrote, "will cost you much less than what you are losing now through neglect and the French merchants' bad faith. What I propose is not a favor for a distant nephew in search of work, but a mutually advantageous business arrangement."

Goldstück had not the slightest doubt that his proposition would be accepted; he merely had to wait for the letter of reply, and he allowed himself to borrow some money, which he was sure he could repay. He also bought a new pair of Western-style shoes and a brown felt hat.

―⌀

When the day came for him to check the first cargo arriving from Courland, Goldstück was at the wharf before dawn. He turned up his jacket collar as protection from the dampness the wind brought in from the ocean, and he scanned the greenish horizon of the sky as though it were an omen. The ship, a rather dilapidated wooden three-master, entered the port when the sun was already rising behind the houses on the old shore. Goldstück stood motionless, observing the ship's berthing maneuvers with apparent indifference. He then went to the gangplank and asked to come on board.

He presented his credentials to the Russian captain and politely spoke his language, though his eyes shifted from one point to another on the bridge, sensing a threat. He carefully checked the instruments necessary for the unloading. He scrutinized every detail with an attention as annoying as it was necessary, in order to ensure the crew's efficiency. Then he disembarked and inspected the ship's broadsides to verify that everything complied with the regulations. And all the grain of that transport ended up in the sacks of the buyers. The only detectable weight loss was the physiological one, due to the grain drying out during the voyage.

After that day something changed at the Rouen port, so much so that the little Jew from the East, whom no Frenchman had ever been eager to salute, began to see many hats raised when he passed by.

In the months that followed it was no surprise when other Latvian and Russian cultivators began to ask him to do for them what he had done for his relative. The boy, who had started wearing a mustache and long sideburns to make himself appear older, felt he had invented a new occupation. As ancient as his land and as modern as his flight. Suited to the sharpness of his gaze and the swiftness of his replies. And very Jewish also, seeing that it had to do with commerce and money.

He opened a little office with windows overlooking the wharf where everything had started, where he first had the idea, and he often stood at the window watching the slow maneuvering of the ships, taking in the sounds and smells of the port as the goods were unloaded. He observed them with attention and pleasure, as if in some way those ships belonged to him, were in his sphere of control.

The story of the Jew with eyes too sharp to be deceived made the rounds of the port and a good part of the city. His work kept expanding. Goldstück saw that it was becoming something different; the percentage he asked was low, but if he could make his work seem like a kind of guarantee, an insurance for the person wanting to buy or sell grain without being there, in short, a complete surveillance of the goods, then the earnings could be huge. He realized it was his opportunity to make a different life for himself.

He didn't waste it.

He didn't look for Frenchmen, he didn't trust them, he wanted people like himself, people who had come from somewhere else, who had experienced the same difficulties, and who had the fury of someone wanting to better himself.

First he found Johann Hainzé, a German of few words who had loaned him money those first months at Rouen. He had a mustache as stiff as his back and splendid penmanship. So Goldstück, who had no love for the pen, put him in charge of accounting and correspondence, and kept for himself everything he could do with his eyes and his gift for conversation.

At Rouen, on December 12, 1878, before a notary as thin as Henry but without his flashing eyes, the firm of Goldstück, Hainzé and Company was established.

They left that office on a windy afternoon, in light that was fading but dry as only the cold can make it. His new partner suggested they go have a drink to celebrate the occasion, and he agreed while buttoning up his new overcoat.

But when Hainzé set off, Goldstück did not follow immediately. He watched Hainzé walking, head hunched down to protect himself from the sea wind. Then he looked up at the sky where white threads of clouds ran southward. He felt free from Latvia's grip. It would no longer hold him back. He knew, with absolute certainty, that he was on his way to becoming a wealthy man.

IX

Geneva 1996

Cause and Effect

*T*HIS HAS BEEN a story, over many years, of ports, of sea voyages. Of dreams of water.

As if those Rotterdam canals from which everything departed had continued to affect the lives of the van Straatens, pushing them toward watery places, as if events ran like rivers, or returned like waves, varying in imperceptible and inexorable ways.

In this story, for a long time, there were ships but no trains, canals but no streets, sailors but no soldiers.

Goldstück's destiny was also made of water. His life and fortune were created on and by water. But this is certainly not the reason why I have told his story. Because no two seas are identical, no surface reflections are repeated in the same way.

No, I did it because I was convinced that although the relationship between cause and effect is infinitely more complex than it appears if reconstructed in a laboratory, there exists a connection between his life and mine. This story would not have been written in Italian if his watch business had panned out, or if his distant relative hadn't agreed to be represented by him, or in short if in Rouen one day in December, Henry Goldstück had not decided to establish his grain surveillance firm.

The years pass so rapidly: Those that we live flatten out, those that do not concern us distance themselves with fissures so wide and deep as to appear impassable. In my family Goldstück's life had become a vague legend, indefinite, almost illegible, even if it was not much farther removed than a man's lifetime.

Only the name, which for my benefit was translated as "piece of gold," and which I found very suitable for a man of fabulous wealth, only that was certain. All the rest fell into obscurity, was fogged with uncertainty. It was fading away forever.

Sometimes even frescoes, especially those on building facades, seem totally lost. Rain, variations of temperature, automobile exhaust provoke chemical reactions that spread like a patina over the paint until nothing can be seen but gray stucco; nothing to make one think that something was once painted there. It takes the patience and precision of restorers and the competence of scientists to make the artwork reemerge, to find its colors. And to the viewer it seems a miracle, a conjuring trick. Almost as if another hand had come to paint frescoes identical to those that were obliterated. Instead it is the originals that were hidden, as though dozing, under the surface.

A corporation, especially if Swiss, is also patient and precise, though not for the same reasons as a restorer. Its memory is located in papers and files, and therefore can be recovered and reconstructed.

In fact it was through the last descendant of Goldstück, Hainzé and Co., a solid multinational firm with headquarters in Geneva, on the lakeshore a few yards from the water, that I was able to obtain information about the life and history of Henry Goldstück. I found it in two typescripts, results of the research commissioned for the company's centenary celebration and never published. But kept, oh yes, in some cabinet for the sake of good order.

As for the chemicals I used to recover the brightness of the original colors, I won't say. It is, after all, a professional secret.

From among the many coincidences that I could choose, since basically they exist only through our will to find them, the one I emphasize here concerns the year 1878: the year of the foundation of Goldstück, Hainzé and Co., but also the year George van Straaten was born.

George was Hartog's fourth child. He was nine years old when his mother died, and only two years older when his father was remarried to Marie Bloch of Winschoten, a little village in northwest Holland, on the border with Germany.

I believe these circumstances forced George to draw on the strength that children generally keep hidden or do not know they possess. To show a self-confidence that Emanuel, his older brother, the one bearing the family name, was incapable of finding in himself. In short, George had to grow up in a hurry, and then forget he had done so.

The growth of Goldstück, Hainzé and Co. was also very rapid. The first branch was opened at Le Havre, where Goldstück met the girl who would become his wife and the mother of his only child. But soon other branches were opened outside France. One, for example, at Rotterdam.

It is from there, from the same canals where I began this story, that I must start again in order to connect Goldstück's story with that of my family. To find again Hartog and his numerous children now grown. And afterward, to move eastward, in the direction opposite that taken by Goldstück, and many years away from his voyage at the beginning of the new century.

At least that is what I should do and will do, but not immediately. Because haste in restorations causes irreparable damage, and it is good to finish working on one fresco before moving to the next. But above all, because every story should be told as if it were unique, the last one and the best. Otherwise the respect that the pen must have, the gentle touch that should be used in bringing to light the lives of others, would be useless.

So it is necessary to give a conclusion to what I have said about Henry Goldstück so far.

X

Monte Carlo 1928

The Arrival of the Rally

*A*LL THINGS considered, he could say that the world had not shown itself to be any less hospitable than that ship en route from Saint Petersburg to London more than fifty years earlier. So it had not been too difficult to deal with men and lead them in the desired direction, as he had done with Martin Abbott, nor too complicated to find Anja's suspicious curiosity in the conduct of other women.

Not that everything was always so clear-cut and obvious, nor everything recognizable, similar to other things already seen, and therefore easy to classify in its proper file. In fact, surprise had been part of his life, had made it better; even now that he was more than seventy years old, even the previous evening in a dark movie theater.

But Henry Goldstück had managed to deal with every situation, to respond with the necessary effectiveness, always finding the right action, the appropriate words, the best demeanor. In this way his had been a happy journey.

Sitting in a spacious wicker armchair on the sunny terrace of his apartment on the fourth floor of a building on Boulevard des

Moulins, he looked at the sea as he had done thousands of times in his life.

But this was not the gray sea of his early days; it did not know the relentless tides of the English Channel or the lakelike stillness of the Baltic. It was a warm sea, intense as the blue of the sky, serene. A southern sea.

Even the port was different from the many he had known through his work: made for rich men's ships that unloaded only passengers and sailors, a port of almost transparent water and fashionable restaurants.

That afternoon, just back from Paris, he had been led to the terrace by Renée, and had remained in silence, almost aloof, well aware that she would not understand the reason for that distance and would wonder if it was caused by the torpor of old age or by embarrassment over his negative opinion of the movie.

Renée was young, only twenty-seven, and appeared much younger once she had stopped behaving like a sophisticated lady of the Parisian theater. Goldstück had felt a tenderness for her, seeing her squirming in her chair during the projection of the film, lighting and snuffing out her long cigarettes. He, however, had been still. And afterward, when supper had been suggested, he had let Renée go alone. He was asleep when she returned to the hotel.

Renée woke him and begged to leave immediately for the south, with an insistence that made Goldstück immediately comply. This time it was she who slept, for the entire length of the trip. So they had not yet discussed the movie between themselves, and the more time passed the more difficult it became.

Now, while Renée leaned against the railing with her face turned to the sea, those arms crossed over her chest, those hands gripping her elbows, she expressed the same nervousness as during the showing of the film — her impatience in waiting for Henry's opinion.

How could he explain to her that for him it wasn't as much a matter of judging something as remembering a life from which she was unavoidably excluded, a world that she did not know and could never understand?

Memory, for Goldstück, was an old-people's vice, something he had always ignored having: a defect that must not harm Renée's youth.

Over the years, for decades, the small firm of Goldstück, Hainzé and Co. had become a conglomeration of companies scattered around various countries, with branches in the major ports of the world. Its growth had been unstoppable amid terrible economic crises; it had even brilliantly survived a world war and had enriched Goldstück and all his associates. For some time there had been no need for his serpent's eyes and intuition; stability and organization were more useful. And Goldstück had become bored. Little by little he delegated the management of the business to others and decided it would be worthwhile to spend the money he had accumulated over the years, or at least part of it.

For him, play and serious activities had always been intertwined, ultimately becoming indistinguishable and giving a purpose to his life: that of participating in a challenge. In the end it was a challenge that had brought him to that terrace facing the Mediterranean Sea.

The first time he saw Monte Carlo, Henry had been at the wheel of a Hispano-Suiza, participating in the rally that went from Paris to the principality of Monaco. He had been traveling all night, hunched over the wheel, straining to see unexpected deviations in the road.

Then he started to descend. Down the Esterel, plunging his foot down on the brake pedal only for the curves, to gain some time.

The fact that those brakes gave out only after the last curve, on the first flat stretch for miles, Goldstück always considered a miracle. He had let the wheels continue turning silently until the car stopped by itself at the side of the road. Ahead of him was Monte Carlo. He got out of the car, trying to catch his breath, to quiet the terror that still pounded in his temples, and he had looked at the city as though it were a mirage, a lucky destiny.

From that time on he knew he belonged to Monte Carlo, owed it something, and in a few years he moved there.

_o_

Renée felt herself trembling. She didn't think she could hold a cigarette in her hand, though she wanted to smoke. Images of the movie had again aroused in her the same power, the same uncontrollable tension she had felt during its filming. Why didn't Henry stop her trembling now, why didn't he find the words and gestures necessary to make her feel like her normal self again?

The movie had taken months to make, sheer torture, a continual tension, and the frivolity of her Parisian evenings, of theater life, had vanished. Now she knew it hadn't been something fleeting, but for always, because watching the screening had made her fall back into that state of uncertainty, almost of madness.

Facing the sun, warm and sinking lower on the horizon, she tried to hold herself tightly with her own hands, as if they could thaw the deep inner chill that was making her shake so violently.

Henry remained seated in his wicker chair in silence, that intolerable silence that had been with them since the end of the showing. But she needed to be saved, and put aside her pride. She turned, smiled in desperation, and blurted out the first foolish thing that came to mind, knowing if she thought about it she wouldn't be able to do it; she was trembling too much. She said, "Dreyer is very satisfied with the movie."

Goldstück nodded. "Oh, it really is an excellent film," he said, "and you were very good."

More false words, Renée thought. Why was he so distant, why didn't he help her? Didn't he see that icy chill gripping her, strangling her?

She turned again toward the sea. She looked at her fingers and saw they were steady, as if the trembling hadn't reached her extremities; perhaps it had settled in her throat, therefore allowing her to use her hands. She took a cigarette, put it in her mouth, and lit it.

Did it matter if Goldstück's words were sincere or not? Wasn't it enough that he had said them, that he had broken that intangible silence that enveloped him?

She looked at the sun, still bright enough to dazzle and to

allow her to ask a question, as though it were natural to start again from the same point, pretending that nothing had happened.

Because she was trembling, but he didn't see her trembling.

꙳

Renée turned and smiled. Goldstück remembered how he had seen her ten years earlier on a stage, seduced by those high cheekbones that had a particular meaning only to him.

He wanted to explain the reason for his silence, to calm her fears about her acting ability, as he had done many times before, but he was forty-five years older than she and couldn't explain the melancholy instilled in him by the film, empty as the anguish of time gone by, and at the same time sweet with the symmetry of the circumstances it portrayed.

"Dreyer is very satisfied with the movie," Renée said, no longer possessing the strength to stop herself.

"Oh," Goldstück said, "it really is an excellent film. And you were very good."

He felt he was lying, even if, in part, he was telling the truth. In part, because he didn't understand many things in the movie, and he wondered how the audience could understand them, wondered what sense it made to hide what should be revealed. But he really thought Renée was good.

She turned back to the sea and lit a cigarette. Goldstück saw her bare neck; after her hair had been shaved for the movie she hadn't let it grow back like before. It was for her, for Renée Falconetti, that he had taken part in financing the movie, although in the beginning he had never even heard of this great Danish director everyone was talking about. He had accepted the risk as a challenge, reassured because the production company's name, Société Générale de Films, recalled one of his most important insurance companies: Société Générale de Surveillance.

But most of all he had welcomed the director's idea for the subject, without remembering that Joan of Arc's trial had taken place at Rouen, like the beginning of his adventure.

What did a holy warrior have to do with a little green-eyed Jew? What did a battle of faith and principles have to do with his conquest of a place in the grain industry?

And yet that symmetry with his own life struck him, as if before and after these two interludes at Rouen nothing important had happened — years to be forgotten, or perhaps not even lived. And in the middle, a perceived normalcy that the death of his wife had interrupted.

That was what he had seen in the film, what he had found again in the projection room; that was why he had been silent, incapable of a trite comment or an affectionate gesture. But how could he have explained that to Renée? There was no way to describe what he felt, no one would understand, just as there was no one who could see that his present-day lover's cheekbones were the same as Anja's; no one who could know that those two girls were the same age when he met them. The most people could say was that the actress was just a little older than his granddaughter, the daughter of his daughter, and judge the affair to be an old man's folly. No, no one could understand. His secrets were contained in the belly of an English ship demolished for some time now.

"Do you really believe what you just said?" Renée asked him.

Goldstück suspected he had spoken out loud without realizing it. So he replied with another question.

"About what?"

"About the movie and me."

He motioned for her to come nearer, trying to ignore the light trembling of his own hand, the swollen veins, the tendons showing through his dry skin.

"Have I ever lied?" he said. But even that was a hackneyed phrase, a way out. Goldstück knew that everyone lied, that men didn't exist without lies, little or big as they may be.

She shook her head, then crouched down next to him and leaned her forehead against his legs. That contact, the warmth of the sun, and the sparkling water flowed into him like a hot breeze.

"Renée," was all he said, in a whisper, almost absentmindedly. *It's madness, really,* he thought, *our madness. But it's still the only thing worth living for.*

She raised her face and looked at him.

"I like your eyes," she said.

And he was reminded that the green in his eyes was fading, that his eyes were almost always too bright, with the whites reddened, and they seemed smaller. He thought they still had the same power: snake's eyes, a magnet. He closed them.

Her hand rose slowly along his inner thigh, to where the hot breath became blood. And Goldstück did not move, did not open his eyes, said nothing.

When he awoke he was lying in bed. Outside it was growing dark. He felt cold and covered himself with the sheet. Renée was not there.

How much time did he have left? What should he have renounced in order to save his life? He was not a saint, he was inclined to surrender. But when an adversary's cards are guessed instead of known already, then the hand is lost. His intuition had dimmed like the color of his eyes. And now the final accounting had arrived: Memory was really a defect, an illness of old age, serious and deadly.

Perhaps it was something he had dreamed, even if he couldn't remember, that had left him with this feeling of anxiety, almost blocking out Renée's gestures, the pleasure she had given him. He had a bitter taste in his mouth, and he would have liked to cover it with a sweeter flavor.

From Rouen to Rouen. It was better to keep seeing it like that, to feel the fullness of a life made of what he had wanted. Of work and women, primarily. To say it could seem trivial, even common, but it depended on what work, what women. As far as he was concerned it seemed worth the effort. For that amount of money. Or for a question of cheekbones, perhaps.

He dressed without looking at his body, almost happily, now that the drowsiness had dissipated and the thought of what had happened between the terrace and the bedroom had returned to him, now that he heard Renée's footsteps in the next room.

He had tricked Martin Abbott, he had held tight to life. Let others try to do something better.

He burst out laughing.

—☙

She got up and sat looking at him from the edge of the bed. In his half-open mouth, in his heavy breathing, she seemed to recognize for the first time the signs of approaching death. Goldstück was old and Renée was aware of it, even though she would have preferred to ignore this frightening realization. Because if even Henry's strength and certainty were subject to the laws of time, then who could protect her?

She felt envious of him, for his independence, for everything that others didn't know about his life, for his ability to travel so far from the place where he was born. And she envied him also because she knew his most important possession was his ability to face life on his own terms; he had never given in to anyone, not even to her.

Now she would like to turn back, to before that damned movie, before those long months of filming had turned her upside down. To the time when Goldstück had been only a part of her daily performance in the Parisian world. It was ridiculous, after all, that for her, an actress, it had become impossible to pretend.

She stood up and left the room. Out on the terrace she leaned again on the railing and looked at the sea spread before her. The sun had completely disappeared beyond the horizon; daylight was fading. A light, almost cold, breeze came from the hills at her back. Renée understood the freedom granted to foreigners, to strangers, and understood that she would have to leave, that only a journey, at least as long as Goldstück's first one, would save her from the phantoms eating her alive. But she also wondered if she would ever have the strength to leave.

The world was losing the sharpness and precision that objects have in the daytime. Soon it would be suppertime. The maid in the kitchen must have already begun her preparations.

Renée went back into the house to wake Henry. She was crossing the parlor when she heard his laughter coming from the bedroom. For a moment she thought everything would get better.

Henry Goldstück died at Monte Carlo, satisfied with himself and his life, in January of 1929.

Renée Falconetti never performed in another movie after *The Passion of Joan of Arc*. She died in Buenos Aires in 1946.

PART II

The Time of Family Life

The Book of Family Life

_—ᴗ XI ᴗ—_

Rotterdam 1901

The Shame

*I*N THE BEGINNING there were no thoughts, only desperation.
Nothing that might be cured: a dull wound whose pain
overwhelmed all reason. He saw no solution, but only the shame
that had returned like a family curse.

Hartog could not speak or move. He remained seated, his
hand resting on the arm of the divan, his wife in front of him
talking, uselessly repeating what she had already said many times.

"I didn't notice anything. I didn't understand."

She had met him at the door on his return from the office, and
had almost pushed him into the parlor: There was news, terrible
news.

Marie's hair was down and she grasped at it as though wanting
to pull it out by the roots. Nothing like this had ever happened before in their quiet and regular life, a life made up of restrained
and routine gestures, without hidden meaning.

There they were, alone in their small parlor, with Marie trying
to talk to him, to explain, but the words wouldn't come out of her
mouth.

Hartog asked which of his eight children — the seven from his
first marriage plus Gerrit, the only child they had together —

which one was dead and how did it happen. He could not imagine anything else to justify such anguish. He shouted, "Who is it! Tell me! Who is dead?"

But no one was dead.

The story came out of Marie's mouth a bit at a time, interrupted by sobs, by justifications, and by that continually repeated phrase: *I didn't notice anything.* Hartog knew he had always asked a great deal from her; he knew her life had not been easy, dealing every day with another woman's seven children, whom she had to raise as though her own. And some so old as to be nearly adults.

She had taken to Emanuel, for even though he was the oldest, he faced the world with the dreamy casualness of the weak. And it wasn't by chance that he had ended up marrying one of Marie's nieces. But with the girls, Zippora and Rosa, everything had been more complicated.

The older girl had a strong temperament, a desire for freedom that often brought her in direct conflict with Marie. It had been she, after Mina's death and before her father's remarriage, who acted almost as a mother to her younger brothers and sisters, and in fact they called her *moesje,* little mama. Perhaps this was what alienated her from Marie, who certainly would have tried to placate the girl's anger and encourage a better attitude. For a long time it seemed this was not possible; the oldest of Hartog's daughters had made a vocation of smoldering with an inextinguishable resentment toward her own fate.

But in the end an answer had come, brought by a slender and intelligent boy, Levie Fles: It's not our parents we must fight, but the injustices of the world. The answer was called socialism, or something like it, and it overcame every obstacle — even that of their religion, their belonging to a people always separated from others. And now every boundary must be abolished, and diversity used as an instrument for enriching others and themselves, until every distinction was erased. Thus they decided to take different names: Zippora became Celine and Levie became Louis. Marie and Hartog hadn't understood this change, so different from their habits and values, and yet they had accepted it because Celine seemed happy.

Rosa, on the other hand, seemed calmer and less rebellious. Reserved, at times peevish, but not intentionally so. She stayed home and didn't have many friends. This didn't worry Marie much, except when she remembered that Rosa was no longer a girl and no one had yet asked for her hand. Aside from that, everything seemed to be running smoothly; that was why she hadn't noticed, why she hadn't understood.

Hartog sat motionless, as though crushed by a responsibility he had not foreseen, for which he was not prepared. He needed help, but had no one to advise him. How could it have happened? Perhaps everything had begun to unravel when one of his sons left Rotterdam, left what was known and familiar: the world as it had always appeared to the van Straaten family. He sorely missed George. He wished that he were there, that he might see his happy face, that George would, as always, find a solution. But he was far away, in an unknown city, on the shore of a sea that Hartog could not even imagine.

And now all the rules and the values that had shaped Hartog's life seemed to have lost their hold. Perhaps it was that new century of the Christian calendar that was harming the Jews, even those like him who kept aloof in order to avoid problems and indiscreet looks.

When she finished recounting what had happened to Rosa, Marie remained silent, hands over her face, as though not wishing to see her husband. Hartog lifted his arm and stretched it toward her. But he did not touch her; it seemed impossible to do. He was more than sixty years old and felt tired. That was why the news had shattered him, why he couldn't find thoughts, but only desperation.

His hand stopped a short distance from Marie's face and then fell back on the arm of the divan.

"It's my fault," Hartog said, "and it's up to me to set it right."

They could not have known, they could not have understood. And Rosa did not have the strength, nor would she ever, to explain. Perhaps if Peter had been different, if in addition to his eyes, his broad shoulders, his wide smile, she had seen the courage and will to undertake together a painful and necessary discussion, then she might have been able to talk with her father.

But Peter was not that kind of boy; he had the decisiveness, certainly, of an energetic youth, but was so irresponsible and rash that he could never, even had he wanted to, wade into a battle with an uncertain outcome. A battle, perhaps, that he had no intention of winning in the first place.

Peter was like the countryside beyond the Rotterdam gates: beautiful, level, and oblivious. That was why Rosa had said yes. Not even said, she had merely accepted his gestures silently, such as when he forcefully took her hand to lead her, almost drag her, past the streets and houses, where the canals seemed like orderly streams.

She knew she had taken the first, imperceptible step. Or perhaps she did not know it, but certainly felt she had, and this too made her weak, incapable of reacting. Because she could not lay the blame on Peter.

It had happened in the morning, on many of those mornings when she left the house unhurried, unanxious, and yet with a feeling of oppression, or more precisely, annoyance, only annoyance, with a sense of emptiness she could not define.

She had never shared Zippora's anger, her rebelliousness that came from some certainty unknown to her. Yet there existed an emptiness, an absence, an inconsequential accumulation of years, as if life consisted only of identical days continually repeated. Perhaps Rosa had thought for a long time that that was just the way it was, that there was nothing more to expect, not even a husband.

But something, even that emptiness itself, evidently filled her eyes at times, on the street while accompanying her stepmother, or when she went alone on some errand. Perhaps for that reason, beyond her shabby dresses, her curly hair already a little sparse, Peter had seen something that urged him on.

He stood behind the counter in his father's shop selling skeins of wool and cotton, passementerie and spools of thread, and carefully observing those who entered. Peter almost always waited on the girls, and the girls were happy that he did. Rosa, without meaning to, without being aware of it, had offered him her emptiness and even a slight sign, a barely noticeable contact. It was she who beckoned him to come closer, until she barely touched him with her hand, but then she became confused, and almost ran away.

The fact that it had been he, with an air of complicity and arrogance, with the certainty of one who believes he has chosen, who invited her in a low voice to the shop doorway, asking for a meeting far from that counter and the watchful eyes; the fact that in the end it had been he who took the final step, who decided the time and place, was actually of little importance.

"Rosa is pregnant," Marie finally said in a weak voice.

Hartog felt he was dying, and yet he found the strength to ask one last question.

"Who is the father?"

Marie wrung her hands with such force that her knuckles turned white. She did not answer immediately. And when she did she could not look him in the eyes.

"Peter," she said in a voice almost hoarse from the effort. "Peter, the haberdasher's son."

"But he's not Jewish," Hartog said.

Marie made no reply.

"He's not Jewish," Hartog shouted.

It was then that the shame rose with the strength of the wind when it blows from the north, when the gale compels sailors to stay home, when the port stops dead and water rises in the canals from the rush of the tide. Hartog no longer felt anger, only desperation.

Marie remained silent, bent, her face in her hands. Hartog moved his hand, almost to caress her face, but let it fall once again on the arm of her chair.

"It's my fault," he said, "and it's up to me to set it right."

How he would do it he did not know. Marie, however, thought he had found a solution and looked at him, a slight glimmer of hope in her eyes. Hartog could not stand her gaze and wanted her to go away.

"Call Rosa and tell her to come here. But first leave me alone for a few minutes."

Marie nodded, got out of the chair, and left the room.

She looked for words to express her feelings and realized there were none; it was impossible to link the happiness she felt with Peter to the desperation of her stony father facing her. Unconsciously Rosa's hands went to her stomach. She could almost feel the roundness of her pregnancy begun only three months ago.

"I thought the shame brought on the family by your uncle Benjamin had not touched this house. That the work, the instruction I've tried to give you, my example, could help you choose a just life.

"Certainly your mother's death . . . and yet Marie has done everything, everything she could, with affection and devotion . . . and I, as much as I could.

"No! Neither she nor I deserve what we must bear today."

Rosa listened but did not understand. Because in spite of the innuendos over the years, she had never understood exactly what had caused her uncle Benjamin's shame. Above all, she didn't believe it possible that the joy and pleasure that Peter gave her, that intensity of feeling experienced previously only in the grief over her mother's death, could provoke shame and desperation. And yet she knew, she understood now, that no one would allow her to accept that pregnancy as a natural fact, and that Peter wouldn't marry her.

So she bowed her head and did not reply to her father's words, merely saying, "I'll do what you decide for me, whatever it is."

Her father rose from the divan and placed a hand on her head, almost timidly. Then, as though regretting his own weakness, he took her by an arm and raised her up.

"You will stay in the house," he said angrily. "You will see no one, talk to no one. This thing must be kept secret."

—◌

If the elderly Polak were still alive perhaps he could have talked to him. But the owner of the fabric company had been dead for some time, and his sons, though serious and scrupulous, lacked their father's authoritativeness. Hartog also thought of turning to Emanuel, who now lived in Amsterdam, or of contacting George, who must be in Odessa or Rostov-on-Don, but Rosa's situation could not be summarized in a telegram.

Hartog slept little that night, forcing himself to lie quietly in bed so as not to disturb Marie, who had finally fallen asleep next to him, destroyed by tension and anxiety. Hartog thought at length; simple, linear thoughts. He thought about his grandfather, Hartog Alexander, and their name that was almost identical, which in some way had been entrusted to him; he thought it his duty to remedy this situation and save his family's reputation; he thought he must assume his responsibilities, as he had done on the day he went to work in place of his brother Benjamin. Hartog thought at length, and then toward dawn he slept.

In the morning he sent a note to the office saying he didn't feel well and would not be able to go to work that day, one of the few times in more than forty years that he had missed work. Still, he was sorry to have lied. He dressed in his dark suit, put on his stiff hat to keep his head covered in the rabbi's presence, and went to the synagogue.

He was not a very observant Jew, but he felt he belonged to a people, and belonging was a privilege. So he had decided that the rabbi, known by all as a studious and just man, was the only person who could give him counsel, who could offer him the best solution.

In the street the noise and movement of people and objects surprised him, as if the interruption caused by the shame in his soul should have spread over the entire city. Instead Rotterdam was proceeding with the same rhythm as any other day of the year, moving about in the canals and streets, with its barges and trams, indifferent and calm as if nothing had happened.

Hartog, too, wore the same expression as always, so no one

could have guessed how different this day was from all the others for him. He walked with his usual pace, with the silent reserve that made him almost transparent, that allowed him to pass unobserved among people. And the shame, there in that confusion, became so secret that Hartog managed to forget it for long stretches at a time.

The rabbi bade him to sit across from him, with the strange, unsmiling kindness that Hartog knew so well. He was a German Jew, Aaron Fink, who had officiated for many years in the Rotterdam synagogue. By now he spoke good Dutch, but the way in which he aspirated the consonants, with the dry hardness of his mother tongue, betrayed his origins.

"Well, Hartog, you asked to see me and I am happy you are here. You haven't been to the synagogue for some time, and it's already something that you haven't forgotten your poor rabbi."

Hartog expected the reproach and didn't reply, knowing he was in the wrong, and at the same time he was certain the rabbi would not have understood his reasons, and rightfully so. So he limited himself to a nod.

The rabbi had received him in his house, amid massive, dark furniture that intimidated Hartog even more than the words of blame. He remained reticent to speak, while the rabbi remained silent.

Finally Fink spoke again, trying to overcome Hartog's embarrassment.

"How are your children?" he asked.

Hartog did not yet feel ready to face the reason he had come. But he had eight children, four boys and four girls, so it was not difficult for him to gain time.

"They are already leaving home," Hartog said. "Zippora and Emanuel are married and live in Amsterdam. And George has been working in Russia for a year. I was so used to having them around that I miss them a lot."

The rabbi nodded. He knew Hartog's family well. He had presided at each boy's bar mitzvah and recited the Kaddish for Mina's death. He knew more about them than Hartog imagined, but he looked interested, almost as if that information were new to him. Then he said, "Don't forget that other children still live with you. And that marriages guarantee the continuation of your descendants, the continuation of your name. Doesn't Emanuel have a son named after you?"

Thus Hartog understood that Fink knew everything he had just said, that the man knew every Jew in the Rotterdam community, and he decided it was not possible to vie with a rabbi.

"His name is not exactly like mine," he said. "They call him Henry, which is the same name, but according to their . . ."

The rabbi stopped him with a motion of his hand, as if the explanation were unnecessary.

"It is up to you," he continued. "It is up to you to keep the family united as it should be. To do it you don't need to live in the same house or even in the same city."

Hartog knew the rabbi was right, but he also felt that his calm reasonableness arose from the distance that separated his world from the daily life of a clerk like him, from a life in which transcendence kept its distance and did not manifest itself except for rare and sudden epiphanies, only to disappear again. But certainly it was true that it was still up to Hartog to keep the family united and to resolve the problem that tormented him.

Five children were still at home, and he had to speak about one of them to the rabbi, who was now looking at him with an almost imperceptible smile as he stroked his beard. That man, now elderly, was waiting for Hartog to say what he had to say, he was waiting patiently, as his role required.

And Hartog, in his dark suit and hat, tried to escape his eyes, moving his own gaze to the candlestick with seven branches that stood on a chest against the wall. For the rabbi was scrutinizing him so intensely he could not conquer his timidity and get the words out of his mouth.

Hartog would have preferred everything to unfold after a question from the rabbi, but that question did not come. He turned uncertainly toward Fink, speaking before their eyes met.

"I came about Rosa."

He said this without being able to add another thing.

"What happened to her?" the rabbi asked, almost sweetly, leaning toward him.

"She is pregnant," Hartog said.

Aaron Fink lowered his gaze. And only then did Hartog find the strength to tell everything. "The person responsible is a boy I don't know much about, but what little I know I don't like. He is frivolous and unmotivated. I don't think he has any intention of marrying her, and even if he had"— he lowered his voice until it became a whisper —"he is not Jewish."

Rosa left with Marie for Winschoten two days later, following the rabbi's suggestion to send her away from Rotterdam. She would spend the term of her pregnancy there. In the meantime a husband had to be found, a good Jewish boy who was also willing to take on the unborn child.

Almost all of Marie's family still lived there, in that little village in the north, and they were well acquainted with other families in the Jewish community, so Marie did not feel it would be difficult to find someone interested in marrying Rosa.

Rosa had made no objection, convinced that it wouldn't be right, that she must accept the decisions of others, as if that were the only way to lessen their pain, even though that pain remained distant and incomprehensible to her. And this cost her only mild suffering, as if her life had been split into two separate parts, one made up of an indelible memory, the other of the same opaque sensation that had accompanied her existence before she met Peter.

Marie stayed with Rosa in the persistent silence she always maintained with Hartog's children, but with an additional sweetness, new for her, that arose from feeling in some way to blame for everything that had happened, for things she had not noticed.

The choice, assuming there were alternatives, fell on Jacob de Levie, a young Jew from a modest family, who did not seem to have found a definite direction in life. But Rosa didn't have one, either, and perhaps the two children could help each other. At least that is what Marie had written Hartog, inviting him to join them as soon as possible.

Hartog was compelled once more to ask for some days of leave, a few months after his little lie when he met with the rabbi. He left for Winschoten with a sense of oppression, for he was unaccustomed to spending days away from his office routine.

He found Marie waiting for him at the station, and seeing her so shoddy in her dark, shapeless dress, so unattractive with her disheveled hair and thin lips, he could not help thinking for a moment of his dead wife, of her beauty that had touched his life without his being sufficiently aware. And he felt the loss as an incurable wound.

He immediately shook off this pain, kissed his wife on both cheeks, and accompanied her to the house where she was staying with Rosa.

Neither Marie's uncertainty as she talked about the prospective husband nor Rosa's timidity when receiving her father added to the oppression Hartog felt upon his departure. In fact, they dissolved it. He found within himself a patriarchal strength, the resources to do that which was expected of him: make a decision. He thought that if his father could see him he would be proud of his son, and almost without thinking, he put his hand in his vest pocket where he kept the watch Emanuel Hartog had given him many years ago. He wondered whom he would pass it on to, whether to his firstborn or to another son, but he asked himself without anxiety, knowing that this was not the decision he was being asked to make.

He sat in the upholstered armchair in the parlor and told Marie to ask that blessed boy to come — what was his name? That Jacob de Levie.

Hartog's self-assurance had another source as well, for he brought an offer of work to this new Saint Joseph. Sitting in the armchair he savored the taste of a resourcefulness that even Marie did not know about. The future bride and groom were destined to move away from their hometowns: neither Rotterdam nor Winschoten, but Utrecht.

The boy came into the room: He had a great bush of red hair, and held a soft cap tightly in his hands. His blue eyes could not stay still. They darted around the room as though subject to a nervous tic. Hartog, who now felt like some kind of benevolent patron, motioned for him to sit down.

"Now, then, you intend to marry my daughter Rosa?" he asked in a tone of voice that tried to imitate the pride and condescension of the elderly Polak.

"Yes," Jacob said, turning to the sideboard.

"And how do you think you will support her and the baby when it arrives?"

"With God's help," the boy replied, with eyes so downcast he seemed to be speaking to the legs of the armchair.

Hartog shook his head, but with a smile.

"God's help is not enough," he said. "But they are looking for a clerk at the Utrecht branch of Polak and Sons. I gave them your name. You could leave right after the wedding."

The boy looked at him with gratitude, yet unable to say a single word.

The wedding took place a few days later in the presence of close relatives and without special celebration.

After returning to Rotterdam with Marie, Hartog telegraphed the news to George. The most important thing was that the family's honor had been saved, but he didn't include that fact in his message. Just as no mention was ever made about what actually took place to cause the gradual estrangement of Rosa, Jacob, and their six children from the other van Straatens, almost as the result of forgetfulness and lack of attention.

That same day the newlyweds left for Utrecht. During the trip Rosa slept. Her head resting against the window of the carriage, she saw, as she had seen an infinite number of times before, the landscape of the countryside just outside the Rotterdam walls. She felt the swaying of the gig, Peter's kisses in rhythm with the horse.

She dreamed of the bed in that house that would have welcomed them silently, and of Peter's blue eyes, his long hair, his heavy and curious hands. She even recalled his odor, a mixture of sweat and dampness and wildflowers that lingered for a long time in the folds of that dress she had decided never to wash again.

And she lifted her skirt again to let Peter untie her petticoat, and felt again that fear that grew into pleasure, that terror of something unknown that she could never have stopped.

No sound came from her mouth while she dreamed in the carriage, just as she had kept silent, biting her lip until it bled, when Peter lifted himself onto her, almost crushing her, and things happened inside her that no woman, the first time, could ever imagine.

She dreamed a dream that would return many times during the secret moments of her life; she dreamed until Jacob touched her on the shoulder. Then she shook herself and smiled at him, because she felt no sense of guilt or resentment. And Jacob smiled, too, not knowing then or ever the reason for that apparent happiness.

XII

Odessa 1903

The Frozen Port

*I*T WAS A VERY heavy camera, one of the first of its kind allowing pictures to be taken quickly and without a tripod. George was very proud of it. According to him, it had been the best way to spend the first earnings he wasn't obliged to turn over to his father, the first wages he had earned far from home.

He had bought it in Venice, one of his destinations after Rotterdam. A few months in every branch, and then a telegram informing him of the next place. He deemed the rapid moves to mean appreciation for his work. But George hadn't been entirely sure until he assumed responsibility for the grain sent from central Russia.

And the camera, the first pictures he took, served to remind him of that beautiful city, white and wet, monumental and marine, as full of canals as the town he came from.

From that time he had always taken it with him, even though it was not easy to buy good film in Odessa (or Adièssa, as the inhabitants called it). And now, in his hotel room waiting for someone to call him from the office to give him the latest news about the temperature and ice conditions, he kept it on the bed, as if that would protect it from everything outside the door.

As soon as he woke up he thought about going to a café, perhaps to Robinat, which was always full of people. A better way to spend his time than gazing endlessly at the ceiling. But when he got up and looked in the mirror, with that large camera in his hand, he decided it would be better to wait for a while. Because he didn't like what he had seen reflected there: a face without its usual smile.

There had been a time, some years earlier, when an inexplicable joy would often come over him, as if freedom were equated with the end of a day in the office.

Like his father, he had been very young when he started working, just fourteen years old, but with a difference, as he was convinced his life would not repeat itself forever in the same way, marked by the identical days of a clerk lost in recording fabric orders.

That joy was the mark of a will, of a decision not to feed on the same aimlessness as the boys he walked with on the streets of Rotterdam, or those he drank with at the tables in the cafés. His laughter indicated a future, a direction.

And yet he had begun with the humblest of jobs. Hired as an errand boy, he had even swept offices as soon as he arrived in the morning. The company was called Max Engers and it dealt with transporting and insuring goods; a rival of Goldstück, Hainzé and Co., but smaller.

Soon they entrusted him with more responsibility. George learned quickly, and was friendly with everyone. What became laughter in the evening was an open, persuasive smile during the day. And it was not mere chance that brought him one day to the office of John Kahn, manager of the Rotterdam branch of the Goldstück firm.

George had met him at the port and had challenged him with almost adolescent insolence when one of Goldstück's customers walked away from the wharf, complaining about something. George had then approached the customer and offered his services. He hadn't closed the deal, of course, because contracts are not broken by a momentary peeve, but he had established a contact, sowed a doubt. And from the edge of the wharf John Kahn had watched with his mouth set and his eyes curious.

Some time passed before he was called upon, a period of hard work and joyous evenings. Kahn, an elegant man, with cane in hand, an impeccable suit and monocle, had greeted him on that same wharf, and with a certain nonchalance had suggested a meeting at his office the following day.

George talked it over with Samuel Swaab, a coworker who shared his hopes and ambitions. Samuel had been the first to make him realize that Holland was too small and provincial for them. He loved Germany, and for this reason called himself Siegfried. But if not Germany, he would have gone willingly to England or France. The important thing was to move, to get away.

"Goldstück's firm is the oldest and largest company in our business. I think you should go."

That is what he told him one evening after a long discussion and before asking, with apparent indifference, about his sister Rachel.

"I don't like people who steal my customers," Kahn told him, when he had been brought to his office after a calculated wait. "But you behaved so calmly and naturally, right before my eyes, that you aroused my curiosity. Enterprise, even a certain amount of rashness, is considered a good thing in our work. I asked around and everyone spoke well of you. Very young, certainly, but we have many young men with us."

Only at the conclusion of these words did he motion for him to sit down.

Then he continued. "To get to the point, are you satisfied with your work at Engers?"

For a few months they kept him in Rotterdam, almost as though under observation. Even Hartog, his father, watched him, inquisitive and concerned that his abrupt and premature change could be a symptom of belonging to the wrong side of the family.

But George was only happy and ambitious. He would never

fall into the same trap as his uncle Benjamin, and Hartog once again experienced the same proud yet sometimes intimidated affection for his son that he had felt since George was a child.

As for the company, George realized immediately that what they expected from him, as from everyone, was initiative, will, and passion.

Henry Goldstück had said as much himself the time he visited the branch, and he said it with a look that left no room for doubt. But George had never had any worries on that score, and soon he was able to pour into his workdays the same joyful certainty that carried him through his nights.

In Odessa lately, however, that certainty of his and the ease with which he made friends did not seem enough to handle the situation. Even the Russian he had learned almost perfectly — so well, in fact, that he was often asked what region he came from because his accent was slightly different from the local speech — even this did not make him feel comfortable.

He was a foreigner, a Dutchman; no one had ever considered him a Jew, but nevertheless the persistent rumors of anti-Semitic acts worried him. In the censored newspapers he didn't find news of it, but he heard in various conversations, in a casual way, that in the north, in some little town, shops had been sacked, houses burned, and yes, it seemed someone had even died.

In Odessa a third of the population was Jewish, and although George did not associate with them, much less go to the synagogue, he still felt that the vague threat could in the end affect him.

Consequently, those surly peasant faces, as impenetrable as always, accompanied by subdued and apparently humble gestures, but with a sullenness behind them, with wrinkles of hate around their eyes, transmitted to George a sense of tension that spread over the houses, over the streets; tension exhaled like vapors from the *ovragi*, the crevasses in the natural terraces upon which the city was built, fifty yards above the level of the Black Sea. And it wasn't something that worried only the Jews, because those peasants, in reality, hated their masters most of all.

Even the old man who polished his shoes; beyond the bows and compliments he addressed to him in his whiny voice, even toothless Ivan seemed to have put him on guard.

"Bad times, sir, bad times."

Rumors, always more rumors. While he worked with the loads of grain on the ships, George listened to the worries of the landowners who feared revolt, or he picked up news about the threat of a war in the Orient. He informed the company about all this and waited for instructions that did not arrive.

Ultimately the ice, which had blocked the port for two days, and had closed down the whole city along with the port, became a kind of symbol, as if the moment for reflection had arrived, the opportunity to look around and understand.

His hotel, the Hotel Bristol, was on Puškinskaja Street. From the window of his room on the second floor he could see nothing but the people and vehicles on the street below, and the buildings across the street.

But if he left the hotel and went a short way down the street, he could see Nikolaevskij Boulevard opening up before him, and beyond that the abstract vault of the sky. As he continued to walk the view would enlarge even more, and after a few steps George would find himself at the top of a stairway leading down to the port. From this point he could take in the entire bay in a single glance, with the moored ships and the city that sloped down from a height almost to the wharves.

That morning, however, George could not make up his mind to go out. He was waiting in that room for a signal, the merest sign, to inform him that something outside was changing, that Odessa's unreal standstill had been broken.

While he waited he turned to look at himself in the mirror, holding the camera in his hands. He saw his unsmiling face reflected again, looking almost lost.

Then, only then, did he snap the picture.

Reproduced in the photograph was the striped wallpaper with its flowered cornice just below the ceiling, a dark, massive wardrobe, a lamp on top of the wardrobe that extended its glass shade over George's head, and finally he himself, with rather long hair pulled back, longer than he had ever worn it in his life, his nose small and regular like his other features, a pleasant face, especially when it broadened into a smile, a mustache and goatee that soon would be shaved, eyeglasses with metal frames so thin as to be almost invisible, a white shirt with a soft French-style collar. And with his two hands tight around the camera as if this were the only means of keeping a hold on reality.

From his family in Holland he received fragmentary news in between long lulls in communication. In the beginning his sister Zippora wrote him most often, the one everyone was now calling Celine. She had become more than an older sister to George, almost a mother, after Mina's death. So her letters truly provided a semblance of continuity, like a telegraph line joining two distant cities. After she moved to Amsterdam with her husband, Louis, though, it was difficult to garner a precise picture of the situation even from her, and all those children — there were four already — must have kept her very busy.

He knew about Rosa, far away and almost forgotten after three years of absence and another child, this time Jacob's. George was amazed to think that his brother and two older sisters were already married and it would soon be his turn; amazed because in spite of his twenty-five years he still felt like a child.

With an uncharacteristic melancholy, he sometimes sensed his mother's face reemerging from the past, a barely perceptible image. He couldn't tell if it was a memory of her, or only the memory of the picture he had seen many times in the Speyer home. That pale, delicate face, so beautiful, her upswept hairstyle, simple dress, with its velvet bodice of a dark violet, almost black, closed by little buttons. When he stopped in front of the portrait he would try to superimpose the features he could remember from his childhood. But little by little everything had become confused, and his mother's beauty became a symbol of her sacrifice, of the injustice of her death; it ultimately sanctified her, making her an abstraction. So George wondered if he maintained a true image of his mother, or if the reality of her had disappeared inside him forever.

He thought about writing his father, taking advantage of that lost workday to strengthen the ties he felt had been weakened by distance and time. But perhaps he was not in the right mood and it would only increase the emptiness that made him feel anxious. He went to the window and looked up at the sky. It was clear and blue, almost transparent. It wasn't the time for melancholy.

So he went back to the mirror, fashioned a smile on the reflected image and also inside himself. He left the camera on the bed where he had put it after snapping the picture, and then he took the room keys from the table and went out.

The hotel porter spoke a French as affected as his thin mustache. A nice man, without a doubt, but also false, as hotel porters often are by habit and profession.

He bowed slightly, and then said there were no messages for George van Straaten, and if there had been, he would have had them sent immediately to his room.

George thanked him, and after buttoning up his coat and putting the broad-brimmed hat on his head he passed through the revolving door and into the open. This time he did not go in the direction of Nikolaevskij Boulevard. He did not want to see the frozen sea spread out before him; instead he turned right for Deribasovskaja Street, looking absently into the shop window displays that seemed to ignore the cold and the fears that gripped him.

Almost unconsciously he headed toward the post and telegraph office in the Ulitza Stolypina, as if the sign that Odessa seemed incapable of giving him might come from somewhere else.

In the large hall there was a strange calm, as if the ice had suddenly slowed down the rhythm. At the telegram window he recognized someone, although he couldn't remember his name.

The clerk looked up at him in surprise and motioned for him to come closer. As he headed in that direction George felt a touch on his arm. He turned and saw someone he knew very well.

—୦

The man's name was Izaak Rabinovic, a person who worked less than George and drank much more. As a result, his paunch hung over his trousers and his jackets always seemed a size too small. His coloring was too red, and his aquiline nose was a map of damaged capillaries. George knew that Izaak would never make a place for himself. But at times his way of being both happy and melancholy — a Russian characteristic, certainly, but also a trait of adolescence, like that of his Rotterdam friends — attracted him. And when the winter cold dried the alcohol in Izaak's veins, that Russian Jew picked up his violin and his hands revealed an agility unknown to the other parts of his body, like the white hands of a mime in contrast to the rest of his body clad in black, as if possessed by a frantic and magical power.

Finally, one winter evening after many vodkas for Izaak and a few for George, he had asked, "Will you teach me?"

Izaak raised his glass in a silent toast. "Have you discovered something worth living for besides shipping grain?" he said. "Good! I am at your service."

Izaak embraced him. His breath smelled bad and his eyes were redder than usual. George hadn't seen him in town for some time. People said he was sick and staying in the country.

"I come and go. I never stay long in the same place," Izaak said. "Something big is getting ready to happen. Something big and dangerous."

He had truly taught him to play. And well, because George was an excellent student. And now George knew he would take something, one thing at least, back from Russia: his love for the violin, his pleasure in playing.

But even if this were a reason for gratitude toward Izaak, George could not stand the man's air of complicity and defeat there before him in the Odessa Post Office.

"Well, then," George said, with the seeming carelessness he had decided to exhibit that day in order not to lose his smile, "why have you come back to us right now when the sea is frozen and nothing will move for at least another week?"

Izaak looked past George's shoulders and didn't answer his question. Instead he said, "A clerk at the telegram window is trying to get your attention."

"I know, I'll go now," George said and turned toward the window.

Izaak stopped him, faced with the prospect of being left alone again, and replied to his earlier question.

"Why am I here? Because I am curious. And besides, I don't have much to lose, not much life or money. So I've come to look. In the country everything seems the same, unchanging. Change goes on in the cities."

After weeks of mulling over thoughts almost identical to what he was hearing from Izaak, George would have liked to contradict him, irritated by the fatalism hidden behind those words. But he didn't do it. He wanted to know what the clerk at the telegram window had to say to him. And he hated the sickness he read deep in Izaak's eyes.

"Excuse me, now I really have to go. Look me up if you stay in town, and we'll spend an evening together."

Rabinovic nodded, but said nothing. He passed a hand over his stomach, as though reflecting. George moved toward the telegrapher.

"And the violin?" Izaak tried to stop him.

But George only made a vague gesture with his hand.

George never saw the last of the ice in the Odessa port, nor did he spend another evening with Izaak Rabinovic. Not because the ice lasted longer than usual; in fact, it melted over the next ten days. That wasn't the reason.

The sense of foreboding George experienced that morning on awakening was not realized, either. Or at least if something happened it was much later, when the news was nothing more than headlines in a newspaper.

The reason he did not see the solid ice turn to water, or the ships set sail and moor as usual in the Odessa port — the reason he did not see the progression of Izaak's illness, or ever know what happened to his violin teacher — was handed to him by the telegrapher that strange morning in the hall of Odessa's post and telegraph office.

"I was about to send a porter to your office. A telegram just arrived for you."

George signed the receipt, took the envelope, and put it in his pocket. He left the hall with his eyes downcast, hoping Izaak wouldn't stop him again. But Izaak seemed to have disappeared.

As soon as he was outside he stopped, took a cigar out of his jacket, and lit it. Then he took the envelope out of his pocket and opened it. The telegram came from Rotterdam.

> Goldstück very pleased with your work there STOP Partners have examined your position STOP Accept my proposal to name you director our Italian company STOP Necessary to go to Genoa as soon as possible STOP Instructions follow STOP Congratulations signed John Kahn.

George looked up at the sky: solid blue, sharp, distant. He saw the smoke of his cigar slowly spiraling upward. At his back, beyond the city limits, stretched the enormous expanse of the steppe, the wheat fields he had crossed many times, which finally he could leave behind him. Forever.

There were no more forebodings, only the joy of victory and the taste of the cigar. George knew an important piece of his destiny had been realized that morning.

He didn't know it would be mine, too.

XIII

Winschoten 1906

The Wedding

*T*HEN A LETTER disappeared. An innocuous, useless, maybe tiresome letter. It was lost for convenience' sake and because no one was aware of its presence in the Dutch lexicon. It was still there during the nuptials and not there immediately after the ceremony.

"Mr. and Mrs. Keizer," said the card, printed in French, "have the honor of announcing the marriage of Miss Henriette Keizer, their daughter, to Mr. George Henry van Straaten, and request your presence at the nuptial blessing that shall take place Wednesday, August 8, 1906, at 2:30 in the afternoon in Harmony Hall at Winschoten (Holland)."

But the birth certificate issued by the Jewish Community of Rotterdam, a necessary preliminary for the ceremony, recorded a George Henry, son of Hartog Emanuel van Straten, with only one *a*. And so in the wedding book the local administration gave to the newly married couple after the wedding there was only one *a* in the family name of that young grain inspector, for this was his profession, resident of Genoa, Italy, who had married Henriette, three years younger than he, without a profession, that is, housewife, who lived in Winschoten, the city where she was born and raised.

Thus the name was modified; in a barely perceptible way, but it was changed, as though their departure from Rotterdam, where George's great-grandfather had made his choice almost a century earlier, had to produce a variation not only in their lives but also in their name.

And that *a* was lost permanently.

Henriette was twenty-five years old and had curly hair that she could never comb symmetrically from a part in the middle: It always puffed out on one side and stayed flat on the other. She had round, blue, slightly protruding eyes, a large nose, and fleshy lips. Already at that age she had begun to gain weight and her dresses could barely contain her enormous breasts. In short, Henriette was not at all pretty.

Even now as she was dressing for the wedding ceremony, as she was trying with the help of her mother, Petronella, to appear as a companion worthy to George, that brilliant and handsome man whom many envied, even at that moment she was aware of her unattractive appearance. She felt quite ill at ease in that high-necked white gown, a beautifully embroidered, full-length dress, narrow-waisted so as to make her large breasts even more prominent.

She still wondered how it all had come to pass — who or what had convinced her future husband to ask her to marry him. She knew she was strong, could sometimes bend events to her will, but in this case she had expressed no more than a vague desire. So how had it happened?

Certainly Marie Bloch had had something to do with it. She, George's stepmother and the sister of Henriette's mother, must have said something to make that young man with the transparent and happy smile come to Winschoten so often over the past few summers. Otherwise, why wouldn't he have just stayed in that beautiful Italian city on the sea where he worked? What had persuaded him to spend his vacations in that town where life monotonously repeated itself and there was nothing worth seeing?

Henriette — Jet, as they called her at home — vaguely remembered the first time George had come to visit: It had been for his brother Emanuel's marriage to one of her cousins. After that he started coming every summer.

The first few times, she had seen him with his father, that small man who almost seemed to look to his son for protection, for confirmation. But she had also noticed how keen George was for his approval; as if a clerk of a fabric company, now retired, never out of Holland, could teach anything to a twenty-eight-year-old man who had already traveled the world and who earned much more than his father had ever imagined possible.

And yet behind George's laughter and self-assurance, behind his happy and energetic way of facing life, Henriette sensed the wish to be head of a family; even though he was not the oldest son, he wanted to become the most trustworthy and responsible.

Perhaps it was Hartog himself who had pushed his son in her direction, out of family custom. Whatever the case, George certainly let himself be led, as though it were regulation, a matter of obedience, a secret agreement and a reward.

While Petronella was lacing up the bride's embroidered gown, her father came into the room, a man with definite features, with a big nose, thick and arched eyebrows, a mustache, and flowing goatee.

Izaak Keizer had studied to become a rabbi, but he had come to doubt God's existence in the course of his studies and so had given them up. For the family, being Jewish had become a way of regarding themselves that had almost nothing to do with religion. An identity separate from faith, but one that remained solid and sure. So a Keizer or Bloch would never have married a Gentile, and there would never have been any need for a veto, because no one would ever have thought of doing it.

Izaak approached his daughter, looked at her sweetly, and passed a hand over her hair, which immediately rearranged itself. "You look very nice," he told her.

Henriette smiled at him, but her smile was distant. A coldness often came over her, separating her from other people, even from those she felt closest to, and this happened almost without her realizing it, as though out of habit. It was a distance she easily masked amid the repeated everyday gestures of their shared lives, but what would happen once her world expanded, once the cities and language and people were not the same?

The thought that this was her wedding day frightened her. She would have to leave everything she knew, the customs she had learned to respect, the streets and houses that belonged to her in their ancient familiarity; she would have to follow George and she didn't know if she was ready.

Hartog and Marie had taken advantage of George's first vacation after his appointment as manager of the Italian branch of Gold-stück, Hainzé and Co. by bringing him with them to Winschoten to become better acquainted with Marie's family. Hartog hoped to find an attachment for his son in his own country, and felt if he succeeded he would be acting in accordance with the rabbi's words; he would keep his family united. Thus by marrying a Dutch woman, George would create a strong tie; although living far away, he would keep their lives connected in spite of the distance.

It seemed George understood, and with a sense of satisfaction Hartog saw his son stop often to talk to one of Marie's many nieces in particular: a quiet girl, and not especially pretty, but unconventional enough to be one of the few girls who went out alone with her friends, whether men or women.

George even seemed taken by her family, by the sweetness of her mother, Petronella, a small and tenacious woman, and by the kindness of her brother David. He admired the simplicity of their lives together, the steadfastness of their feelings, and the stability of their economic situation. And when his son left, promising to return the following year, Hartog believed his objective was growing closer.

Over the years Hartog had been afraid that the Italian life and warm climate would corrupt the ways of an exuberant boy like his son, carrying him off in a different, easier direction. As a good Dutchman he could only vaguely imagine that life, but to him it seemed dangerous. George, however, had decided long ago not to disappoint his father, not to cause him regret.

Hartog had waited, and now the moment of the wedding had arrived. The old clerk, he who had been the sensible son, even a little boring, and perhaps the one less loved, the man who had been entrusted with the family continuity, was in the parlor of the Blochs' home waiting for George to come down from the upstairs room where he was dressing. He asked himself if it would have been better to give Benjamin's watch to him instead of to Emanuel. But that was the way it had gone; tradition had won, the power of the firstborn. And now he had nothing to confirm his affection for that son who had made his choice in accordance with his father's wishes.

George possessed the determination that Hartog had always sought, but it was a joyous determination, as luminous as his mother's face. While Hartog, in the end, had only Marie's pale presence.

He heard the creak of the stairs leading down from the floor above. George was coming. Hartog rose from the chair and went to him. He had many things to say, but could only embrace him without a word.

His father had waited patiently for him to fall in love, and now he was sure his hopes had been realized. But George had actually never been in love, not the first year nor in the years that followed, if being in love means a sudden acceleration of feeling, a sense of helplessness that upsets everyday existence. With George everything had been much calmer, more rational. A choice, or rather, an implicit suggestion to which he consented.

It was a natural process without deviations or impetuousness, summer after summer, until finally, returning from a trip to Groningen, the only city near Winschoten that had shops of high quality, he had appeared at the Keizers' house with a diamond ring.

Henriette was waiting for him in the parlor.

"Jet," he said, using the familiar diminutive, "I would like to marry you."

She looked down and whispered her consent.

"You'll have to come to Italy with me."

"I know," she replied.

Their words fell into a silence that insinuated small doubts into George's mind, but not into his eyes or gestures.

"In Genoa, they will call you Enrichetta," he said then, as a way out of the embarrassment. For the first time she looked at him in surprise.

"And what do they call you?"

"They call me Giorgio."

She laughed. "What strange sounds," she said.

"You'll get used to them. They are strange, certainly. Full of sweet vowels. Beautiful, more beautiful than ours."

As for George, he would have to get used to having a wife and then a family. Meeting the challenge was what counted. And he was calmed by the continuity he felt he had chosen with his preceding life, with his family's history, as if it diminished the unknowns of the changes facing him.

He pulled away from his father's embrace, straightened his formal jacket and the knot of his pearl-gray tie, and felt ready.

The tables in the hall had been pushed up against the walls, covered with white tablecloths, and then laden with bottles and glasses. There were chairs and small tables for the guests' comfort, and in the middle of the large room was a bandstand where the dance orchestra would later play.

The newlyweds arrived around three o'clock, when the hall was already full and the conversation had swelled to a din. Henriette held on to George's arm, as if this gave her a certain dignity. She seemed embarrassed but happy.

George escorted her into the room, proud and sure, while voices trailed off, giving in to the curiosity of watching the new couple enter. The guests applauded and cheered. As people gathered to kiss and embrace them after they were seated, their closest friends began to ascend the bandstand.

Each guest took a card from a jacket pocket, raised an arm for silence, and read a short poem dedicated to the bride and groom; these were witty sayings, rich with double entendres, but at times also touching and affectionate.

Most pleasing of all was the poem read by Louis Fles, Celine's husband. It was admired for its tone, for the way each phrase gracefully led to the next, and also for its sentiment, which had no antireligious overtones this time, as so often happened. Louis was a freethinker, but also an honest and successful man. His office machine business was doing very well. The applause that followed was an indication of how much the family appreciated him.

Each time a speaker finished reading, the children took the card to the couple.

These were the children of George's brother and sister: Henry, Emanuel's boy, now almost adolescent, tall and delicate, and Celine's brood of four wild girls.

The girls, especially, ran continuously from the stand to their uncle's table, cards in hand, emitting sharp and repeated cries. Their mother let them run free while proudly holding her first male child, who was only five months old.

George's brothers and sisters were all there, except Rosa and Gerrit. Bernard came without his wife, as she had just had a baby and wasn't up to the trip from Amsterdam to Winschoten.

Emanuel and Louise were there, and above all Rachel, the beauty of the family, swept away by the joy and wonder of being only twenty-two years old. She wore a low-necked dress and long, elbow-length gloves, a gift from her fiancé, Siegfried Swaab, an old friend of George's from the Max Engers days.

Rachel was not interested in the poems or the speeches, but was waiting anxiously for the reunion to turn into a real party. She also endured the rabbi's speech, his good wishes and reminders of the scriptures and the duties of husband and wife. At last her wishes were realized and the musicians appeared on the bandstand, tuned their instruments, and struck up a waltz. Finally, Rachel could dance.

Waiters circulated with trays, offering the guests cakes and pastries. But the attention was focused on the dancers and the small orchestra filling the hall with polkas and mazurkas. Even those who didn't dance, who sat at the tables, perhaps smoking a cigar, couldn't take their eyes from those men and women who swayed, turned, laughed, clapped, in rhythm to the music.

Even Hartog, father of the groom, looked at that different world, at the wealth of a festive occasion seemingly made just for his amazement. The Keizers certainly were better off than the van Straatens, and wanted to show it. But he had his dignity and knew how to conduct himself. Suddenly the elderly clerk, who had spent most of his life with his eyes downcast, looked up. He walked up to his daughter-in-law, bowed, and invited her to dance.

Henriette turned to George, who replied with a smile and a casual wave of his hand.

"The first dance always goes to the father of the groom," Hartog said.

He took his daughter-in-law by the waist and walked her to the center of the hall. He was slightly taller than she, and without a doubt more frail, but he led the dance with pronounced agility, making Henriette feel lighter on her feet and able to follow her companion's moves as he guided her closer to the stand. He didn't even notice the other dancers moving aside to let them pass; some of them stopped, smiling. Henriette noticed nothing, having distanced herself, but the distance was not cold this time. It was a joyous exception.

The waltz ended. Everyone clapped. Someone gave a shout. The bride looked at Hartog, who squeezed her hands happily and held on to her while he caught his breath. Henriette passed a hand through her hair, disheveled once more, and felt perspiration dripping from her forehead, but it didn't bother her at all, it wasn't important. Looking over at the table she met George's eyes, watching her as he clapped. Then she freed herself from her father-in-law's grasp and began to applaud, too.

Had it been up to Rachel they never would have stopped. But Siegfried fell into a chair, resisting her efforts to return him to his feet.

"That means I'll have to cheat on you," she said, leaving him alone.

He laughed, but shivered when someone put a hand on his shoulder. He turned and saw it was George.

"Well?" asked the groom, overhearing his sister's last words.

"I don't think she'll really do it," Siegfried answered mildly, continuing to look in the direction Rachel had disappeared.

"At my wedding?" George said, laughing. "I would be the first to stop her."

Siegfried laughed with him, then stopped, lowering his gaze.

"I want to marry her," he said.

"And you will. But she is still very young."

Siegfried spread his arms. He stood up and whispered in his friend's ear.

"I don't have time," he said. "Engers has offered me the manager's job at the London office. I don't want to leave Rachel here."

George was happy for Siegfried. He knew how important it was to move, to discover new and different places. It wasn't out of arrogance that he looked around with a self-assurance that many interpreted as a sense of superiority. It was just that many of those in that hall had never been on a train, had only seen the North Sea and a few Dutch cities. Foreign cities, for the few who had been out of Holland, were identified with Germany or Belgium. The most fortunate had visited Paris.

Only George knew how different the world could be, how vast the choice of attitudes and words. These experiences made one feel better and, sometimes, lonely. Now Siegfried was about to take to the sea; no one remained the same after crossing it.

"Take her with you," George said. "You'll both be happy."

"Thanks," said Siegfried, then added, "And you?"

George laughed and spread his arms as if indicating the hall, and the people, and the music. "I?" he said. "I've already done it."

The party was almost over. The orchestra was no longer playing and the guests were saluting the couple and slowly departing. The relatives stayed on, as though their custom and affection required a different kind of leave-taking, a longer, calmer time before separating.

George felt tired, and an abstract melancholy made him think of his mother, though not of the image in the photograph, or of the vague memory of his childhood. Now George looked for something of her in her family, asking himself if perhaps she continued to live, after all, to be present in the manner in which some of the family members thought; or maybe even in the fibers of their bodies, ready to reproduce herself in the distant future, to survive in their spirit by leaving her imprint in her descendants, continuing on in the expression of their eyes, in the cadence of their voices, in the gesture of a hand. In this way the family was destined to grow, to extend itself not only in space but also in time.

And now, while thinking of her, it seemed to George that eternity was compressed into a single point, in that unique, actual moment, in that ceremonial hall that was slowly becoming empty.

He took Henriette's hand and squeezed it. "Let's go," he said. "Let's tell everyone good-bye and leave."

XIV

Florence 1997

A Second-Rate Restorer

I CAN'T DO IT, I don't know how to stop myself. That's why I'll never be a good restorer.

It's a matter of detachment. Not emotional detachment, which is hardly likely for someone restoring a painting; I mean physical detachment — because the painting always remains a separate and distinct entity from the restorer. On the other hand, the stories I go about recovering, that seem to be reviving now without my help, end up belonging to me, staying inside me, mixing with everything that no one outside can see. So if I decide to paint what has been lost, who will be the wiser?

In short, I will never be a good restorer because I am unable, in spite of all my good intentions, to avoid using my brush.

Of course, I have left parts of the plaster white, according to the rules I have imposed on myself, and I have often resorted to simple dabs of color, but sometimes I end by completing what should not be completed. In other words, I invent.

And if when I began I was able to distinguish clearly what was true from what was simply probable, what was mine and what belonged to the people I was speaking about, now I no longer have this clarity. Things are intermixed, they are superimposed, until they pass into a picture that, fortunately, is assuming the perspective and depth of life.

Because what was forgotten, covered with dust, which I as an imprudent apprentice magician have resuscitated, is an obstacle requiring the persistence of the most dogged archivist to overcome. Flesh and blood ask their due, they demand that these phantoms not remain vague and pale figures. Life does not stop with a commanding gesture, much less for a question of correctness.

Besides, hasn't even the best restorer for a moment, even a single moment, had the desire to cover the gap, to repaint what has been lost and could perhaps be found again? Is what we see in a picture always true?

Now I am beginning to write about people who lived closer to my time — people known and remembered by others. All this will certainly require greater attention and delicacy.

The available details become more plentiful, and therefore I must try to impose a greater objectivity. But the opposite happens: I feel I am called to account. The gaps cannot be left white any longer; they require a completeness that did not seem necessary at the beginning of this narration.

This also happens to the historian. The closer he comes to his own epoch, the more difficult it is to remain objective, even if the sources, documents, testimonies are so numerous as to seem infinite and are therefore useful for resolving any question whatever; yet something appeals to us to take a position, compelling us to take sides, at the risk of forcing the elements of experience. Historians of contemporary times participate in the event, or at least express judgments that are conditioned by that event.

In the wedding book *(Trouwboekje)* with the blue cover issued by the municipality of Winschoten, which was given to George van Straten after the marriage ceremony, there was also a place for registering the birth of children at the nearest Dutch consulate. The first was a boy born in Genoa on July 23, 1907. His name was the same as his other firstborn cousins, Henry, but no one called him

Henry. Because he immediately became Enrico, Italian-style.

This event was memorialized in a photograph, probably taken in Holland a few months later. To the left, sitting in an armchair, is David, Henriette's brother, gently resting a hand on the shoulder of his own first child. This girl, who is just over a year old, manages to stand only by propping herself against her father's leg. She is wearing a long white dress with embroidered hem and a ribbon around her waist. Near them, standing, is David's wife, her left hand resting on a tall table, art-deco-style, and next to her hand is Enrico, sitting with legs sprawled, he, too, in a white dress, with bald head, arms limp, and what seems to me an ironic smile. George is holding him with one hand, looking at something beyond the camera, with the self-assurance of someone pleased with his own appearance. He wears a pince-nez, a mustache with upturned tips, a stiff collar, tie, and a perfect-fitting suit with vest. At the edge of the photograph, on the right, in an unflattering light-colored blouse and a dark skirt that envelops her, as if trying to hide her incipient largeness, without effect, is Henriette, sitting on a chair, her curly hair shorter than it was at the time of the wedding, puffed out on her head. She looks at the lens with a lethargic and serene air.

On October 3, 1909, another son was born. And in 1911, Nelly, their first daughter. The boy was called Ivan, a name taken from the Bloch-Keizer tradition. And to a great extent that child inherited his physical characteristics and way of doing things from his mother's family.

There are no photographs of his first months. None that preceded Nelly's birth have come down to me. I must therefore begin to invent them, and in inventing them put in something of myself.

That is what I mean when I speak of the difficulty in maintaining the necessary detachment, and not confusing what is true with what is merely imagined.

Because that little boy is my father.

XV

Genoa 1913

Childhood

*T*HAT CITY HAD never become hers, that world did not belong to her. Not even when a north wind blew from the hills, gripping the city with cold, not even when fog covered houses and roofs until the port and sea disappeared. Even then she knew she was not at home.

Henriette did not forget Winschoten, and could not make Genoa resemble the flat Dutch horizons. She could try not to notice, certainly, she could in the end forget how far she was from home, but that cost her a great deal of effort and fatigue.

The van Stratens lived on the first floor of a two-story house in an area where the city began to climb the hills. Behind the house, below street level, they also had a garden, or better, a little piece of land scattered with gravel, separated from other houses by a black iron grating covered with vines.

Now Henriette was sitting there in the garden, even though the pale and hazy sun was unable to heat the February air. She held Nelly in her arms and watched Enrico and Ivan as they ran around the narrow space hurling inarticulate shouts at the sky.

This was not her world and would never be. But she had strength; enough strength and determination to allow her to proceed as if none of that mattered. She could wait for George to return home from work, show him the house in order and the children ready for bed, and she could listen to his joy as if it were natural to share it.

George tried to teach her Italian, which he could now speak without an accent, and listening to it she could find again the sweetness she heard many years ago in their translated names, but when she tried to repeat it there was always something she could not control; she mangled the stresses, aspirated the consonants, was ignorant of the many particles of that language.

George shook his head and smiled at her mistakes, and he pretended to commiserate with her.

"Now I'll talk to you in Genovese dialect, Jetje," he would say.

That was when Henriette would hold her ears in mock desperation, and he would burst into one of his hearty laughs.

She defended herself with rules, giving to the days, to their life, an order that was respected; not for the certainty that it was the right one, but because repetition, the assumption of habits, seemed a plausible protection from the unknown surrounding her.

Others had to conform to her rules: Giovanna, the live-in maid, the deliverymen, and above all the children. From the beginning she had decided, for example, that food could not be refused; what one did not eat, one would find at the next meal, until hunger overcame resistance.

Henriette exhibited an inflexibility about her rules that was relentless, unfaltering. There was no room for argument, so that George did not dare intercede for anyone who broke them.

In any case the children knew that in the space and time unoccupied by her rules they were free. Because the effort their mamma put into conducting their life according to those intangible dictates would suddenly give way to moments of withdrawal, which they took advantage of without risk.

At those times, with Nelly in her arms, weightless and silent, Henriette did not hear the children's shouts, did not feel the biting cold, but continued to stare fixedly at some indefinite point in the black grating.

—☙

In the meanwhile she grew fat, following the tendency she had shown from childhood, but now without any resistance, as though it were inevitable. The more George groomed his appearance, the less attention Henriette devoted to her own: Her dresses continued growing wider, but no dressmaker seemed capable of giving them a shape that could flatter her buxomness. The most those dresses could manage was to conceal her breasts.

She grew heavy during her pregnancies and afterward did not return to her previous weight. Moreover, she did not even try; she grew accustomed to her ever-expanding figure, to her ever more uncontrollable hair, now with some white strands.

She watched her children grow, and accepted the idea that Genoa was their city, and she even accepted the fact that they had begun to speak more Italian than Dutch at home. She preserved, but without particular emphasis, family traditions in food, in songs like the lullaby *"Roe, Roe, Kindje,"* and in the calendar of all her relatives' birthdays that she kept hanging in the bathroom. Apart from that, she let go of her relatives; while still loving them, she sometimes found them alien and different. She knew they did not belong to her, just as no human being belongs entirely to another, and this impeded her familiarity and gestures of tenderness.

The maid called to her while she was in the little garden, with Nelly asleep on her shoulder and the two boys sitting on the stone bench, now worn out.

"Signora," the maid said, "Maria is here."

"Show her to the parlor," she replied. "Wait a minute," she added, "you take the baby. I'll go."

Then she went into the house, motioning for the two boys to follow her, while the maid preceded her with Nelly's head reclining on her arm.

Maria was the dressmaker. Henriette had forgotten the appointment for that afternoon, but now she remembered what she had ordered only the week before. And she imagined the contents of those packages put on the table in the entrance hall where she also found Maria waiting for her.

‿◦

When George came home he noticed a different atmosphere and was happy to see the children excited, running around in the entryway and dashing into their room, slamming the door.

Henriette was standing in the middle of the parlor, a slight smile on her lips, with a pinch of the irony that she sometimes, though not often, revealed.

"What is going on, Jetje?" George asked in Dutch.

She spread her arms. "I don't know," she said in the best Italian she could muster.

George did not fear what was outside his house: not his work, which was going well; not money, which was ever more plentiful; not people, who actually piqued his curiosity and to whom he devoted a large part of his charm and his wish to please. At the same time he needed to think that at home, among his family, everything ran on track, that Henriette looked after the things dear to him.

For this he was thankful, and he harbored a sentiment that, while lacking the features of love, which he had never felt for her, did contain a certain solidarity and gratitude. Because of this he would always look after her, just as she looked after the family life. He accepted her moments of absence, the harshness of her rules, and he was amused by her occasional gruff displays of irony.

He removed his bowler hat, handing it to the maid along with his long heavy overcoat and his silver-handled cane. Then he turned to Henriette again.

"What have you concocted?"

She did not reply, only motioned for him to sit in the wide upholstered chair, and then she went out to the hall to gather the children.

George obeyed her and lit a cigar, listening to the excited voices that intermittently reached as far as the parlor as he waited for the preparations to end.

He did not try to imagine what was awaiting him because he knew his surprise was the real purpose of the performance. And he didn't want to disappoint them.

First Jetje came into the room with Nelly in her arms, dressed like a little Dutch girl. The baby was wearing a white cap, a dark bodice, and a wide skirt with a little white apron. Next came Enrico dressed as a sailor, with a round hat, a curved pipe, a large scarf at his neck, wide trousers, and clogs. Last, proud and uncertain, came Ivan dressed as a cossack. Henriette had chosen the costume because of his name, which for her recalled the great expanses of the steppe, and now she was happy about her choice. Ivan had a white furry busby, a makeshift, light-colored caftan, and a cartridge belt across his chest.

George opened his arms and began to laugh. "How beautiful you all are," he said.

Enrico ran and threw himself into his arms.

"Like a real Dutchman," George said, hugging him.

All three of his children had traits that reminded him of his mother, but Enrico and Nelly were fair like the van Stratens. Ivan had the Keizers' pale blue eyes and Henriette's mass of dark, unruly hair. Perhaps he had not been as attentive to him, reflected George, and this saddened him. So he relinquished his armload, raising Enrico high in the air and then setting him feetfirst on the floor, and he went to Ivan, who was standing by the glass door that separated the parlor from the hallway.

"Come here," he called. "Come here next to me, soldier of the czar."

The boy ran toward him, prancing, his mouth open with emotion and a shout in his throat that he did not have the courage to let out.

"This will be an unforgettable show," George said, turning to Henriette. She nodded, while the children clapped enthusiastically, pleased with the success of their performance.

The Italian branch of Goldstück, Hainzé and Co. was now an important firm functioning at maximum capacity and making a great deal of money.

A few months earlier, after Henry Goldstück had sharply reduced his own activity, a man had come to Genoa to assume the most prominent position in the company: Jacques Salmanowitz, a sturdy man with a wide black mustache, originally from Latvia also, although he had lived since childhood in western Europe, first in France, and then in Holland. During that visit Jacques and George had long talks about their experiences on the Black Sea, where Salmanowitz had also worked, though in Romanian territory. They were on familiar terms, and Jacques told George that everyone in Paris was pleased with his work; indeed, they considered him indispensable for the good of the business in Italy.

In fact, the activity was continually expanding, and George's salary also increased, along with the help he gave his Dutch relatives and the pleasures he allowed himself.

So the day after his children's performance, he decided to respond to their surprise with a surprise of his own.

He left the office earlier than usual, around noon, and instead of going home he walked downtown from the port. He walked quickly, inhaling with pleasure the air of a sunny day, warmer than usual.

He went into the best toy store in town and had a clerk show him through the rooms full of marvels. He wanted something for his little soldier of the czar, something to complete his costume.

He found a cannon, as long as Ivan was tall, with its dark metal barrel neatly set on a wooden stock, and wide, lightweight spoke wheels; a cannon that shot blanks, but loudly.

"I'll take this," he said to the clerk without asking the price.

He added some gifts for Enrico and Nelly so as not to disappoint them. But for George, the cannon was the important purchase that day.

He paid the clerk and called for a cab, which like the sled of a tardy Santa Claus took him home loaded with presents.

When Papa put the cannon in front of Ivan, he couldn't believe it. He looked at Mamma and clung to her smile to make certain he wasn't dreaming. Then he touched the cannon with his hand and it felt cold; he liked that dark metal and the feeling on his fingertips. He said nothing, only looked around him again, and he saw his brother.

"Your cannon is beautiful," Enrico said.

Ivan knew it was truly beautiful, the most beautiful thing he had ever seen, but he remained silent, a bit afraid of saying the wrong thing.

"Do you like it?" his father asked.

In the end he spoke. "Yes, very much," he told him.

"What did you say?" his mother asked him in Dutch.

"*Ja*," he replied, "*veel*."

He took the cannon, holding it in both hands this time, and made it move backward and forward on its big wheels. Then he saw a knob at the back of the barrel; he tried to pull it, and noticed it came out, barely resistant, as though restrained by a spring.

Papa bent over him, took the cannon in his large hands, and said to him, "Let's go out to the garden to try it."

Everyone ran behind Papa, dressed in the costumes they had wanted to put on that morning — even Nelly, who walked with her uncertain step, reaching for Mamma's hand.

In the garden Papa made the primer inside the cannon explode. Nelly almost cried, and Ivan jumped at the first shot. Then he realized what happened and hoped they would keep firing all day long.

He also hoped that Papa would always be so close and attentive, that he would bend over him until he could feel his rough mustache, until his glasses fogged from his breath.

Mamma had followed them in her house clothes: one of her stiff, heavy skirts, a white blouse with a collar, and an embroidered, heavy sweater. She, too, seemed happy with all that was happening.

Then the explosions stopped. Papa put the ammunition in his pocket and walked toward the house.

"Wait here," he told the children.

When he came back he had his camera, his tripod, and Giovanna, who trotted behind him carrying two chairs.

Papa made Mamma take a seat, but she did so only with reluctance, saying that she was not suitably dressed, that one should be elegant in a photograph.

"But it's our show," Papa replied.

Ivan was also told to sit down, with the cannon in full view in front of him. Nelly was arranged on Mamma's lap, and Enrico stood behind her.

After fixing the camera settings and instructing Giovanna, Papa stood behind Ivan with a satisfied smile, wearing his splendid double-breasted suit, stiff collar, and perfectly knotted tie. His right hand was buried in the furry busby of the czar's soldier.

Ivan felt the pressure of his father's hand, the sweet strength of his assurance. He saw the cannon in front of him and knew that Papa loved him, that he had given him the most beautiful cannon in the world.

"Now," said Papa. "Now, shoot, Giovanna."

And the photograph was taken. While the others went away and Papa took the camera into the house so it wouldn't be damaged by the humidity, Ivan remained seated for a moment, lost in a feeling that could not be repeated, in total and perfect happiness.

Then he jumped up, leaped over the cannon, and ran toward the house.

"Bang!" he shouted at the top of his lungs.

XVI

Rotterdam 1919

Rites of Passage

*I*T WAS A SLOW journey, just as it had been a slow war. But when he woke up on the third day, when he opened the curtains covering the little window and looked at the flat countryside of Belgium, he realized he was nearly there. He was happy not to have seen the devastation of the French plain: the furrows of the trenches as though left by an enormous plow, the walls remaining after the shelling, and the eyes of windows opening onto nothing.

The war had not touched George. He had only heard about it in the words, in the sorrow, in the tiresome days of those who had stayed home. He had seen it in the desperate and happy eyes of the veterans, in the number of the maimed, in the newspaper headlines. He was a citizen of a neutral country and had continued to work in Genoa, even though the business that occupied him was sharply curtailed.

And as much as it had been impossible to avoid the sense of death that had infiltrated those years, the war had also been a lucky break for him, because in order not to incur the sanctions that every belligerent country applied against foreign corporations with offices in enemy countries, Goldstück, Hainzé and Co. had subdivided into a series of diverse companies. One of them, La

Sorveglianza, had been established in Italy with George's partici-
pation; now that the war was over and Goldstück, Hainzé and Co.
had transferred to Switzerland, changed its name to Société
Générale de Surveillance, and reacquired the various companies,
George van Straten was an important and wealthy man.

The train crossed the plains of Belgium, carrying him toward a
death, and so he was relieved at the idea of having left behind another death, that of the war, unknown and impersonal; it served to
counteract the feeling of emptiness that had settled right under his
breastbone, a physical thing, every time he thought of his father.

A telegram from his brother Bernard had summoned him, and
George had decided to go by himself, leaving Henriette in Italy
with the children, now numbering four. In 1914 Louise Mina
Henriette was born, named after one of his sisters, whom
everyone called Lisetta.

It was the first time George had returned to Holland since the
end of the war, since the borders had reopened. Had it not been for
this, and the difficulties in travel, it would have been better to send
Henriette, who still thought of Holland as her country. He, on the
other hand, wondered where his roots lay: perhaps in a story, or
even in a name. Certainly no longer in a place, in a physical space.

This was a thought that saddened him at times, but above all it
gave him a sense of freedom, knowing life still offered him many
opportunities that he could accept because he could relocate.

A waiter, after announcing himself with a light tap on the door,
opened his compartment door.

"Good morning," he said. "Do you want to eat breakfast here
or in the restaurant car?"

It was the same question and the same waiter who appeared
every morning on the train, and George gave the same answer.
"In the restaurant car."

But this time he added, "When will we be in Rotterdam?"

"In about six hours," the waiter replied, bowing slightly and
closing the door.

He shaved, combed his hair, knotted his tie with sure, precise
movements. He put on his jacket and laced his shoes. In the rep-

etition of these familiar acts he avoided thinking about the reason
for his trip, about what was happening in Rotterdam right at that
moment.

Then he went into the corridor and walked toward the center
of the train with decisive steps, barely hampered by the swaying of
the cars. The restaurant car was crowded, but the waiter had reserved his usual table, the one where Mrs. Horn also sat.

"Good morning, George. You are late this morning," the
woman said in an impudent manner.

She was beautiful, with wavy blond hair just covering her ears,
but short on her neck. She wore an iridescent pink silk dress with
a low-cut neckline, short sleeves, and pleated skirt. Her high waist
accentuated her slender, soft body and round breasts. Around her
neck she wore two strands of pearls.

She was coming from Italy also, where she had spent a restful
time on the Riviera, and was returning to her husband, an American who worked in Rotterdam.

They had met on the train and had become friendly immediately, because they were alone and the waiters had put them at
the same table, and because they both felt the need to transform
those three days into a parenthesis.

The woman's beauty served the same purpose for George as
his routine gestures that morning: a means of keeping himself
from being overcome by the sadness brought on by the purpose of
the trip. It seemed to him that preserving his serenity until the last
possible moment could do no harm; on the contrary, it created a
condition that allowed life to go on as it should, naturally. In fact,
his were not even calculated thoughts, but instinctive behavior.

This game of his was without malice, almost naive, an homage
to that surprise beauty discovered on a train, a woman to whom it
was proper to show respect and appreciation.

Mrs. Horn had enjoyed his attention and now lowered her
eyes with the sureness and coquetry of one who knows that there
is no time for anything else.

"I slept longer than usual," George replied.

"I noticed," the woman said, "and you left me here all alone."

Most of all it was relaxing, that innocuous repetition of words and glances, developed according to known rules, requiring neither obligation nor concentration.

"I have been unforgivable."

She laughed. "You have a few hours to make up for it."

Life, for George, had two speeds, or rather, two levels. That is not to say the superficial amounted to less than the profound; it was only different in its consistency.

Breakfast finished, Mrs. Horn invited him to accompany her to her compartment, and when a swerve of the train forced the woman to stop in the corridor, George bumped into her, just in time to feel her body, to think that a contact between them was possible.

"Sorry," he said, and Mrs. Horn smiled.

In her compartment was the faint smell of her perfume, sweet and spicy.

"Please sit down," the woman said.

There was not much room, because although the bed was made and stored in the wall, almost every space was occupied by open suitcases and a trunk. George managed to sit on the edge of the seat, near the window.

"What a mess!" she said. "Excuse me, and don't judge me harshly."

It had not occurred to George that the game might develop in any direction other than a tribute, chaste and casual, to the woman's beauty. But in that situation, for a moment, he was aware of the reality of her body, as he had felt it in the corridor a few minutes ago. And it embarrassed him.

"Well, Mrs. . . . ," he began, rising from the seat.

"Call me Rebecca," she interrupted.

"Certainly . . . Rebecca. I'm afraid I must leave you. I have to pack my bags."

"Oh, I know. But wait just a few more minutes. It seems that as long as you are here, Italy isn't so far away. And I already know how much I will miss the Riviera in this gray country, even in June," and she pointed out the window.

"I'm Dutch," he said.

"But you seem like an Italian. You have the same gallantry I found there."

So George stayed because he did not want to think of death, and he tried to delude himself that the space separating him from her would not be overstepped.

"All right," he said, "I'll stay a little longer."

Rebecca gave him a satisfied smile and turned to her luggage. With her back to him she continued their easy conversation, her words, however, sounding like flattery.

George stood up and moved closer to her, looking over her shoulder at her tapered fingers rapidly folding clothes and putting them in the suitcase.

Her perfume became more intense. George's breath scalded Rebecca's neck; she put down the dress she had just folded and turned toward him.

George took a step back. Rebecca did not move, but ran a hand through her hair with a gesture that showed she was also embarrassed. Nothing was at stake, certainly, but Rebecca didn't know how to relieve that tension, either.

In her hesitation George found the assurance, the calm, and the rashness of old nights in Rotterdam. He stepped forward and pressed his lips to hers; she closed her eyes and responded to his kiss.

Then Rebecca gently pushed him away.

"I'll keep this Italian flair as a souvenir," she said, and then turned toward the window. "We are almost there."

And while she was not looking, George nodded.

At the back of the platform he recognized Bernard, waving to attract his attention. When he reached him they embraced with the awkward gestures of a lost habit, and at that moment George felt he had arrived and there were no more barriers to protect him from what was happening. So he did not look around, did not see a tall man with wide shoulders and short blond hair who was jumping from one foot to the other as if he were cold, even though it was June; a nervous and impatient man. And he did not see the woman with blond wavy hair and a silk shawl run to the tall man and rise on her tiptoes to kiss him.

George released his brother and looked him in the eye. Bernard shook his head.

"We are all fine," he said. "You came just in time."

No, George did not see the woman's eyes turned toward him as she walked toward the station exit, he did not notice that her husband, surprised by her distraction, touched her arm, smiling. For George there were no farewells or regrets, nor any memories afterward.

He had arrived.

The house was the same, the same odors. The fabric of the chairs and divan in the parlor more worn and shiny, but the furniture still what George had always remembered from his childhood: the gift of the Polak company. It was hot, a heat of bodies and cigarettes, even though a fresh breeze came in from the open window.

He had just arrived and was still exchanging greetings when Marie entered the parlor and took him by the hand. *Wait a moment*, he wanted to tell her, *let me stay a minute with my brothers and sisters*. Instead he remained silent. There were no trains or sleep to save him, this time he had to look.

Hartog was lying on the bed, his mouth open, his breathing labored, his eyes closed. To George he seemed even smaller than he remembered, the flesh thin and barely covering his skull, his hair like lost threads, his hands as still as if he were already dead, or turned to stone.

He bent over him, placing a hand on his. But he felt there was something false in that gesture, as if a puppet were doing it and he was just the one who pulled the strings. That man lying there did not seem like his father, but a stranger lying on his bed, deaf to every contact or word. Marie wept silently at his side.

"Papa," George said in a whisper, "Papa."

"He hasn't responded for three days," Marie said. "He's gone."

George closed his eyes and squeezed Hartog's hand, as if that were a way to recognize him, as if he were a little boy who wanted to go along. Even though he knew that death was an absence, a solitude, which could not be entered together.

He reopened his eyes. His father was so small he felt he could pick him up and carry him away, like a puppy.

He looked at Marie, slumped in a chair with her head in her hands. He wondered what to say to her but nothing came to mind. Then she looked up at him. He let Hartog's hand go and went to her.

"Come on with me," he whispered.

She nodded. Arm in arm they left the room.

It was his brother-in-law Louis, Celine's husband, who woke him. George had fallen asleep on the divan. The arm on which his head had been resting was completely numb. For a second he didn't even know where he was.

They were in darkness; only a yellow light came from the hallway.

"Excuse me, I fell asleep," George said.

But it wasn't Louis he wanted to ask for forgiveness, because he already knew what had happened and was ashamed of being unaware, of not having felt it.

"He's dead, isn't he?"

Louis nodded.

Only then, only at that moment, did he realize just what a devastating, irreparable matter he was dealing with. And again he felt that oppression, that emptiness he had felt on the train, but now without the possibility of forgetting or repressing it.

He braced himself on the arm of the divan to give himself strength, but he couldn't get up. Then Louis sat down next to him and put his arms around him.

When they separated, George looked at his brother-in-law, at his face that seemed to droop downward, his eyebrows that stretched from the bridge of his nose straight to his ears, his too-soft skin that formed some inexplicable wrinkles, his intelligent and melancholy eyes. He waited for his words, his eloquent way of handling every subject. But this time Louis was silent. George knew that without words, his brother-in-law would never have the strength to take him into the other room. Or anyplace.

"Let's go in," George said, and he got up from the divan.

He did not look at his father, did not have the courage to see him right away, motionless and maybe even tinier than he had been a few hours earlier. Instead he looked at his brothers and sisters. Only Rachel was missing, unable to make it from England in time.

Rosa was crouched on the floor beside the bed, her head in her arms, Jacob behind her, one hand on the back of a chair, the other stretched toward his wife, but not touching her, as though wanting to protect her, but not knowing how.

Bernard stood to one side, leaning against the wall next to Marie, who seemed incapable of moving, and Gerrit, the half brother, who even now remained outside, not completely accepted by the others. Celine was standing in the middle of the room, small and hard, her features marked by fatigue and grief. She was the only one to turn to George, motioning him to come near. But still he did not move.

On a chair in the corner was Louise, her body limp, collapsed under her weight, her head against the chair's upholstered back, with her husband, Samson, sitting on the arm of the chair, his arm around her shoulders.

And finally Emanuel. George saw him last and couldn't take his eyes off him. He stood beside the head of the bed, solid, his thick hair now white, on his shoulders a tallith, the prayer shawl. His eyes were half shut, his lips barely moving, and from his mouth came what to George sounded like a child's lullaby from the past, but instead were the words of a Jewish prayer. George recognized sounds he had nearly forgotten, but he did not understand the words; he could no longer recognize them.

Only in the end, only in the end, did he catch something he knew. "*Adonai, Israel . . .*"

Listen, Israel, the Lord is our God, the Lord is one.

"*Adonai, Israel . . .*"

On a pillow in the middle of the bed was a small marble head, inexplicably wrapped in a handkerchief, as if a marble mouth could open. Then the cover, and two suit sleeves, as though empty, and two white lumps on top.

Instead of advancing, George turned toward the door.

"My father is not here," he said to himself and to the others, and he left the room.

Before beginning the ceremony they had to wait for the cemetery guard; otherwise there would not be ten men to recite the Kaddish.

In the little cemetery the gravestones were so crowded together they almost propped each other up. A foggy, humid light fell from above like rain. The simple, undecorated casket was silently lowered into the grave.

Now everything proceeded according to fixed and immutable rules allowing them to distance themselves, at least partially, from grief. Above all, they no longer saw the body, that inert and unrecognizable body that had driven George from Hartog's bedroom.

There was a wooden coffin and the earth. Time had prevailed over the unprepossessing little clerk. In the end hadn't Benjamin's been a better fate, the fate of that mysterious uncle so rarely mentioned, disappeared into nothing, evaporated, and therefore, basically, never dead?

Everyone took three handfuls of earth and threw them into the grave. Next Emanuel and the rabbi intoned the Kaddish, the funeral prayer that does not speak of the dead, and the others followed, with the uncertain words of memory. Marie was still crying, and seemed exhausted.

The rabbi went to George and cut a piece of his shirt with scissors. Then he did the same to the others.

The ceremony was over. The gravestone in its place, and the family motionless around the displaced earth. George didn't believe the ceremony had any meaning, he didn't have the faith to understand it; just the same he felt calmed, because he was familiar with it, and like everything familiar, it served to lessen the anguish.

"Now we can go," Louis said, touching his arm.

The others also moved, single file, like slow ants. George let them pass in front of him, shook the rabbi's hand, and followed them toward the cemetery exit.

That evening they all ate together with a good appetite. George found the potatoes cooked in butter, and the sweet-and-sour meat especially appealing. Bernard had brought a large container of the pickles he produced himself in a small factory in Amsterdam. They were sold there in Rotterdam at the market on Goudschesingel, one of the city's covered canals.

George loved his brothers and sisters, yet the atmosphere struck him as oppressive — not only because Hartog was dead, but also because life seemed to breathe too slowly there, almost hidden in the monotonous days. *What are you waiting for? What are you afraid of?* he wanted to ask them, but he didn't. Instead he went out, as he had done with his dead father. He left the house, crossed the street, and stopped at the edge of the canal.

"What's wrong, George?"

He heard Celine's voice behind him. He turned to face his sister. She, George knew, was one of the few people there who was not afraid. She continued to nourish herself with Louis's hopes. Different hopes from those held by George: distant, collective, as much as his were near and concrete, like a woman on a train. For Celine, instead, there was the world to change, and men, from beginning to end. George knew her words, remembered the talks with Louis, the questions he asked them: *And if you two are mistaken, if your expectations are destined to remain just that, if the world were to continue on in the same way?*

Louis shook his head. *The world is changing all the time. The problem lies in how it changes, and we socialists will be the ones to consciously change it for the better.*

George admired their courage, had contempt for their naiveness, envied their certainty. But most of all he loved them.

Celine loved him as well, and had demonstrated it by naming her last son, the second male, after him. No Henry in the Fles family. Among the van Straten names they had chosen George.

Now Celine was facing him, repeating with her eyes what she had already asked with her voice when she came up behind him.

"Come here, Moesje," George replied, calling her the nickname that went back many years. "Come here next to me. Nothing is wrong, nothing more than what we all feel this evening."

She took his hands and pulled him toward her. "Now let's go back. Emanuel will be looking for you."

First his only son had died of consumption. And a few months after that, at the beginning of the year, his wife. It had been up to him to close the hat store she had managed for many years, up to him, who knew only about the fabrics of the Polak company, and the hats were in the dozens.

Now his father was also dead; but by now his detachment from life lessened the grief, made it remote, almost artificial. The death of old people is a natural fact, it can be accepted. But the death of one's child is inconceivable, and one should have the courage to kill oneself. Otherwise there is nothing to do but hide — from everything.

Now Emanuel was hiding. He had resumed his habit of withdrawing, of leaving to others the responsibility of decisions, and he was learning to ignore his desperation, to forget his thoughts.

So when George joined him in the parlor and sat down next to him, Emanuel looked up in surprise, as though he had not expected him and had not already had his words prepared for some time. Emanuel remained silent, almost as if chance had brought them together and he had nothing to do with it.

"We have thought about you so much, Henriette and I, during these months," George said, putting his arm around him, "and I wanted to tell you, we wanted to tell you, that it would make us very happy if you would visit us in Genoa for a while."

Emanuel ran his hand through his hair. "In Genoa?" he replied. "Why not? After all I wouldn't be leaving anyone here waiting for me."

Only dozens of hats, he thought, *each one in its own box.*

"Then it's decided. You'll come."

"I'll come, I'll come. But that isn't what I wanted to talk to you about."

Emanuel was not yet fifty, but now he seemed wrapped in a quiet wisdom that he could transmit to others, even if it could not be useful to him, because his life was over anyway.

"I have something here," he began with embarrassment, his head down, his hand in his jacket pocket. "Something I can't keep any longer."

George looked at him in surprise.

"Perhaps our father Hartog," he continued, "perhaps he would have preferred it this way. But I waited until he was dead and you were here, because I didn't want, didn't want . . ."

What Emanuel didn't want he didn't have the courage to say. Instead he began to weep silently, with the tears bathing his face and flowing down to his shirt collar. He was weeping for his son, for his wife, for the hats, for the years left to live.

George held him, let him rest his head on his shoulder, and waited for him to regain the strength to speak.

"Now you are the head of this family. I tried to be, I did all I could, you know I did. Even working in the same company as Papa. I accepted it because it seemed right. But it has all been useless. Now you are the head because I no longer have descendants," Emanuel said after a few minutes, still leaning on his brother.

Then he sat up and put his hand in his pocket.

"Here," he said. "You take it."

The next morning began just before daybreak, when the cab that took George to the central station drove up the Coolsingel. George examined the construction of the new town hall, nearly finished, and he realized the city was changing; soon he would no longer recognize many areas.

The train left at seven and George took from his vest pocket the watch that he had attached to his old chain. He checked the time remaining. It was enough.

To his right he noticed the Delft gate, the only one remaining in the old city walls: a historical reminder. He, too, would leave descendants, would carry on a name, because he had two sons. Enrico was the one destined to follow his footsteps; George knew it even though the boy was only twelve years old. He understood it by the way Enrico looked at people, by his sure gestures. Ivan was less sociable and more introverted, like his mother. He loved him, too, but with fewer hopes, fewer expectations.

The cab stopped in front of the central station. George checked the watch for the last time. Then he turned it over, opened the back lid, and read the inscription on the case that he had already read many times in the hotel the previous evening.

In the end the degenerate son had left a lasting sign, as if his wrongdoing, his thoughtless acts, were only an extreme distortion of something in George, inside every van Straten who did not want his own life reduced to the feeble repetition of days.

Sixty-four years after that engraving, Uncle Benjamin's watch had become his.

XVII

Scheveningen 1924

The Vacation

*I*N SUMMERS the family reunited at Scheveningen.

There, for two or three weeks in August, the van Straten brothers and sisters would meet, and the cousins would become better acquainted, or at least some of those twenty-eight cousins, who were the fifth generation to bear the chosen name.

Scheveningen was a town on the North Sea, a few miles from The Hague, and one of the best-known holiday resorts in Holland and northern Europe at the time.

The beach was wide, long, and straight. A stone roadbed separated the beach from the street, the Strandweg, which ran parallel for its entire length. Close to the roadbed, just beyond the entrance to the beach concessions were the tents, white umbrellas enclosed for the greater part of their circumference by sheets of fabric reaching to the ground. Closer to the sea were wicker chairs with high backs that served as shelter from the wind.

The sea was a grayish color; the white of the low, wide waves decorated it with stripes near the shoreline.

Most of the people on the beach remained in street clothes, with many men in ties and jackets. Only the more open-minded, and those less sensitive to the cold, wore bathing costumes, which could be rented from the concessions.

Behind the road, toward the north, stood the large Kurhaus where the vacationers went to eat or listen to music. Toward the south were the dunes, and on the dunes the town.

Ivan still wore short pants, a three-button jacket, and an open shirt with an oversized collar whose points brushed his shoulders. Enrico, though, had begun to wear a tie that year. Both had let their hair grow, short around the ears and neck, but expanding into an undulating and rebellious bush on top. Their sisters, Nelly and Lisetta, wore skirts and blouses, white socks, and flat shoes of the same color.

Ivan felt there was something sad about that summer, which was following the last winter he would spend in Genoa. At the end of the vacation he would leave for Switzerland, to Neuchâtel, where he would attend high school. This thought tempered his enthusiasm at being once again in that warm and festive climate that so little resembled their cold and reserved life in Genoa.

There were the games at Scheveningen: enormous sand castles, bicycle races, and the inventions of *tante* Lou, Aunt Louise van Dijk. Ivan had not forgotten the time two years earlier when she took everyone to the beach on the backs of donkeys: her two children, Paul and Lineke, the four Italian van Stratens, and George Fles, the younger son of Celine and Louis.

And then there were the evenings in Scheveningen, the hours spent together, assembled in the parlor of a house rented for the holiday, listening to *oom* George play the violin, singing songs or *Lieder*, talking to each other in different languages, trying to understand, to learn, and laughing at the others' funny sounds, whether Dutch, English, or Italian.

Ivan wondered if that warmth, that manner of being together had something to do with being Jewish, but he didn't know the answer. That identity seemed of mythic proportions to him, as fascinating as that last summer of his childhood.

Merely being Jewish was mystery enough for him, because

after circumcision he had received no religious education; nor had he participated in the Jewish community or attended the synagogue. Perhaps that coldness of their life in Genoa was also due to being so removed from family traditions, from the customs kept by his Dutch aunts and uncles, aside from the Fles family, who rejected any faith, beginning with their own.

By now that distance was real, it could no longer be bridged by an act of will; during the year it was occasionally attenuated by some choice of food, a wedding, or a relative's visit. Only the summer was capable of hiding it, leaving it aside, ignoring it, covering it with games or music, with their life in common.

The cousins were many, and of such different ages that there were twenty years between the oldest, Mina Fles, and the youngest, Richard Swaab. But the groups were formed not only by age; the relationship between parents also played a part, especially the relationships that were formed over the years during the vacations. Ivan's favorite cousins were Paul van Dijk, who was twelve years old, and George Fles, born in 1908.

Those two were nothing alike. Paul belonged to the light side of the van Stratens. His hair was almost red and stood straight up; he had blue eyes and freckles that were prominent as soon as he got some sun. George had dark hair and coloring, and he wore glasses. Paul was the unruly one; his shirt always wrinkled, the tie that he wore in spite of his age always loosened so he could unbutton his shirt collar, and his energy for every adventure unlimited. George, just the opposite, was timid, his clothes always neat. He spoke little, and was careful to respect his father's wishes. But whenever there was singing, he was always happy to break out in his powerful and slightly out-of-tune voice.

Ivan, Paul, George, and Enrico still went around together as a foursome, even though the oldest was beginning to seek out different company, especially girls, and he no longer spent hours on the beach digging enormous holes with shovels brought from home; by then Enrico was already seventeen years old.

And then there was Harry Fles for Ivan. Nine years older, she certainly had nothing to do with the games and intrigue. That year Harry had arrived with her fiancé, Meijer Vorst, who was more than thirty years old, and this had promoted her definitively to the adult world. But all that had little meaning for Ivan, because Harry's thick, straight eyebrows, her short black hair, her sweet, sad expression, and especially her smile, her way of deferring to him, even without speaking, all added up to a secret sign in Ivan's eyes, a kind of magic from an older, maternal cousin.

"Will you come visit me when I am married?" Harry asked him. "When Meijer and I move to Paris?"

Ivan nodded and dreamed of a world of freedom.

Among the van Stratens there were the ugly and the beautiful, as in all families. But often the ugly, who made up the majority, were very ugly, and the beautiful were very beautiful, and this created a strange contrast.

What was there in common between Henry, *oom* Bernard's oldest son, with the embarrassed scowl on his face, his narrow shoulders, his black hair slicked down with brilliantine, and the big blue eyes and blond, gauzy hair of Betsy, his sister, who seemed so beautiful and unapproachable to Ivan, always wearing flowery dresses, exhibiting her seventeen years as though they were a snare?

Ivan asked himself this, sitting on a bench in the garden of the Hotel Clarence after coming back from the beach, watching the only four cousins who bore his same surname. They were standing around, holding their bicycles, waiting for their mother to appear from the hotel where she had been visiting her sister-in-law Henriette.

With his courteous and easy manner, Enrico had gone over to join them. Ivan, instead, had remained seated on the bench, observing them from a distance, and pondering those strange questions about family aesthetics.

"What are you doing here?" Nelly asked from behind his back.

Ivan turned and saw his sister, her smile a combination of complicity and irony.

—ᴄ᷈

Nelly had been coming out of the hotel with her mother and *tante* Johanna, Bernard's wife, when she saw Ivan and ran over to him. For Ivan, who had to make a great effort with the Dutch language, these Italian interludes were a pleasure.

"Nothing," Ivan said. "I was watching."

"Who?"

Ivan did not answer. In the meanwhile Johanna had joined her children and was on her bicycle, ready to go. The children waved toward Ivan and Nelly. Betsy also waved, with a graceful gesture that revealed a shapely arm issuing from the short sleeve of her flowered dress.

"She's too old for you," Nelly said.

Ivan had found a new intimacy with his sister, now that Enrico seemed to be growing more quickly than he, while Lisetta was still too much a child, and different, anyway, with her joy and capriciousness. Nelly, in spite of her thirteen years, seemed to understand Ivan's melancholy, almost to control it by her easy demeanor, just as she controlled her terrible curly hair in two long braids so it wouldn't be so unruly.

The bicycles disappeared around the bend leading to the park exit, and Enrico went back into the hotel on Henriette's arm.

"Now, little brother," Nelly said, "what are you thinking about?"

What about? About Betsy's beauty or about the fact that the vacation would be over soon and he would have to leave? Or even about Enrico's self-assurance, which seemed so distant from his melancholy?

Something of the eternal sameness in which he had lived up to now, the peaceful repetition of habits that had tranquilized him, was melting in the uncertainty of change. He did not know what awaited him, but he knew it would be different from the past, and that fact alone frightened him.

Suddenly Ivan got up from the bench and started running toward the back of the hotel. What was he thinking about?

"I won't tell you," he shouted to his sister as he turned the corner and crouched against the wall. He waited a moment, listening to his sister's steps on the gravel, and as soon as she appeared he grabbed her.

"That doesn't count," she said. "Did we say it was a game?"

Ivan let her go.

"You really want to know what I was thinking about?" he asked her. "I was thinking that this vacation will be over soon and I'll have to go to Switzerland."

"Why? Don't you want to go?"

"Certainly I want to go," Ivan told her, "but I'll miss you."

Nelly, embarrassed, ran her fingers through his hair.

That same evening after supper Ivan, George, and Paul were sitting on the steps of the house that Louis Fles had rented for the summer.

The sky was full of stars; across its center even the strip of the Milky Way could be seen, and the wind had died down. From inside the house came the sound of a piano and Enrico's cello. Ivan recognized the Beethoven Sonata in C Major that he had heard so often in Genoa. He, unlike his brother, had not learned to play an instrument, but he didn't care much. At times, though, he was sorry not to be able to make music with the others.

After all, wasn't it also music that these three boys were making now, in silence, sitting on the steps of a summer house, looking at the sky and thinking?

"When I grow up I want to travel around the world," Paul said.

The other two were silent.

"I'm serious! Maybe Uncle Louis will send me to Batavia."

He said this because he knew there was a branch of Louis Fles's company there, on the island of Java, and it was the most exotic place that came to mind.

"And you, Sjoppie, do you want to go to Batavia, too?" Ivan asked George, using his Jewish diminutive.

"I don't know. I haven't decided yet."

"Still, there must be something you'd like to do," Paul said.

"Maybe I'd like to see the great events of history up close. I've heard so many stories about war, but I've never seen one. And I wonder about it. Dead people, heroes, and all the rest."

This conversation seemed too serious to Ivan, who interrupted it with a joke.

"And what would your father say about a warrior son?" he asked George.

George did not laugh.

"My father is worried most of all about Barthold, because he's the oldest."

Ivan knew the firstborn had more responsibilities; everyone expected something from Enrico that they didn't ask of him. He did not know whether to be glad or humiliated, whether his father's distance was a gift of freedom or a sign of disinterest.

At that moment, however, it didn't matter, because before them was the future and a starry sky.

"You talk about the sea and the land, about journeys and war," Ivan said, laboring with his uneasy Dutch, "but aren't the stars more beautiful, and the light that travels in space, and the infinite distances that, when I try to imagine them, my head can't even comprehend?" He paused, as if groping for the proper words, then added, "I would like to be a physicist when I grow up."

"What?" Paul asked.

"A physicist, like Einstein," Ivan repeated.

He felt odd, as though the thought had never occurred to him before, at least not with such clarity. His throat was a little sore, and his head was spinning, and not from the stars, but as if he had had too much wine. Actually he had only sipped a beer. He also felt flashes of warmth, as though a fever were coming over him, but he decided to ignore them.

"That's a nice idea," said George, after looking up at the stars. "Really a nice idea."

That night he had nightmares inhabited by strange shapes, bursts of fire, and, worst of all, by something that took his breath away, obstructed his lungs. Ivan awoke in the dark and felt his skin burning with fever, his throat in a vise, as though a claw were blocking and scratching it simultaneously.

He heard Enrico's regular breathing from the next bed and

searched for reassurance in his tranquility, as if the nightmare had caused his malaise, but he still had trouble breathing and it was nearly impossible to swallow because of the pain.

"Enrico," he called, his voice weak and distorted by the swelling in his throat.

"Enrico," he repeated with difficulty, not having received a response.

"What's the matter?" Enrico asked. "What do you want?"

"I feel awful."

The light on the dresser seemed blinding to Ivan, like a flash of lightning penetrating his brain. Enrico rose and put a hand on his forehead.

"You're burning up!" he said. "Your temperature must be over a hundred and three. I'll go get Mamma."

At that precise moment, his throat closed and his breathing became a desperate wheeze. He could not move or speak, because every effort made the air penetrate his lungs. Enrico ran from the room, thinking his brother was about to die.

As soon as she saw him, Henriette knew what it was. That constriction in his throat, those muscular spasms, meant diphtheria.

Ivan was taken to the hospital at once and put in the isolation ward. He was alone, as though abandoned; his mother, who came to see him once a day, could do no more than wave at him through the glass. His brother and Nelly wrote him notes that reflected the outside world too much to be any consolation.

In the hospital Ivan realized there are insurmountable barriers, truths that cannot be explained to someone who does not experience them firsthand. In the next bed a boy who hadn't had a mother to immediately recognize the disease cried out in pain and desperation.

"I don't want to die," he cried.

He repeated it obsessively, over and over, as if it were a magic formula to oppose the concrete certainties around him, such as death in that hospital.

"I don't want to die."

"You won't die," Ivan said, but the boy seemed not to hear him, not to listen to him. He continued repeating those words that echoed around the room, filling everything with that anguish, making Ivan want to shut his ears in order not to hear them, or put his hand over the boy's mouth to keep him from saying them. Until the words became no louder than breathing, reduced to an unintelligible whisper, even though Ivan could still recognize them.

Then the boy died and they took him away. Looking at his empty bed, Ivan thought he would die, too, thought nothing could surmount the barrier to the outside world, the world that went on the same, as though it would last forever. There were no notes or hands waving in the distance that could bring him back to a normal life.

But Ivan was saved. The serotherapy began to take effect, his fever dropped, and the lesions diminished. He felt better, and although he remained in isolation, it was now only to complete his recovery. The inside and outside of the hospital had returned to being part of the same universe.

The holidays ended and his relatives returned to their own towns. Before leaving, his cousins wrote him an affectionate letter. George Fles added at the bottom, "Many good wishes to my scientist friend." Harry sent him some flowers, a small yellow bouquet.

His brothers and sisters also left, and Papa George; and then his mother, too, once it was clear her son was out of danger. So Ivan remained alone in that gray hospital room, thinking about that boy and wondering why Henriette, at least, hadn't stayed with him, while the days grew shorter and the sky became low and dark again.

The classes at Neuchâtel had been in session for several weeks when Ivan finally left the hospital.

He telephoned home from the Hotel Clarence. He hoped it would be possible to postpone his departure for Switzerland for a year, to remain tied to a world that for a few days he had thought would disappear forever. With the help of routine family life, he wanted to forget the wide-open, dazed eyes of the boy in the next bed.

But his father had already given him instructions for reaching Neuchâtel before he could explain his intentions.

"Do you feel better now?" was all that George conceded to the memory of his illness.

"Yes," said Ivan, "much better, Papa."

Thus he did not return to Genoa. He was unable to experience the routines that would attenuate his anguish, did not see any of his family again until the Christmas vacation, and from his mamma he had only a line at the end of a letter from his brother: She hoped he was fine, that his new companions were nice, and that he was not still upset about the poor boy in the hospital. "That death was really being terrible," Henriette wrote, confusing, as usual, the imperfect tense with the past absolute.

Ivan thought anyone who had not been inside that hospital room could never understand what had happened, not even his mother. Otherwise she would know the boy's death had not *been* terrible: It continued to be terrible, every day.

XVIII

São Paolo (Brazil) 1995

Chocolate Letters from *Oom* Emanuel

Now I would like to ask you for something, something I would like for a present. I saw some air rifles at Grandjean's and I would very much like to have one. They are different prices: 58 francs, 48 francs, around thirty francs, 17 or 11 francs. I think the best would be the one for 48 franks, but if you think that is too expensive I could get one for 35 francs or put a little of my savings toward it (I have 60 francs). I hope to receive your consent and money. Greetings to all, greetings and kisses to you from your

Ivan

*I*T'S A SQUARE SHEET of paper, the number three written at the top (but the other two pages are lost). The handwriting is large and childish. My mother found it in a drawer and gave it to me. Something leaped out (even if it is not a message for future memory), and I repeat it all, not because it is very important, but because it is the only thing my father wrote that has been found.

On the right side of the paper are two small drawings: above, a sort of clown with a narrow, long hat. Under that, a thin little man in a pointed hat urinating in a vase. Underneath, in a smaller, adult hand, is written: THE GARDENER.

Did my father draw them? His brother Enrico? A friend at Neuchâtel?

Certainly they must have been added later, if this letter was ever sent, because it would not have been the most auspicious means for obtaining "consent and money."

I also wonder why this is the only piece of writing to survive, this sheet of paper that has the appearance of a first draft, that tells me nothing interesting, and only relates the naive desire of an adolescent sending a letter to his parents from Switzerland during his high school years. Was it perhaps just for those drawings that my father saved it?

There is something I am unable to see under the opaque patina that time has spread over those lives. Facts are not missing. I have a sufficient number of those; but existence is composed of so many different things, of gradations, atmosphere, feelings that I cannot reach.

It is like a polyptych stolen from a church, whose sections have been separated and then come to light centuries later in different places far from one another. Now they cannot be reunited. None of the present owners wants to recognize the fact that he possesses only a part of it, because unlike the tiles in a destroyed mosaic, each of which is only a piece of colored stone, a separate part can be admired. Yet only by putting all the panels together can the polyptych's meaning and worth be fully appreciated.

Then it would take a thief, rather than a restorer, to plan a theft by installment, until every part was in his hands and the altarpiece appeared whole before even one man's eyes: There, leaning against the walls the panels would be reassembled, and that thief could then, after centuries, be the first to grasp a sense of the whole.

São Paolo, Brazil, is a city without limits. Even seen from a plane it never seems to end: first flat with slums and low houses, then sharply pointed by an expanse of skyscrapers that extend to the horizon. No one can calculate exactly how many people live there because the number increases daily.

Memory doesn't seem to have a place in São Paolo. After arriving there I saw only the present: the traffic, the line of slow-moving cars, the air that scratched my throat, the poverty sleeping on the sidewalks, the violence waiting outside barred windows.

I had gone there for work, but I hoped to find a panel of my polyptych, something that would help me understand the life of those adolescents in the mid-'20s.

In the phone book, as though normal in the middle of the chaos that continually transformed the city, I found a name and address that had remained unchanged over the years, identical to what was written in my father's old address book.

Her voice was kind, almost excited, when I told her who I was.

"Please," she replied in an Italian without accent, "come have lunch with us tomorrow."

Then I understood how time could outlive itself; in some niche it can manage to barricade itself, ready to surprise us, and at the same time, to ignore us.

"Will you come?" she insisted.

"With pleasure," I replied.

The signora, that old signora who had courteously answered the telephone, lived in a good neighborhood, in a building separated from the street by a garden and gate. When I rang a porter appeared, asked whom I wanted, and left me waiting on the sidewalk while he talked with the signora and received assurances that I was expected.

I seemed to be entering a place protected from the outside not only for reasons of security, but also to hide the permanence of the past, of objects, people, furniture that no longer resembled the outside reality.

The woman had come directly there after leaving Italy with

her husband as a result of the enactment of the racial laws. She had crossed the ocean, leaving everything she knew to start over again. She had reconstructed a life and seemed to want to protect it from every ulterior change.

Her husband was very old and sick; he seemed to have suspended all communication with others. The woman, however, treated me kindly, and tried to help me reconstruct the past, but she spoke as if everything came from behind glass, as if she were unable to re-create that life within herself.

Smiling, she told me that as a child she had been in love with my father and that my grandfather, being aware of this, had always teased her about it.

"I must have some photos here of a week in the mountains . . ."

But I was unable to imagine anything; I remained inside the bubble of that apartment, isolated like that woman's life.

"And I also remember Uncle Emanuel who often came from Holland and brought us chocolate letters. What do you call them in Italy? *Quaresimali?* It was always a party when he came. He spent a lot of time in Genoa."

And then, only then, perhaps because she was remembering the taste of those cookies, perhaps because she had for a moment heard an echo from that past, she looked at me with her elderly woman's clear eyes, but smiled with a hint of a girl's mischievousness.

"It seemed like the world was young," she said, "that everything was ahead of us. Nice things, extraordinary things never before seen. Evil, if it existed somewhere, had nothing to do with us, could not touch us. So we thought. But instead . . ."

Beyond that *instead* she did not go. I did not want to go there, either. It was not the moment. But that young world, I understood that one, because perhaps all of us have seen such a world, or we have imagined seeing it.

Now, instead, the world is old, it shows its wrinkles and years. Maybe that woman was right: To endure you must find an apartment and pretend there is nothing outside it. But I had to return to the hotel, go out into the streets of São Paolo without any protection for my soul.

Those children of the '20s stayed with me, however; their lives, the magic moment of suspension before the bomb exploded. And they were good company.

Because the polyptych panels dispersed throughout the world, or destroyed, may be created and reassembled in one's own head; in any event, the most detached restorer, like the most devoted thief, must imagine the result of his own work before actually beginning it.

XIX

Pegli 1927

A Common Experience

THE SUMMER OF '27 was not only sea, rocky beach, and big umbrellas crammed together for lack of space. It was not only Pegli, squeezed between the train tracks and the water, its hills with scattered villas and views of the Riviera that on the clearest days stretched from Capo Mele to Portofino.

For Enrico, who had also been ill the previous year, all this certainly would have been enough now that the symptoms of the Malta fever no longer persisted, now that he no longer had to be careful about sweating, now that he could go out evenings, could run and dance. Enrico was cured, and could lead the same life as the other boys.

He and Ivan wore bathing shorts, like all their contemporaries now, and looked with condescension on Uncle Emanuel who still wore an entire costume, like the women. They often laughed about it together.

For Ivan, the time spent with his brother would also be enough to make that July a real summer, a time when he tried to learn to act and talk like a man, now that he was almost eighteen years old.

He wasn't always able to imitate Enrico's self-assurance, his sometimes surprising certainties; his sympathy for Fascism, for instance, especially in the early years, because of the order it had brought Italy, he said. Ivan, meanwhile, questioned the violence and arrogance of those black shirts.

Otherwise he looked to Enrico as a model of what he would like to be, of what his father seemed to ask of a son, and those days together made up for the Swiss winters and gave him hope that even for him it was just a question of time.

No, summer was not only the sea, that summer of '27 in particular. There were also the girls to wile away the hours. In the beginning it was still a game for Ivan, like the glances exchanged with one of Nelly's friends, after his sister let him know that the girl was in love with him.

George van Straten — or Giorgio, as everyone called him now — laughed at the awkward overtures he saw made by those girls, who didn't have the preoccupations and shrewdness of their older sisters. When some girlfriend came to the house looking for Nelly, he would bow like a chivalrous admirer. And he would say to the embarrassed girl, "Don't you think I'm too old for you, Signorina?"

The girl would blush, while Nelly dashed off laughing.

"Oh, Papa!" she would say.

"What did I do?" he would ask, with mock surprise.

Enrico explained to Ivan that women shouldn't be taken too seriously, but it wasn't a game, either. And Ivan felt that life was growing inside him and that time was spreading out in front of him with an unlimited horizon.

The girls arrived that month of July '27, those who wore short skirts and low-necked bathing suits.

So summer was also dances held in the garden of the Grand Hôtel Méditerranée Pegli. The orchestra played the Charleston, Black Bottom, and Slow Fox Trot, the girls wore straight dresses with short pleated skirts and laughed a lot; everyone smoked cigarettes as if they were the passport to becoming an adult.

Lisetta didn't go with them in spite of her pleading, because thirteen was really too young. Nelly met her girlfriends there and left her brothers alone, so Ivan and Enrico could move among the tables with their synchronized step, hands and eyes moving rapidly like a snake's.

Ivan had things to learn, but there was also happiness, and unconscious hours spent without effort or thought. He would invite a girl to dance, usually a casual acquaintance or friend of his sister's, and Nelly watched with affection and pride.

Almost always at the beginning of the dance, when the light still clung to the edges of the sky, he would feel the cool sea breeze blowing lightly from the west. Then the breeze would fall and darkness would descend.

"There is always a first time," Enrico told him laughingly, when he caught him looking at a woman without finding the courage to approach her.

His words seemed an affectionate encouragement. He didn't hear coldness and sarcasm. He was his older brother.

Occasionally Ivan would lose sight of Enrico, then suddenly notice his presence behind him, calling him over to introduce him to some foreign girl.

Ivan would bow slightly, saying, "Mademoiselle."

Enrico would nod in satisfaction and vanish again.

The girl must have been older than he, by at least four or five years. Or perhaps the lipstick, the cigarette holder, and the painted fingernails deceived him.

It wasn't the first time Ivan had seen her at a hotel dance; in fact, he remembered very distinctly his brother introducing her to him. She always came with a group of girlfriends, all from Turin, who were spending the summer in Pegli.

Ivan thought she was beautiful. She had almond-shaped green eyes, black hair cut like a helmet, narrow fingers that fluttered in front of him like wings. But her mouth attracted him most of all, with her heart-shaped red lips; a mouth that also repelled him, almost frightened him, for the expression of scorn and boredom that crossed it occasionally.

"Don't go overboard, little brother," Enrico said when Ivan

told him how much he admired her. "Be careful not to fall in love with Giovanna. The seaside isn't the most suitable place, and she's not the best woman for it."

Ivan hadn't exactly understood what Enrico meant, but he preferred to keep quiet. Being in love with her wasn't the problem, but rather being able to talk to her, because she wasn't a friend of Nelly's, and she seemed to know how both to attract and reject him. Also, she had the advantage of experience over him, or perhaps only the habit of receiving men's attention.

Ivan was afraid of failure, of making a move, such as kissing a woman, only to have her stop him with supreme indifference by a vague and haughty wave of her hand.

Consequently he had decided that when given his first opportunity to kiss a woman, he would do it only if it was a sure thing.

That evening he danced with many of Nelly's friends, especially Augusta, whom Ivan knew admired him. It gave him confidence to lead those girls to the dance floor, knowing the right steps and rhythms, in the hope that Giovanna would notice him.

Ivan was dressed in white, with a wide-collared open shirt, lightweight linen trousers, and shoes of the same color.

Between dances he went to the bar and had something to drink, better if alcoholic because he hoped it would give him the necessary courage to start a conversation with Giovanna should the occasion present itself.

"You are in great form tonight, my brother," Enrico said at a certain point, and then he introduced him to a rather ugly English girl with dull hair and very white skin sprinkled with freckles.

"Do you want to be a little company to Margot?" he asked, going away.

The girl smiled and Ivan held out his arm to escort her to the dance floor.

Later George arrived to escort Nelly back to her room. She waved good-bye to Ivan, who had freed himself from the English girl and was again drinking at the bar. Nelly had grown up. She wore her hair shorter now, with a part on the right, the other side puffing out like a cloud, which irritated her. Her face looked serene and she had wide hips.

Ivan waved back, then turned, trying to find Enrico among the dancers or the people gathered around the tables. But Enrico seemed to have disappeared, dissolved into nothing.

Then Ivan looked up in an effort to distinguish the stars and constellations beyond the bulbs hung like festoons in the garden trees. He saw little, though, because the luminous halo of the artificial lighting obscured the sky.

After their dance, the young Englishwoman sat down at a table by herself. Ivan, feeling guilty that his brother had left her in that fashion, ordered another drink and started walking toward her with it.

He was halfway between the bar and the English girl's table when he saw Enrico moving, almost parallel to him, toward Margot. He had red cheeks and tufts of hair in disorder in spite of the brilliantine.

Ivan stopped to call to him. He had just turned in his brother's direction when he was surprised by a voice behind him.

"Are you bringing me a drink?" Giovanna asked him.

He wheeled around to find her looking at him, smiling, and she continued speaking.

"I saw you with two glasses in your hand, and I hoped one of them was for me."

Ivan handed it to her.

"Who are you two-timing right now?" asked Giovanna. "Because this can't be for me. You didn't even see me. Or have you become prophetic?"

"No, but I always keep one in reserve," Ivan said.

Sometimes a few words can change the course of events, at least those trifling ones that, when put together, form an entire life. That reply seemed to Ivan to suffice, putting an end to his embarrassment and allowing him to feel more secure, capable of leading the dance even with this young woman with the red lips and short skirt.

Giovanna took the glass and drank down the contents in a single gulp, her head thrown back. Ivan looked at her long, slender neck, and as she put the glass down on the next table, indifferent to whomever might be sitting there, he looked into her eyes. "Shall we dance?" he asked her.

It must not have been her first drink of the evening, because as she said yes she leaned on his arm with the strength of one who has some doubt about her ability to maintain her equilibrium.

She laughed when Ivan pulled her toward the edge of the garden, toward the wall where a group of trees and the dark protected them from being seen by the others. She laughed and ran, almost leaping in her high heels.

Then there they were, next to the crumbling plaster wall, with Giovanna leaning against it, her hands behind her back. She wasn't laughing anymore; she was looking into his eyes, her lips slightly open, still breathless from their run.

But there was also a challenge in the way she looked at him, and in her barely open lips. He came closer, but was still slightly hesitant, afraid of feeling her hand on his chest to push him away.

Instead she did not move.

"What are you doing?" was all she said, in a deep voice, a bit hoarse from breathing.

What was he doing? Ivan bent over her face, no longer looking at her, incapable of focusing on anything but her mouth.

When his lips found hers he closed his eyes.

He waited until he was in the room with Enrico before saying anything. He felt he had something important to divulge about his admittance into adult life, and he rehearsed the moment when he would surprise his brother with the news.

He had succeeded in kissing Giovanna, there, against the wall, pressing her lips, finding her tongue, passing his hand over her light dress.

As soon as he entered the room, Enrico threw himself on the bed, his shoes hanging off the edge, his arms crossed behind his head.

"I had a good time this evening," he said.

Ivan was standing near the door. He felt slightly dizzy, a mixture of alcohol and tiredness.

"What are you doing there?" Enrico asked him. "Don't you want to go to the bathroom first?"

That was their routine when they slept together.

"I kissed Giovanna a little while ago. After dancing with her. Near the wall."

"Bravo, little brother," Enrico said with no apparent surprise. "So tonight we both kissed her."

"You, too?" Ivan asked.

Enrico did not reply but began laughing. He seemed happy about that pleasure shared with his brother, as if he had participated in his initiation. And Ivan laughed with him, hoping to cover something he immediately wanted to forget.

So they had a good laugh together, though not in the same way.

Naples 1928

In a Hotel Bathroom

*T*HERE ARE MANY ways to be twenty years old. Enrico's way was made of combed-back hair, so thick it formed a wave on top of his head, and of elegant suits and a pearl stickpin; it was made of a sweet look, a small mouth, a full face, and a prominent nose.

Most of all it was made of rules he imposed on himself, almost without his realizing it, to resemble the man he expected to become, that is, a young manager of an important company.

There are many ways to be twenty years old; Enrico's was an adult way.

He worked at Sorveglianza of Naples, lived in a hotel, and had stopped worrying about his health. He played tennis and soccer, perspired without concern, was happy and enjoyed himself, had a social life and liked girls. He loved to skim the surface of things, just brushing them, because everything was easier that way, less complicated; besides, that was the way he had learned one must be, the way he had interpreted his father's behavior, which he used as a model. Around him existed a world to be observed with curiosity, but without becoming too involved, in order to avoid unexpected surprises.

Life seemed so fragile to him that only by following the rules, only by respecting the role he had been assigned, could he hope not to spoil it. Sometimes he worried about his brother in this regard, about his abstract melancholy, and he tried to bring him down to earth with the letters he sent to Neuchâtel, with trivial descriptions of a billiard game or a jaunt to the sea. He thought this part of his duty as the older brother, heir to the family tradition: He would teach Ivan how to face the world without getting hurt.

In the meanwhile he was getting his life ready, marking its stages without forcing their passage, and when he was uncertain about something he tried to imagine what his father would have done under the same circumstances and then he acted accordingly.

"You are charming, van Straten."

That's how Marcel Levy put it, a French friend who worked in Naples, when he opened the door to Enrico's room and found him sitting on the edge of the bed looking out the window.

"And you, dear Levy, enter without knocking," Enrico replied, rising quickly and trying to straighten the papers on the desk.

"I see you have written a letter," Marcel pressed on, smiling.

"And I imagine you want to know to whom. The answer is easy. You know. To Kissina. But what I write is no business of yours."

Kissina played a part in his future plans. He had met her at Gressoney the previous summer, at the Grand Hôtel Miravalle. In the beginning he had watched her from a distance while she walked her dog Kiss; in order to speak about her to his friends, and in the absence of any other information, her nickname had come from the name he heard her call the little pet. In time he met and courted her, and finally kissed her in the doorway of an abandoned hut. He continued to write her, and thought they might become engaged. But there was time for this also.

"Certainly what you write in your letters is none of my business, but I have the right to worry about arriving on time for appointments," Levy said. "Get dressed because the Boruchowitzes are expecting us."

After supper the hosts and many guests began playing poker,

but Enrico preferred to watch. He soon left the tables and began telling Levy, Charles Lièvre, and Signorina Cori, a blue-eyed Neapolitan, stories about conjurers and a trip to the mountains, where a house that many said was haunted by ghosts was inhabited only by two cats. Enrico was in an excellent mood, but toward the end of the evening he became laconic, absentminded.

"What's wrong?" Marcel asked him.

"Nothing. Only a little headache."

"You need a purge!" Charles Lièvre told him. Lièvre was distinguished for his pedantry, and for an absolute lack of wit that was accompanied by the conviction of having one.

Enrico, out of kindness, began to laugh.

At twelve-thirty he left with Marcel Levy to return to the boardinghouse on Piazza Amedeo. They went by foot, sniffing the air like hunting dogs, trying to identify the odors of spring.

Naples had the breath of the south, the fascination of mature fruit just before spoiling. Enrico could remember nothing like it, was unfamiliar with the world of the scirocco.

"You'll get used to it," Marcel had told him many times. Born in Normandy, he posed as a southerner but continued to speak to him only in French.

That time, too, before parting at the boardinghouse door, Marcel repeated one of his syrupy phrases: "It's the most beautiful city in the world."

Enrico agreed. At the same time the perspiration that was standing like beads on his forehead frightened him, reminding him of the danger it had signaled at the time of his illness. It also seemed as if that climate could lay something bare, draw out the mysteries buried in every man. Enrico didn't want this to happen, because he didn't know what he might find in himself.

"Do you want to come get me tomorrow so we can go to Signor Hakim's house together?" he asked Marcel as he left him at the boardinghouse.

"All right. I'll be at your place at twelve-thirty."

Enrico remained in the doorway until Marcel disappeared behind the corner of the piazza, then went inside.

He woke up early, a little after eight, still with that pressure in his
head and a slight feeling of hunger. He stayed in bed, hoping the
discomfort would pass. Behind the heavy curtain appeared the
veiled light of a spring Sunday morning.

At nine-thirty he requested breakfast and ate it in bed: two eggs,
bread and butter, the usual tea. The food and daylight made him
feel better, and Enrico savored the delights of a tranquil Sunday, of
the not-very-demanding performance awaiting him. Training and
experience had taught him there was an appropriate gesture or
word for every situation, and one could develop the ability to reproduce them automatically, therefore completely naturally.

But the real, personal words and gestures, those of Enrico van
Straten and no one else, what were they? Who had ever seen them?

At ten-thirty he called the maid to turn on the hot-water
heater. The girl, waiting for the tub to fill, stood near the room's
window. She seemed almost embarrassed to have to stay there
with a man more or less her age, and she kept playing with a lock
of hair, looking toward the piazza.

"You can go," Enrico told her with a slight smile, kind but
mocking. "I can turn the water heater off when it's hot enough."

After ten minutes the maid knocked on the door:

"Excuse me, Signore," she said, "but I didn't give you clean
towels."

Enrico, already in the bathroom, opened the door a crack and
took the towels the maid handed him. Perhaps something else was
seen through that crack, but the girl acted as if nothing happened,
and gave a barely perceptible bow when Enrico thanked her.

He watched her walk away from the room with her silent and
undulating step, and he turned the key in the door again. The tub
was almost full, so he turned off the water heater. Once more he
had the sensation, barely perceptible, that something was not
right, that he might be coming down with something, that there

was some sign to be heeded, a warning. But it lasted only a matter of a second, and Enrico didn't understand what it meant.

He slipped into the tub, immersing his legs first, and then the rest of his body. The water, a little too hot, enveloped his limbs in a welcoming embrace.

It was a Sunday, a typical Sunday in the spring of 1928. Enrico had nothing more to do than kill time until the midday meal, letting his body recover the efficiency everyone recognized, which at the moment seemed slightly affected. Maybe those last few days had been too tiring. He thought he would go to Capri the following weekend to relax, and if it was sunny he would have his first swim of the season in the sea.

Marcel Levy was a very precise fellow, as unimaginative men often are, with his shirts always ironed and his bow tie, which he frequently wore, always perfectly straight. He was also very punctual, so it often happened that he arrived early. In such cases, punctuality being only one aspect of his upbringing, he would take a walk in front of the place of appointment and wait for the exact time.

That Sunday morning he knew that in spite of the long walk he would arrive at the boardinghouse on Piazza Amedeo half an hour before the predetermined time. Nevertheless he decided not to slow his pace and not to wait outside. He thought Enrico, too, would like the idea of having an aperitif before joining their host.

So at noon he entered the lobby and asked for Signor van Straten.

"He is still in his room," they told him at the reception desk.

"I'll go call him," said the young maid who was passing by the desk at that moment.

Marcel looked at her and smiled at her sense of timing, convinced it wasn't due only to professional zeal.

"Fine," he said. "Tell Signor van Straten that I'll be waiting for him here in the lobby."

The maid went upstairs, but came back down almost immediately.

"That's strange," she said to Marcel. "He's still in the bathroom. He went in at ten-thirty and hasn't come out."

Levy ascends the staircase, enters the room, and automatically looks at the desk where the letter for Kissina had been placed the evening before. The desk is clear. He knocks on the bathroom door, but receives no reply.

"Enrico," he calls.

Nothing.

"Enrico, what's going on?"

Still silence.

Marcel raises his voice and shouts, "Enrico, open up."

The maid, who has followed him into the room, stands behind him, clenching her fists.

Levy tries to open the bathroom door, but it is locked. He turns to the girl, as though to ask what he should do, but she looks at him without expression. Marcel tries the handle again without success, and then hurls his shoulder against the door, forcing it open.

Enrico is in the tub. His head and neck are above water, he has the serene expression of someone taking a bath, but his eyes are wide open and he is not moving. Levy comes closer and touches him. His body is still warm.

The maid is in the doorway, hands to her mouth, but she does not scream, does not make a sound. Marcel takes hold of Enrico, mindless as he drenches his suit and musses his bow tie, and he lifts him out of the water. He drags him to the bed with great effort.

"Is there a doctor here?" he asks the maid, out of breath.

She nods but does not speak.

"Quick, run and call him. Don't stand there like a half-wit."

The girl runs out of the room and her voice, like a scream, echoes in the hallway. Marcel passes a hand over his wet jacket lapel, then looks at his friend and covers his body with a towel. *Enrico is dead*, Marcel thinks, as though inside an opaque shell, as though those words had suddenly changed meaning.

The doctor arrives. He looks at Enrico, bends over his chest, puts an ear to his sternum, and says there is nothing to do.

"He's been dead for at least half an hour."

"But he is still warm," Marcel says. "He's still warm."

The doctor shakes his head.

"Only because he was in the water."

The maid leaves the room, sobbing, and Marcel stands looking at the empty doorway where the girl passed just an instant before, as if perhaps a reply could come from there.

Levy telephoned two friends of the van Stratens: Charles Boruchowitz, the manager of the Neapolitan branch of Sorveglianza, and Charles Lièvre. The men came at once, and together they decided to call Dr. Guglielmo Tobino, a well-known physician who had given Enrico a checkup a year earlier. They went to pick him up at Vomero and brought him back to the boardinghouse. In the meantime the police had arrived and the bathroom door was again locked, awaiting the magistrate's investigation.

As though overcome by a useless and uncontrollable frenzy, the three men went out again, found the magistrate, and brought him to Enrico's room. There they found the forensics doctor, the magistrate's clerk, and an engineer who had been summoned to check the hot-water heater. The doctors were unanimous: Death was not due to gas poisoning, because there was no odor, nor was it congestion, because his face was calm and relaxed. His heart had perhaps been undermined without his knowing it by the Malta fever. An aneurysm or embolism. A sudden death. Enrico didn't even have time to ring the bell next to the tub.

Marcel left Boruchowitz and Lièvre in the room, numb and motionless after their frenetic anxiety a short time earlier. He went down to the lobby of the boardinghouse and asked to call Signor George van Straten in Genoa. While he waited for the call to be put through, he thought about what to say. But nothing seemed right.

"Genoa on the line," the porter told him.

Marcel Levy took the receiver from his hands and began speaking. "This is Marcel Levy. Yes, Marcel Levy. Do you remember me? I am a friend of Enrico's. I am calling from Naples . . ."

It was Sunday. Sunday, April 1, 1928.

The Time of History

Stettin 1928

The Substitution

THE WORLD WAS contained by an enormous gray membrane, a foggy sphere that kept everyone from seeing past its boundary. And inside that ball it rained all day without letting up, a rain of dense little drops that ran down the windowpanes.

Frau Guterman prepared a strong black coffee and poured it in a cup that she set on the little table next to him, while he sat looking through the window at what could be seen outside: the gray membrane, fog, and rain.

The steam from the coffee spiraled toward the ceiling and soon could not be distinguished from the smoke from Ivan's umpteenth cigarette. Strong cigarettes, like Frau Guterman's coffee, unfiltered, of American tobacco consumed persistently and desperately, never for pleasure, but rather as a matter of principle, as if finishing two packs a day were a goal to achieve, a mission.

This was the way it went on Saturday afternoons and on Sundays, the only times of the week he didn't work.

Frau Guterman shook her head.

"There's never been an autumn like this one, where it didn't stop raining," she said.

There really never had been such an autumn; but Ivan, who knew that well enough, though for other reasons, did not reply. Frau Guterman left the room, still shaking her head over the rain, but also over a boy who spent his days in such a way and who barely said two words.

His father had called him into his study a few hours after Enrico's funeral, a few hours before he took the train for Switzerland. Ivan didn't want to see or talk to anyone because he felt that any human contact, any communication with the world, served to make his brother's death more concrete and real. He wanted to get back on the train, in the compartment, surrounded by people who seemed to look at life as a normal, daily fact, where he could believe that it had all been a mistake, that the announcement was a joke and Enrico was still alive.

But his father had called him into his study because he wanted to talk to him, and this brought the pain back to its unbearable essence.

When he entered the room he smelled the familiar odor, sweet and intense, of his father's cigar.

George was sitting in an armchair and only the slackness of his body, as though shattered, gave any indication of what had happened. His face, meanwhile, showed no traces of desperation or grief.

Ivan remained standing. He wasn't tall, but his stiff, lean figure made one forget his five feet seven inches. George looked at him, still smoking his cigar, unable to bring himself to speak; Ivan would have liked to smoke one of his cigarettes, but he refrained, since the family didn't know he had taken up the vice.

There was a question in his father's look, a silent query, a desire to find in Ivan what until then he had never imagined in his younger son, in the one who now was the only male.

They remained facing each other in silence until George stood up and placed his cigar on the edge of the ashtray. He went to Ivan and drew him close. It was a strange gesture, unexpected, because there had never been the physical closeness between them that his father was now displaying. Ivan wanted to cry, but shame restrained him, and he pulled away without the courage to look George in the face. Instead his eyes fell on the cigar that continued to smolder in the ashtray, and on the clean, colorful light of the sunset outside the window. Ivan knew that only a frenzy of movement could mitigate the pain, only a succession of superfluous gestures could check the desperation, but he felt paralyzed.

"Now things are different. Nothing can be like it was before. Not my life, not yours," George had begun.

Ivan had already imagined what it would be about, but the violence of that affirmation, its inevitability, had struck him with such a force as to make him lose the words that followed. He could not hear them. At that moment he understood the impossibility of remaining on the sidelines, of avoiding attention, as he had done up to now; one of the foundations of his life was crumbling.

"You are the family heir," his father was saying when Ivan could hear his words again. "And the heir must assume his responsibilities. Those that Enrico had readily accepted; now they are up to you."

Ivan's mind had turned to an evening with Paul van Dijk and George Fles under the stars at Scheveningen. The youngest of Celine's children was unhappy about the lack of attention he received from his father, Louis, although it offered him, without his understanding, a freedom of choice. Ivan had been aware of that advantage. "I would like to be a scientist," he had said.

"I have faith in you. I'm sure you can do it," his father added.

Ivan doubted that was true. He was afraid George had no faith; he didn't have it, either, and that profession wasn't what he wanted. The only option, for everyone's sake, was to tell his father no. It was the best thing, the only possible way for everyone to recover, albeit slowly. Each one of them had to continue his life as he had started it.

"I have already spoken to Salmanowitz. He agrees there should be another van Straten working in the business," George continued.

Ivan felt he should stop him before the events gained the upper hand over thought and reason. It was difficult to deny his father anything, to upset his habit of getting what he wanted, and yet this time he had to do it.

"But high school . . . ," he said, to gain time.

"Certainly, you must finish it. You will stay until July. After that come the holidays, and in the autumn you can start work."

It was wrong, Ivan knew it. He was not Enrico and had never been. But he didn't say so.

His choices, his desires, suddenly seemed the product of small-mindedness, selfishness. Enrico had not been able to choose, not before, not after. Didn't he owe him something? And his father, and the whole family?

"All right," he said. "I hope I won't disappoint you and can be worthy of your faith."

George had nodded in agreement, though his expression seemed to deny that consensus, or at least to make it questionable from where Ivan stood.

"There is a position in Stettin," his father concluded. "You will start there."

When he arrived in Stettin, Ivan didn't want to live in a hotel. He had looked for a room to rent and had found it in Frau Guterman's apartment on Grabower Strasse. It was a nice building, near the botanical gardens, and the woman was very kind. Her husband, an officer of a merchant ship, was at sea, and her daughter had recently married.

Rosa Guterman was a fat and affectionate Jew with large blue eyes who tried to the best of her ability to look after that boy with the lost expression. Someone told her what had happened, but she had never spoken to him about it, nor had Ivan confided in her.

With a naturalness slightly veiled by amazement, Rosa accepted the strange behaviors of her guest, such as his habit of announcing every time he went into the bathroom. What need was there, she asked herself, to inform her of this each time?

But she never asked him about it, even though she should

have guessed something the day she absentmindedly entered while Ivan was in the tub.

"I'm sorry," Frau Guterman said, retreating in embarrassment, "but why didn't you lock the door?"

As she closed the door she waited for an answer that did not come.

That summer, the summer of 1928, the van Stratens went on vacation as though nothing had happened. First to Pegli, again with *oom* Emanuel, then to the mountains, at Combloux, near Megève, and finally to Wengen, in the Bernese Alps. They also took a trip up the Jungfrau, for an excursion on the glacier: George, Lisetta, and Ivan. He wore plus fours, boots, a jacket with a high zippered collar, a beret, and dark glasses with round lenses and thin frames. He looked elegant, almost handsome.

In the wide mountain spaces it seemed possible to elude the ambushes of time. Memories faded into the present, as if Enrico were in another room, or at the most in a town nearby. Henriette's hair, now completely white, could be attributed to the passage of years, and when George took a photograph everyone managed to smile as though it were natural.

Ivan thought he could probably do it, could comply with his father's wishes; facing the immutability of the mountains, he was convinced that life was made of marked roads that, once taken, would lead in the desired direction without apparent difficulty.

But when the vacation was over and Ivan went to Stettin, the world had exploded; he had doubled over without a sound, breaking into tiny, irreparable pieces. In the enormous gray membrane of the north everything turned out to be muffled, deformed, unrecognizable. And the roads that Ivan had glimpsed going up the Jungfrau had disintegrated.

The daily work seemed incomprehensible and pointless; his colleagues were faded figures who took no interest in him. He had waited futilely for some signs from home that would bring back the serenity of the summer, but all that arrived were the typical laconic letters like those he had known at Neuchâtel, and a postcard from Grandma Keizer for his birthday, sent from Winschoten.

It rained in Stettin as though it would never stop, and even when it stopped that gray patina remained in the air, that low, oppressive sky. Ivan concentrated all his efforts on the single objective of surviving.

The days accumulated without order, so alike as to be rapidly confused with each other, and so long as to appear infinite. There was no solution, no way out. Ivan multiplied the days by the cigarettes smoked and came up with frightening numbers. His life was besieged with numbers: prices, tons of merchandise, records to be filed.

If only the sea were in Stettin, even metallic and abstract as the Baltic. But the sea was forty miles to the north, at the mouth of the Oder, the wide, slow river that the inhabitants of the city had transformed into a port, made navigable by locks as far as Berlin.

Ivan would have liked to see the ocean, and he often thought about organizing an expedition to go there; but every weekend he shut himself up in his room without finding the energy for a trip as far away as the Gulf of Pomerania.

The autumn grew chilly, and darkness fell progressively earlier.

"Why don't you go out?" Frau Guterman asked him. "Why don't you have a little fun?"

"I'm tired," Ivan replied.

There was, in effect, something that oppressed him, drained his energy, kept him in his room. He ate little and slept a lot; he never lost a night's sleep, yet he always woke up tired, and often late in the afternoon, before supper, he would fall in bed again and sleep.

At the end of November the wind rose, the clouds ran toward the east, the skies cleared.

Frau Guterman felt relieved. Hers was a tranquil life; her daughter was settled, her husband sent long letters from ports where he landed, and Poland, where her ancestors had suffered so, was beyond a border. She was a Jew living in Germany and felt secure.

But that boy worried her, and now she hoped the blue sky that spread over them would allow him some respite. And so she waited for him with more confidence that evening, convinced it was only the rain and the distance from home that disturbed him, because Frau Guterman was a simple, honest woman.

But when she saw him come in wearing his gray raincoat as if the rain were still falling, with his eyes bright, almost feverish, a cigarette between his lips, she understood that it was not a question of atmospheric conditions.

So that evening, after giving him his dinner, she took a piece of stationery, one of those blue sheets she kept carefully stored in the desk in the parlor, and wrote to Signor van Straten in Genoa, because someone had to inform him of his son's condition. She wrote it in her elementary German, a letter of only one page. She sent it the next morning and hoped she had done the right thing.

Something had been broken forever, and even if someone could be found to fix it, the world would never function the same again. An enormous machine had jammed; Ivan was aware of it and marveled that the others could go on living as if nothing had happened. Yet the crisis did not pertain only to him, it did not come only with Enrico's death.

In those months of madness he seemed to have moments of intense, almost prophetic, lucidity, as if time opened up before and behind him. Perhaps the visions experienced by his ancestor Hartog Alexander more than a century earlier in a Rotterdam square passed through his mind; if so, those images had now come closer and were more frightening. They became nightmares. And Ivan forgot them, too, just as his ancestor had.

The cold arrived. Ice formed on the banks of the Oder and began to grow toward the middle of the river. Soon the port would be impassable. Ivan's thoughts continued to expand, formless, loaded with an incommunicable complexity, and he retreated ever more into silence and cigarette smoke.

"They'll make you sick," Frau Guterman told him during a fit of coughing.

"It's the cold," Ivan replied, "not the cigarettes."

She would have liked to tell him that it was neither, but rather the desperation that enveloped him and would not give him rest. But she was only the landlady, and there were limits to how much she could say.

"I'll fix you some hot milk," she said, hoping there was someone in Genoa more helpful than she.

George kept Frau Guterman's letter on the table for some time, but he didn't show it to Henriette. In those lines he had read the announcement of a wager lost, with no one at fault. The son in whom he had put all his hopes and expectations was dead, the strong son; the other one, shy and smiling little Ivan, the one he had often felt a responsibility to defend from the cruelty of the world, didn't have shoulders strong enough to carry the burden he had entrusted him.

Yet for weeks he did nothing but send him two or three post-cards written with the wide letters of his fountain pen and ending with "affectionate kisses from your Papa" — the only means by which George could let him know he loved him. Those postcards went unanswered.

Finally he turned to the director in Geneva, hoping to find out how things were going from the manager of the Stettin branch. He did it in a cordial tone, yet he made it clear, given the level of his position in the company, that he expected his son to be given special consideration.

He was told the head of the office in Stettin gave Ivan a good report, though the boy seemed absentminded, little interested in the work or in the other workers. The manager asked if Signor van Straten's son might not by chance be dissatisfied with his situation because he was already able to take on more demanding work.

George knew that was not the case. So he took Frau Guterman's letter from the desk and threw it in the wastebasket. He no longer needed it because he knew it was true.

He had never felt lost, even when his mother died, even during his solitude in Odessa. But now he had to recognize that Ivan was different from him, and different from Enrico.

That evening he spoke to Henriette with the necessary prudence, without letting her know more than was necessary, especially since she navigated at a distance, returning from it only occasionally. She never showed grief; in fact, she behaved as though nothing had happened. And yet George knew her behavior was a strategy for survival.

So he said to her, "We all need a vacation. I made reservations at Andermatt for February. And I'd like to have Ivan come, too. It can't be easy for him up there alone. Stettin is not Neuchâtel."

"Did he write you?" Henriette asked.

George thought about the postcards that Henriette had also signed, those postcards without a reply.

"No."

"Well, then, how do you know?"

How did he know? George did not want to tell her about the letter or the news coming from Geneva.

"I imagine so. It happened to me when I was his age. At that time no one in my family could offer me the opportunity to come back for a vacation. But we can do it."

Finally Ivan wrote a letter, a detailed list of the necessary mountain clothes and ski equipment he would need at Andermatt.

When he went to the manager to ask for two weeks off, he could tell from the quick consent that the request hadn't exactly come as a surprise. His father had evidently laid the groundwork. He was happy about it; for the first time he understood that those months in Stettin had nearly driven him crazy.

Frau Guterman, too, was happy when she heard that the van Straten boy would be taking a vacation, and that Saturday she invited her daughter and son-in-law to dinner to celebrate. Ivan still noticed the heaviness in his head and limbs that had been with him for months, but at least now he could feel something, as when an object is touched with a numb but healthy hand.

Then the world turned gray again, this time with ice and dirty snow. It was mid-January and Ivan's departure was growing nearer. He thought his own salvation had something to do with escaping from that place and its inclemency. A different life was possible, a regeneration. That mistaken beginning was remediable; it could give way to something different. But not at Stettin, because at Stettin it would not be possible.

Leaning on the railing that separated the sidewalk from the river, Ivan lit a cigarette and inhaled it with the attention that for some time he had not devoted to the warmth of the smoke, to the flavor that filled his mouth. Perhaps there was still a solution, a means of escape.

So he hoped, without reason, like a child seized by the most abstract terror, never to return to that remote corner of Germany. He was convinced this was one of the last times he would see the Oder, was certain different landscapes awaited him: luminous seas, clear skies.

He left Stettin with the melancholy that comes from leaving places one believes never to see again.

Instead he returned at the end of February, and aside from a few months spent in the Trieste office between the end of that year and the beginning of the next, he remained there for three more years.

London 1932

George Fles Departs for the Orient

*I*N EVERY SEASIDE town, in every city that rises from the banks of a navigable river, there is always an observation point from which the entire port can be seen, where the water follows the man-made coastline in an abstract yet uniform design. From there one can understand how the wharves, the shipyards, the dry docks are the center of the life of that city, of all the cities on the sea and rivers.

Ivan thought it was that way in every part of the world, except London, where the port mingled with everything else, subdivided by living quarters at staggered intervals, and yet separated from everything, excluded, hidden behind walls and buildings. Thus it was possible to live in London and be unaware of its port, and a vision of the whole was not possible.

Even he knew only one part, the part he customarily frequented, where the shiploads of grain arrived and departed. It was in a basin called Millwall Dock, part of the Isle of Dogs at the last loop of the river before the city center, just beyond the West India Docks. There, in a long, gray building by a railroad sideline, were the company offices.

What he couldn't see, what remained hidden, was of no interest to Ivan. He did his work diligently, but as if it were a marginal part of his life.

No, it was not the port that interested him. After his exile in Stettin and a short stint in Hamburg, London had seemed to Ivan an absurd, unlivable place, and at the same time the center of the world, the city where everything happened, where everything was possible. The air was almost unbreathable, the fog of pollution attacked the throat. In the evenings and on weekends, anyone who could escape to the green areas surrounding the city or to the open country would do so. He, too, had found a place to live in a beautiful residential neighborhood, as the guest of his Swaab aunt and uncle, and yet he often returned to the center of the city where life had the mystery of the unknown, each time different, in the pubs, fashionable restaurants, theaters, dance halls.

It seemed as though London were a magnet that attracted people of different races, colors, and cultures from all parts of the world, and then enjoyed mixing them to see what might come out. And the result was a surprise to everyone.

Ivan avoided only the poorest neighborhoods, not because of the danger as much as his irritation with those who looked for the exotic in other people's misery. But this irritation was not political. He did not view a city made of contrasts and divisions as the symbol of a world in need of change. London only represented life as it usually functions, with many imperfections and great fascinations.

George Fles appeared in Ivan's office one morning in the late spring of 1932. He arrived in a rumpled three-button tweed jacket, plus fours with stockings to match, and laced boots. Ivan, who had begun to dress English-fashion, with high-collared shirts of impeccable material, was a bit perplexed at the sight of him, but embraced him with the warmth that grew out of their intermittent relationship as the younger brothers in their respective families.

George was a restless, dissatisfied young man who put much enthusiasm into life and very little perseverance. He had lived not only in Holland, but also in Germany and France, first becoming involved with the socialists, and after that with the Communists, and changing work every few months. Now he was living in London, where he got by on his translation work, because in his wanderings he had at least mastered some languages, and he was engaged to Pearl, an English girl.

His restlessness expressed itself in nervous gestures and constant swings between states of euphoria and depression, as though there were no shades of gray in his world. Ivan, on the other hand, had come out of his desperation at Stettin only by dulling his view of external things, by blunting, at least partially, his own perceptive capacities. As if his feelings were like the soles of his feet after a summer on the rocks, hardened and nearly insensitive.

The rare encounters between the two cousins were different for the two of them, because either Ivan would find George's excitement amusing and George would ease Ivan's sense of isolation, or both would be put off by the other's differences and they would part with angry gestures and bitter words.

But that morning Ivan saw George Fles as he had always known him: generous, restless, and ineffectual, certainly, but also hell-bent in his desire to find a place in the world. And he decided that whatever might happen, he would give him all the help he could.

Ivan understood at once that something was new, because his cousin seemed unable to contain himself and jumped around the room as though trying to warm himself.

"Sit down," Ivan told him, in an attempt to curb his growing irritation over his cousin's exaggerated behavior. "Tell me what you are doing."

Certainly George had a problem to resolve, a big and difficult one, but he didn't want Ivan to think it the only reason for his visit. George had always felt an affection for his Italian cousin, as well as confidence in him, convinced that his silences originated from the same restlessness, even if skillfully hidden, or maybe even extinguished by now.

In fact, although they were nearly contemporaries, George saw

Ivan as a younger brother, still uncertain about his own destiny, yet at the same time obliged to follow a fate imposed by circumstance. Enrico's death had been a trauma for all the van Stratens, but for Ivan it had represented a definite break.

That was why George wanted his visit, their first encounter in some time, not to seem the result of necessity, but as a wish to see each other again.

"You are really elegant," he said when he finally sat down and forced his hands to hold still on his knees. "Now I understand what it means to have rich relatives."

The Fles family was also well off, but Louis had given up his business and seemed disinclined to give much help to his children; nor did George want to ask his father for help, perhaps to avoid being considered a failure in his professional life. In fact he was too proud to turn to anyone. So he convinced himself he had come to Ivan merely to lay out his problem and see if the solution he had in mind could really work.

Actually, George was also looking for a backer.

"They want to throw me out of this country. That's how things are. They say I am undesirable and that I must leave England as soon as possible."

Ivan looked at George as if he were crazy.

"I got a letter from some government agency. It says: Out! Away from this country!"

"Why?"

"I don't know why, they don't say. But I'm sure it's for political reasons. They don't like Communists."

They spoke a mixture of German and Dutch. George, to be gracious, tossed in some Italian, but he didn't feel well enough versed to tackle an entire conversation in that language.

"I can hear *oom* Siegfreid: *If you know someone . . .*"

Siegfreid Swaab had been the manager of the London branch of the company when Engers was taken over by Goldstück, Hainzé and Co.

"Uncle Siegfried, Uncle George, the company . . . you always have to find a solution in the family, an answer from your parents. Can't we ever do anything for ourselves?"

Ivan tried to sidestep George's provocation.

"Even Paul, our van Dijk cousin, has begun to work for the company. They've taken him on in Rotterdam and I think he's happy. It might be possible for you to find a place where . . ."

"Never mind. It's not important," George went on, raising the tone of his voice and beginning to pace around the room again. "In fact, I'll tell you, it is better this way, better that they send me away from this decadent country. This old Europe is on its last legs, dear cousin. The depression is only the beginning of the end."

George walked over to Ivan and squeezed his arm. His eyes were feverish, sharp, full of an excitement strange to Ivan, alien to his way of thinking, but also fascinating, because Ivan envied that passion, just as his father had envied *tante* Celine's passion, but with a difference, because Ivan lacked the detachment that comes from self-assurance, from the certainty of being right.

"The future is not here, Ivan, it's not in this part of the world."

Ivan rose and closed his office door. He felt George's words had veered in a direction that not even his youth would excuse in the eyes of some of his German-speaking colleagues.

"And where is this future, then?" he asked, leaning against the door, and for a few seconds he waited for the answer with the irrational conviction that this future concerned him, too.

"Where they are building socialism: in the Soviet Union. The future is there, and that's where I want to go."

So George had his dreams. He had them in his head and would transform them into reality. Maybe he was crazy, or maybe he only had more hope than Ivan did.

"If I find the money and a recommendation that helps me get a visa and a job, I'm leaving," George concluded, and he smiled with the air of a sweet and bewildered boy, the air that boys who wear glasses so often have.

Ivan chose hope. Not his own. That he could not invent. The socialist country did not inspire it, either, because nothing could be aroused, it had dried up inside him. No, Ivan chose George's hope, as if he could be warmed by its reflection just by observing it.

He wrote his father, whose name Celine had in fact given her son because George van Straten was her favorite brother. Now he could return that affection by making his nephew's dream come true.

Besides, *oom* George had always helped his relatives, as if it were natural to share with them a part of the fortune that life had reserved for him. *And he certainly wouldn't refuse,* thought Ivan, *now that it was only a matter of paying for one ship passage from London to Leningrad.*

Ivan did not want George Fles to know anything until the moment was right, so he remained silent as he listened to the plan. He let the unexpressed demand for help go by, as if he hadn't understood, and George had enough pride not to persist.

When Ivan met George again he was with Pearl. Ivan saw at once how much in love he was. He could tell by the way his cousin looked at her, by the way he turned to her for signs of approval. Pearl loved him, too, but she was not yet twenty, and with one so young it is never clear whether it is the person or the idea that is loved, whether a man or the supposition of a particular existence is being married. They were two enthusiastic and involved Jewish Communists. Ivan regretted never having had an unconscious age, an age of making choices based on impulse.

"Communism is young, like us," George said. "It has the strong blood of youth; it is unstoppable. This world of ours is a cadaver, at the very least a decrepit old man, barely alive. Every age has a heart, ours is in Moscow."

What George and Pearl said had a declamatory, even rhetorical aspect that Ivan did not like, but at the same time he had to recognize they both wholeheartedly believed every word. Pearl, with her vivacious eyes and beaver teeth, her flimsy dress reaching slightly below her knees, believed it. George, with his dark shirt, no tie and plus fours, believed it. Perhaps even Ivan believed it for a moment.

For that reason he had thrown away the letter from his father, who had agreed to help George, but whose words were biting: "Wherever he lives, he must work hard to succeed. George is not used to work and doesn't have the patience to learn. The place counts, but the person counts even more. Russia is no different from Rotterdam or Genoa; success depends mostly, if not totally, on ourselves." He wrote as though the revolution had never taken place.

He was probably right, as usual. Yet Ivan felt like ignoring his instructions for a day at least. So he went to the bank and withdrew the necessary money. Next he went to a travel agency, Dean & Dawson in Piccadilly, and bought a ticket for a steamship that left the day before the deadline George had been given to leave England.

"Every age has a heart: Ours is in Moscow," George had concluded as the three of them walked quickly through the streets of London, headed for the opening of an art gallery.

"I think for now you will have to be content with Leningrad," Ivan replied.

Then he put his hand in his pocket, took out the envelope, and handed it to George.

He opened it and began to shout, while Pearl expressed her excitement in her own way, hiding her tears behind a brusque hug.

Their plans changed on the spot, and they went to an Italian restaurant in Soho to celebrate. Ivan was paying and so chose one of the best, the Tuscan on Shaftesbury Avenue.

Those were frantic weeks. George got the visa from Intourist of London, but he also needed a letter of recommendation that would allow him to find work in Moscow. For this he went to the English Communist Party office.

The building had a shabby, gray look, and the people George saw there came and went with the assurance of those who know what they are doing and do it according to the rules. But he didn't know what he should do, and in his uncertainty he turned to a girl sitting behind a desk at the entrance.

"At the moment, the only person you can see is Henry Pollitt," she said after listening to George's confused explanation. She pointed to some stairs and added, "Third floor."

Henry Pollitt was not eager to receive him, and made him stand and wait in a narrow hallway for almost half an hour before admitting him to a small smoke-filled office. The man remained seated on the other side of the desk, looking at the papers George had put in front of him while running his hand over his nearly bald head. The documents consisted of some letters in French and an introduction signed by the secretary of the Communist cell where George had enrolled immediately after arriving in London. Everything was in order, but Pollitt didn't seem to care for that restless Dutchman who hadn't even accepted his invitation to sit down, and who was in such a hurry to leave.

"You are right, Comrade," George told him. "I am in a hurry, but the expulsion order doesn't give me much time."

"I don't know you," Pollitt said to him, continuing to turn the papers over in his hands, as if they might change from one moment to the next.

"But I am a comrade. Convinced and faithful," George insisted, "and I'm sure the Soviet Union will know how to make me useful."

Pollitt distrusted nervous men. It was his belief that true Communists should be cold, should not make an obvious display, should be careful not to call attention to themselves. This man, on the other hand, seemed like a dangerous enthusiast. But it was hot in London that July, and Pollitt, who didn't want to prolong the discussion, finally wrote the letter.

"Don't make me sorry," he said as he gave it to him.

"You can be sure of that," George replied, barely able to keep from giving him a hug.

The steamships usually departed from docks below those used for transport ships, at the city's outskirts where the Thames becomes wider at its mouth. Ivan and Pearl had gone on board with George and had accompanied him to his cabin to leave his luggage. Then they all went up on deck to wait for the announcement requesting all those not sailing to leave the ship.

George Fles was happy. It didn't bother him at all that he would not see Pearl for a long time, maybe for a couple of years, until he was settled in the Soviet Union and she could join him. There, on the bridge of the steamship, he seemed to have finally reached a point that gave his life a sense of completion.

Only a few minutes now separated him from a departure marking the passage between two periods of his life: that of uncertainty, of aimless search, and the new life where everything would be logical and full of meaning. George had no doubts or hesitations, not even a moment of sadness. He wanted that moment to be preserved for the future, so he stopped a passenger and asked him to take a picture with Pearl's camera. He called Ivan over, too, but his cousin stayed to the side, sitting on some equipment covered by canvas.

"It's a picture for the two of you. What do I have to do with it?" he replied to George's request.

George embraced Pearl, who laughed in the direction of the lens, infected by his enthusiasm, and he bent his head until it touched hers. He felt a sense of beatitude and abandon that translated not into a smile, but into a relaxed face revealing his serenity.

The passenger took the picture. In the photograph were not only the couple embracing, but also Ivan sitting on the canvas, elegant and distracted, and an unknown girl who had stopped to watch while passing by.

Time remained suspended on the film, unique and complete. Every possibility open, the future still to be written, as it reappears at times in our memory when we ask ourselves how our life might have turned out differently.

In reality the whistle blew and the guests were invited to leave the ship. From the wharf Pearl and Ivan continued to wave until the ship set sail.

That is how George Fles left for the Orient.

૮ XXIII ๑

Florence 1998

Exhumation and Delicacy

*I*DON'T KNOW IF my father would be happy about all this. After all, to remember is also to lay bare, to unveil, to bring to light what was hidden and perhaps forgotten. The writer is free to do that, but don't those who are being written about have the right to keep their secret? Especially someone like my father, who certainly did not like to draw attention to himself, who in fact had chosen to appear as seldom as possible, even to the point of forgetting his own aspirations?

In preserving my father's memory and his name, I am approaching the present. I begin to speak of facts that others remember, about people who are still alive. By so doing I could injure someone. Even if this were to happen, it should come as no surprise, because a writer is always selfish and easily forgets the others, those facts of flesh and bone who continue to move around him. Often the writer asks them to be quiet because they disturb him. And yet it is from them that he draws the strength to write, it is of them that he speaks.

Someone could ask me why I used real names, why I did not camouflage, at least in part, the identity of the men and women of whom I speak. I don't believe it would make sense to tell the story of a name, down through the generations, by falsifying it. No, I can invent many things, and have already done so, but the names must be exact, because only then can I save them and wipe out the debt I have with those who have borne them.

But I feel I must make a promise: to proceed from now on with the greatest caution; life is too complex and delicate for someone to harm it out of arrogance. The canvas of the painting is worn and could disintegrate under careless handling; the entire image runs the risk of being destroyed, and I do not want that to happen.

Therefore I shall use the necessary caution, even if the doubt remains that my father's silence was not entirely of his own choosing — to the point that today I wonder if it was he who did not wish to speak or I who did not ask him to. Was that lack of information the consequence of a choice, or something imposed on him by life, even without anyone pestering him with questions?

My father had started to tell me about some of the events. In a calm and somewhat detached tone, he had tried to tell me about George Fles, for example, but I hadn't encouraged him. He talked to me at a time when I didn't listen much, and the circumstances made me think it was a sermon. Instead it was a true story, which I later found by chance thanks to the research of a distant relative. But some details that my father could have remembered are lost forever. And this is my fault.

The names, as I said, I cannot change, especially at this point in my narrative, because the time of the history is now, a time I could not invent even if I wanted. It is the time of dates and certainties, the time I must accept, that I must bear with the effort of memory.

Now is the time for the material preserved in the archives, political police records, censuses, and lists: what has been destroyed and what has remained.

As with the castles and walls that make up the background of Renaissance frescoes, I can try to understand where those cities were and place the horseman in the right perspective. But beyond that I am not allowed to go. The brush stops, I can only observe what happens, nothing else; I cannot even destroy that fresco if I don't like it, because the museum guards are watching. The images dreamed by Hartog Alexander are now closer, about to become a reality. They pursue me and have a blinding clarity.

I would like to stop the hand of history, ignore a sheet of paper I keep on my desk with many names and dates, but I cannot do it; my work as a forger has unbridgeable limits. So I can no longer paint on the plaster that in the beginning I wanted to leave white. Others have already carved graffiti on it that asks only to be deciphered. Messages left on my path to be taken to someone, if only to myself.

I cannot stop history, but perhaps I can still allow myself a pause, a pause for a love story before the century — now over, but at that time only thirty years old — turns the lives of the van Stratens upside down.

Ivan was transferred from London to Livorno. He returned to Italy, to a city that had a rather important port, where the sea had the same smell and the same reflections as Genoa.

His sister Nelly, his favorite, had married a year before, in 1933. I have the invitation to a dinner held in Genoa's Hotel Bristol on the fifth of November. So I know what they ate: Canapé alla Marinara, Cup of Consommé, Boiled Sea Bass with Steamed Potatoes, Casserole of Chicken, Veal Mascotte with Endive Salad, Pears Belle-Hélène, Wedding Cake, Baskets of Fruit, and Coffee (the capital letters are not mine, but the typographer's). The wines were a 1928 Soave Bertani, a 1916 Barolo Opera Pia, a Veuve Clicquot Sec champagne. On the last page, blank, are a few words written by my father in blue pencil: "To my beloved, engaged for the second time, from her enamored Ivan." About whom it speaks I have no idea. I doubt it was a joke, and I also wonder why, if the dedication was real, the invitation remained with my father.

That he wrote about love at a wedding celebration, whether seriously or not, seems to me an indication of a state of mind. For that reason I am taking the pause I mentioned to tell a love story.

XXIV

Livorno 1934

A Love Story

ROM PIAZZA CAVOUR, after crossing the bridge over the Fosso Reale, he entered Via Cairoli. To the left was the post and telegraph office, to the right the Galleria building, where the Philological Club was located. It was the part of the city where old buildings had been replaced in recent years with new ones in the fascist style: marble facades, columns, square shapes, long tree-lined streets.

Ivan paid no attention because he knew that part of Livorno well by then. They were the same streets and the same buildings he had seen almost every day for many months, when he left Hotel Corallo, in front of the station, and took the electric tram or a carriage downtown.

It was a rather cold March, and Ivan was wearing heavy, London-style clothes. Many times he had spent late afternoons at the club, the oldest in the city, exchanging a few words and looking at the Livornese girls with their quick eyes and undulating saunters who seemed so different from the English girls, easier and more dangerous.

As he entered the door, he encountered a woman he'd already met, who was accompanied by a girlfriend he had never seen before.

"This is Franca Straccali," the girl told him.

He removed his hat and kissed her hand.

"Ivan van Straten," he said. "Very pleased to meet you."

Franca said nothing, only smiled, with a vaguely mocking air.

She was very young and Ivan thought very beautiful: dark brown eyes, rather short hair, a shade lighter than her eyes, well-shaped lips that opened into that strange smile, a nose that widened slightly at the base.

The girls had already left for Piazza Cavour when Ivan turned and whispered a *buona sera* that came out too weak for them to hear.

He entered the club, where he found a couple of friends drinking liqueur. Ivan took off his coat and smiled as he went up to them.

"I've said many times I will never marry a woman from Livorno, these women are not for me. But if I were to break that vow, it would without a doubt be for the girl who just left."

"Who was she?" asked one of his friends.

"You'll have to tell me. All I know about her is her name."

She began to laugh, holding on to her friend's arm, and couldn't stop.

"Where did that man come from?" she said when she could catch her breath.

"He's a Dutchman who has lived in Livorno for a few months. A nice man."

A *nice man?* Franca thought. *What is Valdina talking about? He wasn't nice, he was just silly, ridiculous.* And she continued laughing.

"But did you see that gray overcoat he had on? And the bowler hat? Imagine, a bowler in Livorno! Where does he think he is?"

"He comes from London, maybe there . . ."

Franca tried to stop her with a motion of her hand, but Valdina was looking at her in surprise, as though she didn't understand. She saw him in another light, evidently. To her he seemed a normal sort, even fascinating, and Franca, with the assurance of her seventeen years, didn't see how that could be possible.

"He knows your aunt," Valdina said, amused but also a little offended by her friend's reaction, "because while their house was being worked on, the Foraboschis stayed at the Hotel Corallo where he lives."

Franca had been in Livorno for a few days as the guest of her Aunt Lina, actually one of her mother's cousins, a forty-year-old woman who still lived with her parents. She was still a beautiful woman, very elegant, who had refused a number of marriage proposals; a nice woman, and strange, who kept covering her nose, as though afraid something might smell bad.

In Florence, where she lived, Franca had finished school and was taking English lessons that didn't interest her much. Still, she liked the prospect of two or three months in Livorno, especially since the MAKπ100* ball — the "mac-pi" ball, as everyone called it — would take place at the end of her visit. It was a celebration for the student officers at the naval academy, one hundred days before the end of the academic year, and her aunt would certainly buy her a new dress so she could attend.

"Do you know a certain Signor van Straten, an odd Dutchman who goes around in a bowler hat?" she asked Lina as soon as she returned to the house.

"Oh, certainly," her aunt said. "A real gentleman."

Franca thought it was a conspiracy against her. Maybe they wanted to play a joke by convincing her they took that funny man seriously, that man whose hair exploded like a bomb, springing up in all directions as soon as he took off his hat.

"In fact," her aunt added, "one of these evenings we should invite him to the house."

Franca looked at her, and Lina gave Franca her usual sweet smile, without leaving any doubt of her sincerity.

They are all crazy, Franca thought, but she didn't say anything.

—ↄ—

---

*Translator's note: The term MAKπ100 comes from an expression in the Piedmontese dialect: *Ai cala mac pi sent dì*, "There are only one hundred more days." Military Academies in several European nations as well as in the United States have similar celebrations.

Perhaps far away, in another world, where families spent the greater part of their time together and lived in the same city or a few miles away, perhaps there it would be all right, without having to prove something, or replace someone who was no longer there. Perhaps this was his Russian revolution, his promised land. Perhaps Livorno counted more than Moscow or Jerusalem.

A seventeen-year-old girl who didn't know who he was, who didn't know his father, was not Jewish, and laughed happily as if her life ended at the door of her house and the rest remained to be discovered. A girl without a past and without secrets, so different from those he had known up to then, a girl who had learned to conquer with those automatic gestures, the kind that once belonged to Enrico. No more continual fog and rain, no gray and silver seas, but a blue sky even in the winter and a sea to dive into.

This Ivan saw in the doorway of the Philological Club, as if he could forget his father and the name he bore. He saw it and then forgot it, because it wasn't even a thought, but a feeling, something that penetrated his stomach and moved on, leaving only the image of a very young girl whom he liked.

And when he learned that Franca was the guest of those very nice, albeit very fascist people who had stayed in his hotel for several weeks, he decided to pay them a visit as he had promised. And so he sent a visiting card and waited for a reply, which came quickly: a telephone call from Signorina Lina inviting him to spend the following evening with them.

She didn't start to laugh when she saw him, although initially, just as Ivan entered the room, she felt she might break into laughter again, though more out of embarrassment than because of his appearance. She wasn't accustomed to compliments, formal gestures, pat phrases, and small talk. She sat apart, in silence, aware of the glances he was sending her way, which made her blush.

Franca asked her friend Valdina to be there also, to help things along, to keep Ivan from getting the wrong idea, from forming expectations of any sort. And he, as a matter of fact, seemed to have understood, because most of the time he talked to Lina, who addressed him politely, but often turned to cover her nose, with what outsiders interpreted as an affectation, ignorant of the real reason.

Every once in a while Franca looked at Ivan, at that man she continued to dislike, with his aquiline nose, his dull blue eyes and thick hair. But since her seventeen years had all been spent in Florence or Livorno, she was still fascinated by the stories he told about other countries and unknown cities, places like Stettin, Hamburg, and London. Perhaps those stories were what made her forget his strange dress and odd ways.

"How long will you be in Livorno?" Franca asked toward the end of the evening, speaking to him for the first time.

"I don't know," he said. "I'm here for work. It could be months or years. It depends on what my company decides."

"And then?"

"Another port," replied Ivan. "I hope still in Italy."

But Franca imagined distant, exotic places, inhabited by mysterious people. Other worlds to dream about, and yet, she realized at that precise moment with great consternation, places that really did exist, places, perhaps, where even she might end up in the indefinite future.

"But they might send you to China," said Franca, laughing.

He laughed, too, but without looking at her.

"Oh, China, China . . . ," giggled Aunt Lina behind her hand. "I would be afraid to travel that far."

"And yet this is a sea town, you must be accustomed to the idea of long voyages," said Ivan.

"I am from Florence," Franca said, wanting to add many other things to distinguish herself from her hosts, such as the fact that her father, Giulio, was not a Fascist and hated Mussolini. But she said no more, and Ivan only nodded.

"It's impossible," said Lina.

"What do you mean, it's impossible?" pleaded Franca. "I don't have a thing to wear to the dance and this is so beautiful!"

The dressmaker stood beside them and looked in the mirror

without opening her mouth. She was afraid of Signorina Fora-
boschi's reaction and did not want to contradict her. Yet this was
now the fashion, whether she knew it or not.

"It's undignified."

The dress fit too tight in the rear; this was the moral dilemma
that bothered her aunt so much, putting the acquisition of that
dress, handmade for her niece, in doubt.

Franca was also looking in the mirror at the girl wearing the
long white dress, and she envied her, afraid she would not be able
to wear the gown outside the dressmaker's shop.

The dress was called Ortensia and at the neck had three fabric
flowers, two pink and one blue.

"Oh, Aunty, please," Franca begged.

"You'll be the prettiest girl at the party," the dressmaker said in
a moment of courage.

The aunt remained silent.

"What will people say?" she finally said.

What will the boys say? Franca thought.

"Will it cause a scandal?" Lina continued.

Franca turned from the mirror to her aunt, her expression one
of gloomy sadness mixed with the hope of not having to suffer.
There was something childish in attributing the choice between
joy and desperation to her aunt's decision.

"All right," Lina said, covering her nose with her gloved right
hand. "We'll take this blessed dress. But you must promise me
you'll behave."

"Me?" Franca said with all the unconscious arrogance of her
age. "I always behave. But this time I want to dance till I drop, I
want to accept every invitation to dance that comes my way."

He had talked to no one but Nelly about her, though only when
they had spoken on the phone; to everyone else he had said
nothing, not even to his Livornese acquaintances. What was there
to say, anyway? He had not done anything that could be interpreted as a courtship, even by the most discreet. Some visits to the
Foraboschis', a few words exchanged on those occasions, but the

rest of the time had been spent at work or taking an aperitif at the club, where they had not met again.

Yet Ivan was convinced he had been too explicit, had given Franca the advantage of knowing his intentions without having to give away anything of herself. This bothered him, giving him the impression that Franca's levity was not just a characteristic of her age, but also a conscious game, and he wanted to believe she was without guile.

So he had become even more detached, had spoken to her as little as possible and with a grimace on his face that made him appear unfriendly. He simply couldn't put himself in the hands of a seventeen-year-old. It didn't seem right.

Then there was the ball. The enormous illuminated ballroom, the cigarette smoke rising toward the high ceiling, the officers' white jackets, the women's hairstyles, the music. The orchestra played traditional rhythms: waltzes, tangos, the fox-trot, and particularly the one-step and other popular songs. Ivan smoked more than usual, in part to conquer the uneasiness that often came over him, but also to occupy his hands, which otherwise did not know what to do. He sat apart, observing the people who moved around the room with an ease that the unfamiliar surroundings did not grant him. Anyway, he didn't want to attach himself to the first person he knew. So he stayed on the sidelines, with the same expression on his face that he assumed, without knowing it, when he talked to Franca.

In the meantime the ballroom kept filling with people, and as the crowd grew, so did the guests' desire to have a good time: young students in their tight uniforms and combed-back hair, civilians, like Ivan, with dinner jackets made to order or rented, girls in their evening dresses, the result of much indecision and questioning before the mirror.

Franca also passed by him, greeting him with a slight wave of her hand and one of her smiles, halfway between teasing and embarrassment. Then she continued on, disappearing among the dancers.

Ivan lit another cigarette.

—ᴄ͡

Travels and adventures were no competition in a world where there was always a party like this one. So thought Franca, proud of her dress and of the stream of overtures coming from the officers, inviting her to dance.

She felt light in their arms, as though something were guiding her amid that whirl of music and glances. There were no worries here, none of the fear that at times she read in her father's eyes when he said he wanted nothing to do with Fascism. She had never even worn the uniform of the Italian girls' organization, but there were moments when she would have preferred life to be less demanding, more natural and easy. Anyway, the navy was not Fascist, even though the orchestra had played the "March of the House of Savoy" and "Giovinezza" at the beginning of the evening; and those boys, soon to be officers, never talked politics.

That was why she accepted their invitations, with the malice and innocence that her age allowed her, and she danced with determination, often forgetting whom she was dancing with, forgetting the faces that seemed so much alike and so handsome. Because the cavaliers mattered less than the ball, less than the repeated yet ever new dance steps she was performing without thinking, as oblivious as the central chandelier that was projecting youthful shadows on the ballroom walls.

She did not think of Ivan, that strange young man who no longer made her laugh, but instead made her curious because of the stories told about him, the legends of wealth and adventure that everyone had manufactured. But not now. She did not want to spend time with him now, to encounter his oblique, almost superior, look that annoyed her so much during his visits. Let him spend time with the other girls who were crowding the room, with someone who had more interest in that foreign face, in that Levantine nose.

So it was he, in the end, who made the move. Compounding the error he had tried to avoid, giving in to the anger he had accumulated in the course of the evening, incapable of controlling it, in spite of the dances with others and the glasses of liqueur.

He went up to her while she was talking with one of the many young officers, so conceited and pleased with the press of their uniforms, as Ivan had described them for the benefit of one of his friends at work, a colleague who often burst into sharp and nervous laughter at his jokes. There, at Franca's back, he waited patiently for the conversation with the officer to end, without drawing attention to himself, almost hiding behind her. Then, as soon as she was alone, her eyes still on the center of the room as if waiting for someone to come up and ask for another dance, her cheeks red, her hand quickly passing over her hair to put it in order, Ivan bent over her shoulder, brushed up against her ear, and said, "Look, Signorina, when I court a girl I don't want her dancing with anyone else."

He said it with an air of impatience, with a hint of anger that compounded Franca's surprise at not seeing him approach, startling her as she turned, and she all but jumped back to get away from him. Then she looked at him, her eyes dilated, her mouth opened as if to say something, but she said nothing.

What point had they reached, almost without noticing? Certainly she had been ignoring Ivan's intentions, never conceding him anything but the small signs of her unconscious coquetry. What had brought him to that unexpected gesture?

They stood there, absolutely still for a few seconds, looking at each other and nothing more while the party went on around them, growing in noise and warmth. Until Ivan, as if he were someone else, as if he had not just spoken a few moments earlier, made a slight bow.

"Would you like to dance?" he asked.

And at that moment she did not even know what music was playing, she couldn't hear it, and she did not know what caused her hands to tremble, or why this new thought had overcome her. She didn't have time to reflect, to understand what was happening to her, because she moved toward him at once and said yes.

XXV

Tbilisi (Georgia) 1936

The End of the Revolution

*L*IEUTENANT VASILIEV, head of the fourth section of the Special Department for Security of the NKVD of Georgia, had blond hair, a large flat nose, small close-set blue eyes. He was a man of few words; outside his work, he never raised his voice, and seemed endowed with a great deal of patience. But in that laconic tranquility there ripened some profound convictions that he was rarely inclined to question.

For instance, on August 19, 1936, he had called in for questioning the foreigner hired as an interpreter by the Observatory of the Academy of Science in Abastumani. He was convinced the man's testimony would prove him worthy of investigation, because Vasiliev had the declarations of other accused men in hand, along with the information that a magazine, *Die Sammlung*, containing an article about Trotsky had been found in the foreigner's house.

But he was a cautious man, as befitted his job as the head of the fourth section of the Special Department for Security, and he would decide how to proceed once he had the Dutchman in front of him, for it was often by looking a man in the face that he could tell if he was dealing with an enemy of the revolution. If the

Dutchman perspired, if he squirmed in his seat, if he stammered his answers, than Vasiliev would certainly think he had something to hide. But even if he was too precise and submissive he could arouse suspicion.

So he began interrogating him in a roundabout way, asking him how he happened to come to the Soviet Union and what work he had done in Moscow.

The Dutchman responded calmly, with long dissertations in his bookish but clear Russian. Yet his eyes avoided Vasiliev's, seeming to hide something behind the glasses he wore for his myopia.

Vasiliev was patient and continued his innocuous questions.

"Why, Comrade, did you decide to move to Tbilisi?"

But he already knew the answer. Fles had never had stable work in Moscow and was looking for something that would give him a better position.

"Working for a while in a remote region," said Fles, "would give me an advantage on my return to Moscow. And my wife thought Georgia seemed the right place given the good weather conditions. Actually, in the beginning I only found work teaching English. The conditions were such that my wife and I decided to go to Iran and then reenter Europe from there. But then Pearl got pregnant and I was offered a job at the observatory, so we stayed."

Vasiliev nodded and never tried to interrupt Fles. He let him continue, listening to him attentively. He saw the effort he was making to answer the questions thoroughly, but this also seemed a sign of difficulty.

Then he asked the Dutchman for a list of people he spent time with, Russian or otherwise. He diligently wrote down their names, because he did not trust the boy who drew up the report, especially when dealing with foreign names. Finally, and with the same indifferent voice, he asked if Fles had ever received Trotskyist literature in the Soviet Union.

Fles surprised him with a strange story of materials received from a Dutch sailor at Arkhangelsk when he had gone there for work — materials, however, that he had turned over to exponents of the Party without obtaining any receipt.

Why, wondered Vasiliev, was he telling this story? Why not look closer, to the origin of the danger in which he found himself? Why not say something about Lydia Gasviani, the woman he had met shortly after arriving, who was now in prison, accused of anti-Soviet activities?

"After that you never received any other Trotskyist literature?" Vasiliev asked him, giving him another chance.

"No, never," replied Fles.

Then Vasiliev shook his head and placed something on the table that he had kept hidden, waiting for the right moment to bring it out.

"Here," he said, "is a magazine, *Die Sammlung*, published in Holland in June 1935. It contains an article by Lev Trotsky. What can you tell me about this?"

Fles looked at it, and then looked at Vasiliev. He remained uncertain for several seconds; a hesitation, from the policeman's point of view, that lasted too long.

"My father, who lives in Holland, sent me this magazine," he said. "I received it in the mail after I was already living here. I don't remember exactly when, maybe at the end of 1935."

But it was too late, Vasiliev knew it, and perhaps George Fles also. The questions that followed became perfunctory. To whom had he given the magazine? Why hadn't he turned it over to the authorities? What did he know about Lydia Gasviani?

The text of the interrogation was read to Fles, who signed it.

"You may go, Comrade Fles," Vasiliev said.

The other man hesitated, as if wanting to add something.

"I said you may go," Vasiliev repeated.

The Dutchman then stood up and left the room.

"This one screwed himself," Vasiliev said to his subordinate, who looked at him in admiration but made no comment.

He had hoped there was a place, however remote and obscure, where things finally would have a meaning, a reason; where their life would take on an understandable order.

Nature had deceived him. The mountains, the woods, the

beauty of that small town, Abastumani, with its wooden houses built early in the century, with the sun warm even in autumn, as when they had first come to Tbilisi.

They had left the anxieties of Moscow, the daily hunt for work and a little bit of money. The revolution was not going well, it was still struggling to grow. Perhaps demonstrating a spirit of sacrifice was a prerequisite for becoming part of it. For that reason George had thought of leaving the capital.

It was there, among those mountains, in their apartment on Makharadze 90, where Pearl became pregnant. That was also a folly, like going to the Soviet Union, and yet George could see in that fact a sign of change. It provided their lives with some stability, or so George thought. Then Pearl had returned to England, where she would enjoy better conditions for the delivery, and a few days later the NKVD, the political police, had called him in.

George left the interrogation feeling like he had done something wrong, yet he was convinced his good faith gave him some kind of immunity.

In a letter of February 1935 he had written to Pearl's sister:

> There is no reason why the Soviet government would kill innocent people; especially at this time. I feel that even our worst enemies cannot claim that our government would do so in order to hide its own failings, because more than ever the almost incredible successes in constructing Socialism have been obvious to anyone who knows anything about Soviet life.

George felt completely innocent. What reason did they have to persecute him? And yet that interrogation was still worrying him after a bad night's sleep, and Vasiliev's narrow eyes had increased his fears. He had been on the verge of asking him if his position was in danger, but had realized at once that it would have been a ridiculous question. And so he had remained silent.

All week long he asked himself what he could expect from that first encounter.

The answer was his arrest on August 26, 1936, by Vasiliev's order. Without recourse to further interrogation, Fles was imprisoned by the NKVD of Tbilisi.

Vasiliev knew that time was on his side; it wouldn't be his questioning that broke Fles, that would not be necessary. The prison, the insufficient food, the poor hygienic conditions, the isolation, the rare news of his family: Everything in the coming days and weeks would make George Fles confess what Vasiliev expected from him.

Furthermore, to the time in his favor the lieutenant added his meticulousness. He had sent Comrade Gabrielov to search the Dutchman's apartment and had carefully inspected the list of every object, letter, and book found there.

What he saw started him thinking that the accusations against Fles could be twofold: counterrevolutionary activities, without a doubt, but also espionage, because he discovered some family connections between Fles and a company whose Moscow office had been closed in 1934, with all its employees arrested.

So in one of the many interrogations he conducted with the Dutchman between September and the first half of November, with calculated breaks, he dropped a question about this firm.

Fles then told him about two of his uncles, George van Straten and Siegfried Swaab, and a cousin, Ivan van Straten, who were executives in that company.

Vasiliev thought it a just and cruel fate for a traitor, the fact that the principal accusations could derive from a magazine sent by his father and by work done by some of his relatives. Vasiliev would not have had sufficient imagination to invent such a thing, nor the humanity to be sorry for it, but he was able to envision the plot being welcomed by his Moscow bosses when the time came to try George Fles.

At first he thought he would go mad quickly, then he thought he might not, and that was worse. He couldn't talk with anyone; he was shown Pearl's letters but not allowed to keep them. All other letters were seized. He could only lie on the wooden board and brood over ways to get out. Every idea was actually insane, an abstract elaboration that ignored every relationship with the outside world.

He had no change of clothes. They had given him none of his belongings: no clothing, no books. He had been arrested at the end of August; three months had passed as if nothing had happened. They kept taking him to the interrogation room where he answered questions that always seemed the same, but Vasiliev listened as though for the first time, and then shuffled through the old statements looking for a slight deviation. And there was a difference every time.

There had to be a way out, George thought when he returned to his cell, a way to speed it all up, for him to be punished, and then it would all be over. There must be a way even if he couldn't imagine it.

Finally a solution occurred to him.

"Vasiliev!" he shouted through the cell bars. "Vasiliev! I want Vasiliev, I want to talk to him!"

They let him yell for hours, until his voice was reduced to a thin, barely perceptible thread. And still he kept on yelling that name.

Not until the following morning did they take him there, to see the head of the fourth section, the authoritative Comrade Vasiliev. George felt as though he had been drinking, his brain reeling and his ideas for resolving the problem seeming so clear and obvious. Vasiliev's face also seemed more friendly. His eyes were still as narrow as two cracks, but his mouth had a slight crease, as if he were happy to see him.

"I want to make a statement," George said. "I want to put an end to this."

Vasiliev nodded. Time had won, as he knew it would. The system had worked as it should, beating the enemy in the end.

"I'm listening," the lieutenant said.

"I imagine you have accused me on the basis of article fifty-eight ten, for counterrevolutionary activities. Fine. Even though I have obviously been loyal from the time I came to the Soviet Union, my actions have not reflected my true nature. I have tried to be a good Soviet citizen, but often I have not succeeded. Before coming to the USSR I associated with Trotskyites and came here with Trotskyist ideas that I held up to the time of my arrest.

"In nineteen thirty-two, when I left England to come to Leningrad, I saw a dirty city full of depressed people, poorly dressed and hungry, dragging themselves through the streets. Then when I arrived in Moscow, at the Ukhtomslaya station, I saw that there was only vodka and matches in the cooperative stores. People complained openly in my presence, and I felt sorry for them."

Fles could not remain still. He repeatedly stood up, then returned to his seat, his arms waving crazily in front of Vasiliev's impassive face. Fles was perspiring even though it was November. He seemed, as Vasiliev wrote in his report, to be in a clear state of exaltation.

"Oh, certainly, the situation has improved, but I still wasn't satisfied. In fact, I believe, in many regards the Soviet Union is too dictatorial."

Vasiliev could not hide a gesture of surprise and annoyance, raising an arm toward George Fles, as if for a moment he had thought of hitting him.

"Yes, that's right," the Dutchman shouted. "Think about it. The law against abortion, the hierarchy and new uniforms of the Red Army. And the architecture of the houses: ugly and needlessly resembling those in the West, particularly what you see in Italy."

"Do you mean," Vasiliev interrupted, "that you can find things in the Soviet Union that resemble those in fascist countries?"

Fles did not reply. He seemed incapable of listening to others, as if he had to follow his own reasoning without interruption or lose his line of thought. Vasiliev interpreted that silence as assent.

"And all these Houses of Culture being built, instead of thinking about housing for the workers!" Fles continued. "Do you want other examples? The closing of the realistic theater in Moscow, and it was the best theater I have ever seen. In general it seems to me that in the USSR they want to make things appear better than they are. At Tbilisi I saw an exhibition of paintings dedicated to the history of the Bolsheviks in Georgia. They were horrible paintings. One of them, titled *Stalin in Kakhetya*, could be in a church with the title *Jesus Christ Gathers the Children*.

"A workers' aristocracy has been created in this country, and some have a hundred times more than others. The new constitution is bourgeois, in fact. Many members of the Party are dishonest and don't say what they think. The behavior of Zinoviev and Kamenev has been disgusting: I would never accuse myself."

Vasiliev stroked his face. Wasn't this exactly what Fles was doing, though shut up in a room under the direction of the NKVD of Georgia instead of in a courtroom? But he didn't realize it; with his bright eyes, his trembling hands, and his nonstop talking, perhaps thinking he might thus end that long torment of silence and hunger, of filth and desperation. And instead it was only beginning.

"Certainly Trotskyism is a mistaken political phenomenon, but in each case it analyzes the situation in the Soviet Union from the workers' point of view.

"I didn't lie before, I just didn't say some of the things I'm saying now. But what's important is that I keep my opinions, those opinions that you consider counterrevolutionary, and that we both think we are right. That is why I refuse to accuse other people who think like me. But on the other hand I won't protect those I consider true enemies of socialism. I will tell you about an Englishman who was expelled from the Soviet Union as a spy, and about another man who works for the *Moscow Daily News* and is also a spy. I'm not worried anymore about what can happen to me. I just want this matter to end."

Then he was silent. The boy who normally transcribed the interviews hadn't touched the typewriter. From Fles came the sharp odor of sweat.

"If you wish, you can write down what you have just said, and add it to your documents as a declaration," Vasiliev said.

George tried to do it. He tried for four straight hours to write what he had said, but the energy, the will he had possessed in that first half hour had melted into nothing. Then Lieutenant Vasiliev tried to make him put his accusation on paper, but George still couldn't do it, perhaps because he was beginning to realize he had made a mistake.

Finally Vasiliev, for the first and last time in the course of the inquiry, lost his proverbial patience. He studied Fles, observed the blank stare that often seemed lost in the void, ever since his glasses had been taken away, and he felt a mixture of anger and pain that made him talk.

"What you are writing isn't the same as what you said. You must be clear. You spoke of fascist features."

"It's not true," said Fles.

"Take him to his cell," Vasiliev said to the guard who had brought him and was waiting outside the door. "We'll continue tomorrow."

But the day after that strange interrogation without questions Vasiliev had already written a statement that contained the expression *fascist features*, a statement that was included with the other documents and became one of the deciding factors in closing the investigation.

Early in December came the indictment. Vasiliev was satisfied with his work, even though he was unable to produce proof for the accusation of espionage, which was therefore abandoned.

With his usual diligence he also took it upon himself to have a doctor visit the accused, so that the transfer to the regular prison of Tbilisi would be done in full respect of the regulations, and no one could later object if something happened to the prisoner.

For an instant he considered informing Fles directly about the outcome of the preliminary inquiry, but that was not allowed under the procedures, and Vasiliev thought it better not to modify them. He was sorry, however, at least as much as it was possible for him to have such a feeling, not to be able to close the relationship personally. After all, he seldom had anything to do with a foreigner in that outpost of the revolution, a place that would remain on the periphery even though it was the homeland of the Supreme Leader.

Nevertheless, Case 8033 was closed brilliantly on December 9, 1936. When the time came, it would be up to the Moscow court to decide what punishment to apply to Fles's crime. Until then, the accused would remain in isolation and could not be assigned work of any kind.

So there was no improvement for George Fles after his declaration. On the contrary, the prison where he was taken turned out to be worse than the previous one. There were no more interrogations, which had at least provided a break in his isolation, he could no longer receive mail, and he was not allowed to have any news about his family.

In early March he sent a letter to the office of the public minister of the Soviet Socialist Republic in Moscow asking to have news of his wife and to let her receive word about him. He requested permission to make some corrections to his preceding depositions, and he asked for some clothes to protect himself from the cold in the unheated building where he was detained at Tbilisi.

He wrote again at the end of the month to Comrade Ezov, commissioner for internal affairs of the USSR, asking again for news and extra clothing, and to be able to clarify his statements, in particular those expressed during the interrogation of mid-November.

He received no reply to these letters.

On April 12, after four months of detention in that prison, prisoner Fles, George Louisevic, was transferred to Baku, on the Caspian Sea. The following day, under escort, he left on train number 7, bound for Rostov-on-Don, where he arrived at four thirty-five in the morning, April 15. On the sixteenth he was put on the rapid train number 75 that reached Moscow at dawn on the eighteenth. George Fles was then taken to the Butyrskaya prison, the main prison of the NKVD.

On that same day, he wrote another desperate request to the commandant of the NKVD in Moscow. He wrote it on a rough, discolored scrap of paper, the only piece he had managed to get his hands on.

1. I have been transferred here from Tbilisi without any explanation about the reason for the transfer, or about the circumstances of my case. I request detailed information on this subject.

2. I was not taken to the bathroom before my departure or during the trip, so it was not possible to wash. Please allow me to do so now. As the NKVD of Tbilisi did not find the time, in eight months, to let me have my personal effects seized in my apartment in Abastumani, and as I am a foreigner without relatives in the city, I have no other means to receive what I need. I have rags for clothes and no clean underwear. I request some underclothes.

On April 26, 1937, a special court instituted by the people's commissioner for internal affairs issued 154 sentences. The judging commission was made up of three men: Belskij, Vyshinskij, and Tsessarskij. George Fles was condemned to five years in prison, from the time of his arrest, for his Trotskyist counterrevolutionary activities.

On June 16, 1937, he was transferred to the Smolensk prison where he was to serve his sentence.

Pearl watched her baby sleeping peacefully in his cradle, and once again realized there was an invisible barrier separating them. She loved him, but at the same time felt there was something unnatural about their life.

She had heard nothing more from George. Months had gone by since his last letter, since the news of his arrest, since her desperate attempts to have some contact with him.

Often she was seized by cold rage, the result of feeling that the mistakes they had committed together had dragged George into that situation. What had happened down there, in those places where for the first time since their arrival in the Soviet Union she had hoped for a peaceful life? Not that they had been unhappy in the beginning. No. There had been feverish moments of excitement, of hope and passion, but always as if things were unfolding in a dream, as if they were under the effects of an illness or a drug. But in Georgia, a different life had begun to open up for them, a real life. What had happened?

Why didn't they send George back, let him be reunited with his family? What was this cruelty that bore no resemblance at all to their idea of Communism?

Until he returned, until she had punished him for the way his intemperance, his nervous exhibitions, had provoked this enormous misunderstanding, until then Pearl would not be able to remove that wall separating her from her son.

Something broke inside her every morning upon rising and becoming conscious: first, the child next to her bed, immediately followed by the memory of George, of the difficult life they shared, and the sentiment that held them together inside a life they could not control. Now Pearl missed that sharing, that common awareness of their difficulties.

It was already summer in London, the summer of 1937, and as Pearl nursed her baby, she tried to overcome the exhaustion brought on by the delivery and from waiting for news from George. The calm she tried to protect herself with while she waited was slipping away, giving way to an unwelcome feeling of desperation.

"Either he comes back or I forget about him," she confessed to her sister one evening. And those invented, untrue words allowed her to survive.

Because George did not return, and Pearl never had news of him.

It was many years later, in 1989, after Pearl had died, that a grandson of George's sister, sent to Russia as a correspondent of a Dutch newspaper, managed to recover Dossier 8033 in Tbilisi, regarding George Fles.

Only then did a part of his story come to light, and it was ascertained that he died May 31, 1939, at Smolensk.

The second part of his dossier, the one kept after his transfer to Smolensk, was never found, and no one was able to reconstruct the cause of his death. The only certainty, according to the documents preserved, is that he was not shot.

XXVI

Rome–Genoa 1939

The Arrest

*I*T RAINED FOR the entire trip. Water ran down the windows, though there was nothing outside to look at but a low fog, an indistinct humidity, and lowering the window created only a wet breath on the back of the hand. It was an autumn rain, one of those silent, slow rains that coats like a patina, seemingly light, yet still soaking everything, penetrating everywhere.

Flora Straccali seemed to ignore that rain. She sat upright in her seat without even touching the velvet backrest or the white cloth behind her head. She looked straight ahead and spoke to no one.

She had put her suitcase on the overhead rack, along with her heavy overcoat with fur collar and her small, black hat with veil. It seemed odd to be traveling alone, to be spending the night in a hotel without Giulio, but she had not wanted him or anyone else to accompany her. She had to find the strength to carry out this task alone, applying the same energy she put into managing the house every day, now that the men had failed and she could play a card no one else possessed.

She thought about her daughter Franca, in Genoa with two daughters, the second one only a few months old, without her parents near her, in that terrible situation she was unable to comprehend, which had become even more difficult over the years: life in unfamiliar cities, first Naples, now Genoa; the racial laws; friends disappearing because Ivan was Jewish, even if converted; fears for her daughters; and now this unexpected turn of events.

But Flora had one possibility, even though she had not yet figured out how to use it. Certainly it was not her physical appearance, since she was now fifty years old and had never been beautiful anyway. But with words perhaps she could succeed, in spite of the fact that her words sometimes turned out to be too cutting and direct, wounding to the point of arousing hostility.

She did not know the best way to tackle the situation, and that is why she sat upright and rigid on the seat, as if dignity were a defense, and distance could help her find the most suitable words. She could not allow herself to be sentimental, could not let herself be infected by the weakness that comes from dependence on others, nor could she be saddened by the dense and subtle rain that followed the train for the whole trip from Florence to Rome on that day at the end of November 1939.

The Marassi prisons rose just beyond the Bisagno, separated from the historical city nucleus of Genoa like a shame. But this was not what bothered Ivan. The accusation that had brought him there, commercial espionage, was not socially disgraceful. What hurt him, what tortured him, was a sense of powerlessness, as if the world had demolished the particulars of his life. Now he was not Ivan van Straten, his history did not count; only the categories he belonged to assumed any meaning. He was a foreigner, a Jew, a manager of a foreign company with offices in Switzerland. Each one of these categories shrieked with the reality of a war, in which Italy was not participating at present, but which was oppressing Europe like a poisonous gas.

Ivan did not know if he could get out, or how. His father, surprised by the same accusation, remained at home, since he had been granted house arrest in consideration of his age, but he could do nothing, not even make a phone call or write a letter. Franca was with their daughters, the little one born at the end of April, in a city not hers, young and frightened in the face of responsibilities that neither her years nor experience allowed her to assume.

For the first time in ages Ivan wanted to shout, to rebel against the cautious, silent steps he had taken to advance over the years, ignoring the sharp edges of reality. He wanted to vent his rage, but instead he lay on his iron cot in the filthy room where they left him alone for entire days, and he didn't move except to light one of his interminable cigarettes.

There was no way out. Either he had to escape his destiny by not calling attention to his existence, or he must face it head-on and surrender in the end anyway. Again, as in Stettin, he felt homeless, without a sense of belonging, but this time without even the idea of a place where he could return. Genoa, his city, theoretically the place from which to start again in his adulthood after his adolescent journey, even Genoa had turned its back, taking on contours of cruelty.

And it was a small-minded cruelty, the routine questions asked him as though only a matter of form, a bureaucratic job to get done in a hurry, as though his guilt were decided, or rather, as though the men who interrogated him were aware of the absurdity of the accusations and wanted to justify the waste of time. And between one series of questions and another came the wide voids of his days in the cell. Weeks like this, without even a variation in tone; only his mother's cold eyes and Franca's tears in the one meeting that had been allowed.

No, there was nothing to do, and so it was better to ignore everything around him, better to think that soon someone or something would come to save him. But the cell was narrow and empty, and Ivan was unable to forget anything.

Flora went to the Hotel Quirinale, an elegant hotel on Via Nazionale where opera singers often stayed. She went up to her room accompanied by a porter carrying her suitcase. She put her change of clothes in the wardrobe, her lingerie in the chest at the foot of the bed, and placed her toilet articles carefully on a shelf in the bathroom. She did everything as though she intended to stay there a long time, not just one night.

Outside the window she could see the wet pavement shining in the lamplight. It had stopped raining, and a cold, biting wind gusted through the street. She was not accustomed to going to bed alone, to not hearing Giulio's regular, heavy breathing next to her, and for a moment was afraid she wouldn't have the strength to enter that building.

"Come on! Come on!" she said aloud as though trying to convince a child frightened of the dark. Then she took off her dress, her slip and stockings, and put on her nightgown.

She was in Rome, near the vertex of the Fascism her husband had taught her to hate.

"People are almost never bad," he had told her. "It's only when they band together, when they act as a group and encourage each other; then they become dangerous."

Just that had happened when several Fascist *squadristi* had entered his Florence office and thrown papers and furniture out the windows. And Giulio had added:

"I make wine, I make a good wine. The papers are not important. But these are bad times."

Flora had come to find a man from that group and convince him. She had come to take him back to other times, make him forget his role for a few minutes, invest him with the same tranquility that Giulio brought to his life, and which she had learned to value.

But before meeting that man she had to get through the night, and without delay. So she lay down in bed, put out the light, and immediately fell asleep.

"We'll leave," George said. "As soon as they let me out of here, we'll go. All of the van Stratens, together. We can't stay in Italy, they don't want us. After all these years they don't want us any longer."

He said it sadly, without his usual energy, as if surrendering to events for the first time, at that very moment. He said it with the surprise of someone who had always believed he was loved by everyone and was proud of being honored by both the king of Italy and the queen of Holland.

Now he found himself caught in a humiliating state, and he was trying to hide it, in part so as not to alarm the two little girls, Lisetta's daughters, who had lived with them since their parents had been transferred to India the year before. It was the only place her husband, a Hungarian Jew, had been able to find work.

Henriette looked at George, wondering if by saying they would go away he had read her mind, had sensed what seemed to her, in their desperation, like a dream, a dream she had not dreamed for years.

"To Holland?" she whispered, with a rare display of anxiety, as it had been so long since she expressed any desires. But at that moment, mistaking George's weakness for a display of longing, she hoped they had the same idea: to return home.

But George shook his head.

"Holland is too close to Germany. What security could we have there?" he said, recovering his energy, almost happy to have caught her by surprise. "No. We'll go to America."

Henriette couldn't catch her breath. The familiar, even when dismal, was always better than the unknown, without rules or points of reference. Everything she had laboriously constructed in the confines of a difficult life now collapsed before an unknown world beyond the ocean. She still didn't know Italian well, and now she would have to learn English.

Yet rebellion did not seem possible. George had always worked for their good, and each one of his decisions had turned out to be right. Once more she must put herself in his hands.

"If you think it best, we'll go," she said in her rudimentary language. "But not before Lisetta comes back, not while Ivan is still in there."

"I said we would all go," concluded George.

She recognized the building, the balcony Mussolini spoke from, the piazza she had imagined would be larger from the newsreels that always showed it crowded with people.

They escorted her down hallways with polished floors, through wide, dark doorways rigorously closed, and she waited in an antechamber furnished with large, comfortable leather armchairs, until a young woman admitted her to the study of the Duce's personal secretary.

Osvaldo Sebastiani was wearing a gray double-breasted suit. His sparse hair was slicked down, and he kept his hands behind his back.

"Flora," he said, "it has been such a long time since we've seen each other."

He invited her in, past the large modern desk of bicolored wood and bright metal finishings, and she walked across the parquet of that spacious room with its window overlooking the piazza and its door leading to Mussolini's study.

"So many years," Osvaldo said again, and he took her hands in an affectionate gesture.

Truly, many years. They had been young together in Livorno and had not seen each other since, but both had fond memories, as if the gatherings at friends' houses, the walks along the sea, the swims taken together had created the conditions for friendship, if not a real friendship itself. As if the amusing way they had met had left a bond between them. It had happened at a party, when Sebastiani had invited her to dance and had tripped on a rug and fallen. Flora couldn't keep from laughing, and Osvaldo, from his position on the floor, had laughed so hard he couldn't get up. Now those feelings from their youth seemed to have intensified with time.

"Do you get to Livorno often?" Osvaldo asked her.

Flora shook her head.

"My husband has property in Chianti and an office in Florence. Only in the summer, when we are at our place in Castiglioncello, we occasionally go as far as Livorno. But that's not often."

"I can't get there more than once or twice a year these days, myself, and always in a hurry."

Flora looked at Osvaldo, trying to judge how much he might

have changed, not physically, but in his way of thinking, and she wondered what she could expect from him. But his eyes were the same, and his sure gestures revealed no hidden intent.

"You already know why I'm here," Flora said, with a dryness she hoped would avoid making her sound like she was begging.

"I know very well," Osvaldo said, and pointed to one of the chairs in front of the desk. "Please sit down."

He turned his back and went to the window, as if there were something on the piazza that might help clarify his ideas. Without looking at Flora he motioned toward his desk.

"On my desk is a dossier pertaining to your son-in-law," he said, still facing the window. "I have examined it very carefully. It comes from the political police, and that is a problem in itself. His name is written in Category A-Sixteen, something that means nothing to you, but for us it means he is dangerous, and we have been following him closely for some time."

Osvaldo returned to his desk and sat down. His face seemed to have no expression, frozen in a mask, with wrinkles appearing that made him look older. Only his eyes continued to give any indication of recognizing Flora, but distantly, as if the two of them were separated by a pane of glass.

"These are difficult times. There is a war, and even if we are not in it yet, it is near; we must be careful. Your son-in-law's firm is suspected of espionage. A Jewish company, with foreign offices. It's not hard to guess which side they are on."

"But can you imagine that Ivan . . . I mean, that my son-in-law is capable of being a spy, he has never been political in his life and . . ."

"It doesn't say he did it deliberately, certainly, I hope from this point of view . . . but even without wanting to, information about goods, what leaves, what arrives . . . Genoa is a strategic port . . . Flora, these questions are out of our hands."

She leaned toward the desk, as if being closer might make things clearer.

"I know only that Ivan is honest and correct, that he couldn't have done anything bad, and now he is in prison."

Osvaldo took the dossier from the pile, placed it in front of him, and opened it.

"Flora, my dear friend, I can only say that the situation is very complex, and that in any case, even if it finishes well, it can take a long time. Not days, not weeks. And if I didn't say that I wouldn't be honest with you."

Flora stood up.

"You are Mussolini's personal secretary, and I came to ask for your help. I did it because I was afraid things would turn out badly . . . even if not as badly as you now say they will. We were young together. Do what you can."

Osvaldo spread his arms.

"Whatever I can . . ."

It happened a few days later, early in December.

A prison guard entered Ivan's cell. He was a stout, unshaven man who stank of sweat even in the winter. He opened the door, letting it bang against the wall, and walked in between the cot and table.

"Get up, Straten," he told him.

That's what they called him, Straten, because he had been booked as Straten, van Ivan Giorgio.

He sat on the edge of the mattress and looked at the man with a puzzled air. He wasn't the one who usually took him to the interrogations.

"What's happening?" he asked.

"What's happening is that you are a lucky man, Straten," he answered. "You are one lucky Jew. Get your things and hurry up. They are letting you out. But be quick about it, because if you don't get out of here fast they might change their minds."

There wasn't much to put in his suitcase, as he had been allowed to bring only a few things with him, yet it took him more than twenty minutes to pack. Ivan did it slowly, without hurrying, while the guard leaned against the wall and watched.

"Anyone in your place would have been out of here by now," he said after a moment. "But maybe habits are different where you come from."

Ivan thought of asking the guard just where, according to him, he did come from, but he let it go. He should have been happy now that he was getting out, but he had a dull ache, a tear that wouldn't mend. His slowness came from an oppression that the open door of his cell could not relieve.

It was a kind of torpor, as if his nerves had quit signaling what was happening around him, a dulling of his senses that befuddled every reaction.

Even when the heavy door of Marassi closed behind him, leaving him alone on Via del Piano, facing the dark and restless water of the Bisagno, even then he felt no impulse to move, in fact it seemed that a profound weariness anchored him to the earth, invited him to sit on the ground in that miserable place. But he didn't do it.

It was afternoon and cold. No blue sky over the gray city. Ivan thought he should begin walking; he started off toward the Monticelli Bridge, crossed it, and took the first tram that came along.

Standing, with his suitcase held between his legs, he noticed he hadn't tied his shoelaces. Shamefully, as though that oversight were a confession of where he had just come from, he bent over to tie them. Only then, breathing heavily from the effort to make the knot while maintaining his balance at every jolt of the tram, did he rediscover the odors that resembled normal life. Rising, he saw the faces of the other passengers, common faces of people who were returning home from work, women with heavy bags, men grasping the straps, their scarves tucked in their jackets.

He, too, after all, had a place where he could go, where he could stay sheltered until winter was over, where he could wait with the same stubborn passivity of those men and women around him.

He got off at Piazza De Ferrari, took another tram to Piazza Corvetto, crossed the public gardens, and at Piazza del Portello went up the elevator to the level stretch of Castelletto. Now he was near Via Accinelli where he lived. There remained only the effort of the final climb, and that effort was so great, so oppressive, he didn't even think of turning to look at the city below, the port, the sea.

He kept walking, wearily dragging his suitcase behind him because that sense of fatigue had never left him. On the contrary, it continued to grow, and only the hope of a bath, the idea of lying on his bed, the expectation of seeing Franca and the girls again allowed him to keep moving. Only the prospect of reaching his den, that dark and warm place to sleep as though in a long hibernation, helped him keep walking.

Now he had arrived. He entered the street door of the building, went up the stairs, and rang the doorbell of his apartment. He waited to hear steps coming to the door; he imagined Franca as she turned the key, threw open the door, and embraced him. But all remained silent. He took the keys from his pocket and opened the door. Inside it was dark. The cold house seemed abandoned, even though each piece of furniture was in its place and nothing had been touched. All he heard were sounds coming from the street. He was alone; no one was there but him.

Many hours later he found out what had happened. The news conveyed by Sebastiani had convinced Flora and Giulio to take Franca and the children back to Florence, where they would at least be near them. Ivan, after all, was still in isolation; remaining in Genoa would be of no help. In fact, it would have only added to his worries. They all agreed it was the best thing to do, even if it seemed to Franca like a betrayal.

Certainly no one had been able to apprise Ivan, who had been released, contrary to all expectations, after only a few days.

So he entered his house and found it deserted. Then he let his suitcase fall to the floor and stood in the middle of the entryway, motionless.

—◦ XXVII ◦—

Amsterdam 1940

A Night in May

*L*OUIS FLES WAS speaking on the radio.

In front of the large gray metal microphone, elbows propped on the table, leaning forward as though doing so would increase the power of his words, he repeated with desperate obstinacy his own convictions: All the peoples of Europe had a mortal enemy, and that enemy was Hitler.

The lines on his face drooped increasingly to the sides, as though only his nose anchored the skin to his skull, giving the impression of total surrender. But a matter of indifference to him, because when he spoke on the radio only his words and the tone of his voice counted; no one could see his face.

And so he talked, and he talked some more in his fluid and fascinating way, his ideas coming forth logically and without hesitation, transmission after transmission, offering an alternative to the apparent invincibility of the Nazis.

He knew the greater part of his listeners did not understand, did not want to understand, what was happening. The war had begun, but on the western front it seemed unreal, more immobile than that of 1914 through 1918. Consequently many thought it would be easy for Holland to stay out of it.

Louis, however, knew it would not be like that, for the neutrality of his country was a deceptive dream. The Nazis were crouching on their borders. There was already the example of Poland to illustrate what the Germans thought of socialism, of Jews and democracy.

"Listen, Dutchmen," Louis Fles said. *Listen*, he thought, *before it's too late.*

But even if they had listened, what good would it have done? The army was mobilized, the government in continual contact with France and England. But Holland was a flat country, almost indefensible, and if it should be attacked it would suffer the same fate as Denmark. Were they not right, then, those who preferred to pretend nothing was happening and went to the park on Sundays, as though that spring were no different from any other?

After eating supper on the evening of Thursday, May 9, Louis waited for his oldest daughter, Mina, who was unmarried and living with them, to leave the kitchen. Seated at the table opposite Celine, his head in his hands, he spoke to his wife.

"I am old, Celine, and I'm afraid."

He said it softly, almost whispering, as though talking to himself, when actually he was asking for help.

Celine also felt the exhaustion of their battles largely lost, her sadness for her daughter Rosine, dead a year ago in the United States, and for George, of whom they had heard nothing since his arrest. Yet she still had the will to resist, to double up her fists, and to hope.

"You can't give up now," she told him. "This country needs all of us in order to survive."

Louis shook his head.

"I'm almost seventy years old," he told her. "I've worn out my voice in front of that microphone, day after day, thousands of words. And I'm beginning to think it's all useless."

"And our children? And Pearl, alone with her son? You don't think of them?"

Pearl was George's wife, his only tie with that lost son, but there was constant disagreement between her and Louis. Nonetheless, he certainly was thinking of them, and too much. Just as he thought about his grandchildren, Harry's and Clara's children, and wondered what would happen, what future awaited them. A leftist Jewish family: What illusions could they have?

"Maybe we should all go to America, or to England," he said, but in saying it he knew it was impossible, because he didn't have enough money to do it. And because you don't start a new life at seventy.

Celine listened to what Louis was saying, remembering how that continuous, soft flow of words had helped her for years to believe in their future and to face life like an adventure. Now, evening after evening, she found herself confronting her husband's weakness, asking herself what was left of their years. Celine felt angered by Louis's attitude, and wanted to shake him, forcing him to react; but she didn't.

As had happened so many other times, Celine rose from her chair and went to Louis. She put a hand on his shoulder and bent over him, mastering her resentment.

"Let's go to bed. It's late," she said.

Celine feared her suggestion would not be accepted and Louis, as usual, would sit up far into the night, reading a book or leafing through the newspapers.

"I can't sleep," he would tell her, "not even if I take something to help me."

But this time Louis stood up and embraced her warmly, a change from their usual distant relationship, and with his arm still around her, he walked her to the kitchen window that looked outside their old house on Van Baerlestraat, onto a little flower garden. There was silence and a starry sky and no moon. It seemed to Celine that nothing bad could happen on an evening like this.

"You're right," Louis said. "It's better if we go to sleep."

They were awakened before dawn by a dull noise in the distance. They didn't understand it immediately; in fact, for a few minutes they pretended not to hear it, hoping it would all end as it had begun, in the silence of a May night.

Louis rose and opened the bedroom window. The sound grew louder, becoming the roar of airplanes, the deep rumbling of explosions. Lower, just above the house rooftops, they saw a reddish flash from the direction of the airport.

To Celine everything seemed to be happening with extraordinary slowness. Their every movement, even the most mindless and ordinary acts — putting on a housecoat, or turning on a light, or shaking Mina, who was sleeping unaware of anything — were done in a void, with no relief or sound other than that which continued to enter through the open window. Neither of them had the courage to speak.

They went downstairs to the parlor to listen to the radio, and heard what they both knew without being told: German troops had invaded Holland.

"I must go to the radio station," Louis said in a flat voice, his words coming out almost robotlike, as though they had been recorded.

"I have to go to the station," he repeated.

Celine, silently, her strength concentrated in her hands and at her temples to keep from crying, followed him upstairs, handed him a shirt and suit, watched him as he removed his pajamas. She saw his narrow chest, the sparse hair, the swollen belly, and it occurred to her that he was old.

She knew they were destined for defeat.

Maarten van Bossum was one of those Amsterdam boys with reddish blond hair and light, almost transparent, skin. He was the technician at the Vrijdenkers Radio-Omroep, the radio for freethinkers, and he had often assisted Louis Fles during his anti-Nazi transmissions, but he hardly recognized him when he arrived at the studios.

Maarten had come down to smoke a cigarette, since no news was coming in upstairs anyway; they were merely rebroadcasting messages from the head of the government and the queen. He was standing in the lobby, where the first gleam of dawn was be-ginning to penetrate and the lights had been turned off for safety. Perhaps that was why he had to ask himself who that little man was coming toward him, his arms open in a gesture of surrender. But it wasn't only because of the dim light that he didn't recog-nize him, it was also because Louis's face was ravaged, devastated by a wild expression that seemed not to belong to him.

"My God," Maarten said. "I didn't recognize you."

"What's the news?" Louis asked, grabbing Maarten's arm. "What is the news?"

It seemed to the boy that Louis Fles was trembling, that he gripped his shirt with an unusual strength.

"Nothing, for now," Maarten said.

"What do you mean, nothing!" Louis shouted. "That's impos-sible, they attacked hours ago and we don't have news? Where are the Germans? What are we doing, our soldiers . . ."

At that moment all the tension and strength seemed to abandon Louis, and he sank on the divan near the copper ashtray where Maarten stood flipping his cigarette ashes. He fell like an empty balloon, like a mannequin whose joints were suddenly loosened.

Then Maarten, too, understood they would be crushed by whatever was happening, and the absence of news signaled the impossibility of any resistance.

"It's hopeless. They are Germans: They will win."

Louis did not respond.

"They'll come here and take all of us," Maarten continued in a faltering voice. "They already know us, each one of us, and they don't forget their enemies."

Louis was looking at him in silence, unable to formulate a reply, when a man raced down the stairs shouting.

"We have opened the dikes; the water will stop them."

Maarten threw his cigarette on the floor and started running up the stairs. Louis followed behind him, but slowly, his body unable to keep pace with the speed of his thoughts. It responded slowly, as if it were a separate entity and every movement a decision.

Slowly Louis went up the stairs, trying to imagine the water flooding out the gates and pouring onto the fields and streets. But he couldn't picture it.

They spent the day glued to the radio, ignoring the sirens calling them to bomb shelters, which proved to be pointless as not one bomb fell on the city. The telephones worked intermittently, and what little news there was went out by telegraph. Only news that could give some hope came over the radio: Here and there the Dutch army had stopped the Germans; in a few areas the water from the dikes had slowed their march. They didn't mention the larger areas where the water had moved more slowly than the Nazis.

Louis understood at once that hidden behind each of their frantic gestures was a sense of powerlessness and the awareness that what was being transmitted were lies and illusions. The war was already lost.

"It's late," Maarten told him. "The curfew begins in two hours. Why not go home and rest for a while? We'll need you tomorrow."

"Tomorrow?" Louis said incredulously, not certain whether the technician was being serious or just trying to get rid of him. How could he be useful now? It was all over, all finished.

Maarten whispered in Louis's ear.

"Run," he said. "Hide. You can't let the Germans take you. Listen to me. Don't come back here."

Louis knew the boy was right.

"I'm going," he said, nodding.

The fatigue he had been trying to ignore for some time was now ravaging him, so tremendous he did not think any amount of sleep would ever overcome it.

He descended the stairs, and realized only at the bottom that he didn't have his jacket. He must have left it upstairs, but he didn't have the strength to go back for it.

Outside was a city he did not recognize. The windows were barred, many store shutters were closed, but people were running from every direction to line up in front of grocery stores. His fellow citizens were stocking up to defend themselves, to survive.

Louis walked around, unable to decide to go home. Instead he left the southern part of the city and headed toward its center. He passed the canals, crossed the dam, saw the flag waving on the royal palace and the guards outside the entrance. He looked at the houses with darkened windows, women and men rushing into their buildings as though finishing a race, bicycles abandoned where they fell. No children in sight and he thought they were safely at home; he hoped his grandchildren were in a safe place.

He took one step after another with methodical regularity, even though his legs were beginning to hurt, as if measuring the city before something made it disappear.

At first he looked around him, then he hunched his shoulders and kept his head down, his eyes on the ground. So he did not see the man coming in the opposite direction as he crossed a bridge over the Prinsengracht. They collided, and Louis lost his balance. His outstretched arms finding no support, he fell to the ground, while the man kept going without turning around, muttering something incomprehensible. For a moment Louis thought of remaining there in surrender on the pavement. But he stood up with effort and started walking again.

The light faded, the curfew hour was approaching, and the confusion seemed to be growing greater, filling the street and his head, and amid that confusion Louis knew that all was lost.

Still, he kept walking as if his steps staved off the moment of decision, until he stopped thinking and every fiber in his body was exhausted, totally exhausted. He halted at the edge of a street he didn't recognize. He felt cold because of the evening air, because of his light shirt, and because he had found no way to escape. Just then he saw a tram pass, the last one before the curfew. He raised a hand to make it stop, and it did. Other passengers helped him on.

"Are you all right?" someone asked him.

Louis shook his head. He was returning home.

But no one was there.

On the kitchen table he found a note from Celine. "We have gone to Harry's. Join us as soon as you can." But to join them seemed impossible. He looked around for a reason to keep moving, but couldn't find it. He turned on the radio and fell into the leather armchair in the parlor, rubbing his hands on the arms to find the warmth from the thousands of times he had made the same gesture, but the warmth had disappeared.

Louis was trembling and still he did not get up, did not decide to go upstairs where he could crawl under the covers and warm himself. The house was dark; outside, too, it was dark, without streetlights. The radio repeated instructions about the curfew, how to behave should the Germans arrive, how to protect the women and children.

All useless. Louis knew he was not in any condition to protect anyone, much less himself.

After what seemed a very long time to him, but was really only a short while, he managed to rise out of his chair and go upstairs. He entered the bathroom without turning on the light and opened the medicine cabinet over the sink. Louis was exhausted and knew he needed to take the sleeping potion his doctor had prescribed many months ago in order to help him sleep. But in the dark room he couldn't find it.

He covered the little window with a towel to keep anyone outside from seeing anything and he turned on the light. At once he saw the bottle he had looked for on the second shelf of the cabinet, and he reached for it. He filled a glass of water and tipped the bottle to count out the ten drops prescribed by the doctor for the necessary sedative effect. But he stopped before the liquid had begun to run into the glass.

He turned out the light, left the bathroom, went into the bedroom, put the glass and bottle on the nightstand, and then lay down on the bed. He tried to think, he tried hard to single out a path, a possible direction toward salvation. But there was none. Maybe he had been wrong about everything, had confused ideas with reality, and had taught this error to his children also, to George who had imagined a Soviet Union that didn't exist. Either the Fles family was wrong, or the world was. In either case the result was the same; there was no way around it.

In the dark it is impossible to count ten drops. They can't be seen as they fall, nor can the faint sound be heard as they mix with the water. Therefore, no sleeping potion. Louis pulled the blanket over his head and breathed under it in search of warmth. It was a night in May, but he shivered for a long time.

After a while he calmed down and hoped to be on the point of falling asleep. He waited, beyond his empty exhaustion, beyond his confused thoughts, but he continued to feel the weft of the blanket on his face, and sleep did not come.

In the dark it is impossible to count ten drops. So Louis pulled the blanket off his head, turned on his side, unscrewed the bottle cap, and emptied its contents in the glass. Raising up on one elbow, he took the glass and drank it all. The bitter taste of the medicine ran down his throat and made him want to vomit.

He managed not to do it.

Celine and Mina found him the afternoon of the following day, Saturday, when they returned home, worried by his silence. Celine looked in from the bedroom doorway and saw him motionless on the bed, still dressed. She thought he had stayed at the station late and had fallen asleep like that. She decided to let him rest.

After an hour she looked in on him again from the doorway, and then entered to try to wake him. Louis was still breathing, his body blindly resisting his decision. Celine shook him forcefully and called his name, but in spite of her efforts he remained inert on the bed, not reacting in any way.

"Mina," Celine cried, "Mina, hurry, run to get the doctor."

The doctor was unable to do anything except note that Louis must have poisoned himself with the sleeping potion. He lived for thirty-six hours, until the morning of May 13, 1940, a Monday. Then he stopped breathing. Present in the house were Mina, Celine, Harry and her husband, Meijer Vorst, and Pearl, George's wife.

Celine did not cry. She felt no sorrow, only hate.

"He left us alone, Mina and I, right now when we most need

him," she said, and Harry, her arms around her shoulders, drew her out of the room. "The coward."

Meanwhile, Mina sobbed without restraint. She thought her whole life, already so banal and insignificant, had been completely emptied, dried up like a piece of forgotten fruit.

"You must come live with us," Meijer said to his sister-in-law.

She did not answer immediately. Bent over the radio, she was listening to the latest news. The queen and the government were taking shelter in England.

"They're all running away," Celine said in a dry, desperate voice. "From Louis to the queen."

"Mama!" Harry interrupted her. "Stop it!"

"I've just begun," Celine retorted. "No, Meijer, thank you for the invitation, but Mina and I will stay here."

And so they did.

On Tuesday, Holland surrendered and German troops entered Amsterdam.

⌒ XXVIII ⌒

Atlantic Ocean 1940

The Flight

THE TRANSATLANTIC liner left the port in the morning; it was early in June of 1940. On board were George, his wife, Henriette, their daughter Lisetta, and her two little daughters, ages two and three, but not her husband, who had remained in India.

So a van Straten had taken to the sea again, following Benjamin's route; once again America had appeared a plausible destination, or rather a destination of salvation.

This time Hartog's descendant was traveling on a liner, the *Rex*, and knew where he was going and what to expect. It had been George's decision. Once again he had thought of life as a series of decisions, which he had imposed on everyone, or almost everyone. The war had become a reality, heating up beyond the Maginot line and spreading like oil over Holland, whose neutrality had been mocked. Italy seemed on the verge of jumping in, as if it were only a matter of taking part in the division of the spoils.

Safety meant distance, putting an ocean between oneself and the threat of danger. George had decided to leave because he did not believe in special cases, because he remembered the guards outside his apartment in Genoa, because racial laws had also been adopted in Italy and had immediately been put into practice. So a foreign Jew was not liked by anyone. Many of his friends had disappeared, and when George met them on the street they pretended not to see him.

Nelly's family had left first, and now that the financial business had been tended to the others were following suit.

Everyone had left, or almost everyone.

George was convinced the van Straten children of that generation were not on a par with their parents. No one, for example, was willing to inherit either his or Siegfried Swaab's position in the company, nor did it seem to him that those who had chosen another path were making much of a place in the world. Quite the opposite. Each of them seemed to be following a very tortuous and irresolute path. Certainly he felt affection for those children now become adults, for that close-knit group who summered in Scheveningen, but George had also come to feel they were hobbled by a vital weakness that kept them from taking advantage of opportunities and pleasures. And the fact that among the grandchildren there was not yet a male with the van Straten name did not seem accidental, but rather a result of that same weakness.

He had boarded an ark, an ark of iron and steam, but he wondered if every species of animal were really represented on board, because there was not one male child from that weak generation on the ship. For the first time, in fact, someone in the family had rejected his wishes, had refused his decision.

If it was Franca who persuaded Ivan, George had no way of knowing; he was inclined, however, to absolve his daughter-in-law of any blame, perhaps because of her lighthearted charm, which left him defenseless, as he always was in the presence of an attractive woman. Besides, he didn't see how a girl of just over twenty could decide anything for a man, no matter how much Ivan lacked his father's decisiveness and self-assurance.

Once through the Strait of Gibraltar on the ship, moving on a sea with a circular horizon, without obstacles or variation, everything seemed vague and distant, the trip merely a cruise. One cannot get off a ship, and the before and after are separated by an insuperable space, as wide as the time elapsed in the crossing. So eventually his anger gave way, his surprise at the unexpected resistance surrendered to a vague feeling of resignation.

Only Henriette, when she looked at him in silence, was able to arouse feelings of guilt in him. *"We will all go,"* George had promised her. But that was not the way it turned out.

He didn't budge from Florence. The geographic distance was protection, a pass to safety. Franca's family was as he had imagined it: a barrier against the outside, a place of genuine welcome.

For the first time Ivan had found, in a life that was crumbling, an excuse for forgetting paternal dictates. Now that there was no work, now that he could freely choose what city to live in while waiting to discover what it was he really wanted, George's unattainable model oppressed him less. He could not be like him, simply could not do it, it was too difficult. But now he could say it, confess it to himself and survive the disappointment.

Of course he had needed the geographic distance, as well as the look on Franca's face, the fear he read in her eyes when the idea of leaving appeared to be getting out of hand.

"We'll stay," he had told his father after the decision had been made and the trip became imminent. "We won't be going."

Actually his resistance had been little more than a formality. Thanks to friends in the Vatican, the girls had obtained a certificate of Aryan lineage, the Straccali family guaranteeing for everyone; the only one at risk was Ivan.

This decision was no surprise to George, but merely a reminder of what he already knew. Ivan was not the one he had put his hopes in, he had known that for a long time, and the latest events only confirmed it. The wrong son had survived, although George would never admit such a conviction, not even to himself.

"Take care of yourself," Henriette said to Ivan.

"Anytime you want to come, you will have a home there," George said to Franca, although certain they were about to avail themselves of one of the last opportunities to escape.

—◌

Every evening George dressed elegantly, and with his four women, as he called them, he went to the dining room. He tried to determine who the other passengers were: Americans leaving Europe, Italians on business trips, or men like himself escaping to their own destiny.

The evenings were fresh and humid, during the days the sun burned their faces. The first-class passengers of the *Rex* seemed just what in effect they were: the privileged, regardless of the reason for their voyage.

The captain often came to the dining room. He had a brush haircut, a row of very white teeth, and he laughed with the affectation of an aristocrat. It was obvious that being in command of the largest Italian liner made him very pleased with himself.

Henriette did not appreciate the presence of that vain man who glided from table to table like the deity of the place. But Lisetta was amused, the part of her most resembling George — her face, especially its coloring, and her gaiety — taking precedence over the characteristics inherited from her mother — her sarcasm and her enormous breasts.

"Come on, *oma*, try to have a good time!" she told her. "Let's just pretend it's a cruise."

What if it really were only that? thought George. *What if I'm mistaken, and remaining in Italy is still an option?*

He observed the captain, asking himself if such a face, projecting such insensitivity, could belong to the eve of war. And the answer seemed to be no. Yet George knew that Louis Fles had killed himself, that German troops were marching through the streets of Amsterdam, that Rotterdam was reduced to rubble.

The girls were too young to realize what was happening. They ran around on the ship's bridge as if it were normal to live in an undulating world. For Henriette, on the other hand, everything seemed outside the norm; rules no longer existed and reality had shattered into a pile of splinters.

She knew George was right this time, too, and she trusted him as the only habit of her life that hadn't failed her. If they had really gone to Holland, as Henriette had dreamed they might, at that very moment they would be at the mercy of a different fate, delivered into Nazi hands. Instead they were on a ship heading for an unknown country, but at least they were safe. Except not everything had gone as she hoped. They had left a son behind, perhaps the son less loved, but this only made him weaker and more in need of help. Yet this time Ivan had not asked for that help, and George had not seemed to feel it necessary to insist, to force him to follow them.

She would have preferred to have all six granddaughters with her, born one a year between 1934 and 1939, leaving no family member behind on the other side of the ocean.

Now she found herself on that ship, on a strange cruise at the crossroads of history and fear, and it seemed unnatural to dress up every evening and enter the main dining room as bright as day to eat supper while the orchestra played dance tunes. But she continued to do so, without asking why, as she had done all her life, convinced the only way to make it through the years was to repeat a series of habits, reconstructing them every time the world threatened to destroy them. In this, the sea was of great help, because it resembled infinity itself.

But Henriette didn't laugh like Lisetta, was unable to follow George's light banter amid the smoke of his cigars. She limited herself to counting the days, to commenting with her cold irony on the thousand oddities of a ship and its passengers, to rejecting the captain's vacuous smile every evening.

So she was surprised when the captain came to supper with a strange look on his face, strict and serious, on one of the last days of the trip.

"What's the matter with the captain this evening?" she asked George.

But he hadn't noticed anything.

"What do you mean?" he asked.

"He's not laughing," she said brusquely.

The captain went to the platform where the musicians sat in silence, their instruments resting on their laps. He stood in front of them as though to direct the orchestra, but he faced the room, and his arm was raised not to give them the beat, but to invite the passengers to be still.

George observed him carefully, surprised by his seriousness and his dress uniform, which he seemed to be wearing with an uncustomary martial bearing.

"I have the duty and honor," he began, "to inform all of you of the news I received only moments ago."

He paused while George sought Henriette's hand across the table and squeezed it.

"Benito Mussolini, the duce of Italy, our great nation, whose flag waves over this ship, Benito Mussolini, in whom the entire country trusts, speaking to the crowd in Piazza Venezia, announced that a declaration of war has been delivered to the French and English ambassadors."

He stopped as if emotion had overcome his natural detachment. Someone in the room applauded.

"This is a great moment," he went on. "I certainly understand the worries that some could have, but our ship is a passenger ship, and furthermore, we are entering the territorial waters of a neutral country. Therefore, there is no danger for anyone. There is only, for all Italians, the pride of belonging to our country."

He raised his arm again and the orchestra started playing, as if he were truly capable of conducting it. The "March of the House of Savoy" resounded in the room, and the applause grew in intensity.

George, who until that moment had not taken his eyes from the captain, almost seeking a confirmation of what he had heard, turned to Henriette but did not meet her eyes. She sat motionless, her hardened and impassible face turned toward the platform, challenging those who were applauding, a silent revolt against the one who had changed her life. Lisetta, meanwhile, was already on her feet, holding the girls by the hand.

"I'm taking them to the cabin," she said to her father.

"Sit down," he replied.

Lisetta seemed on the point of tears.

"Stay here," Henriette also said.

George gave his wife's hand a stronger squeeze. He had discovered again what gave solidity to their marriage, what cemented their relationship over all those years: their similar way of facing adversity by ignoring it, he by character and she by will.

"Let's all stay here. Everyone," confirmed George. "We have to eat."

And they did, as if nothing had changed, as if the toasts at the other tables did not concern them. As if that trip had not become different, even though the direction they were headed was now irreversible.

This is how it appeared: It grew out of the sea like an enormous canebrake; from a bottomland without natural irregularities it rose into a series of geometric, indented shapes. The tallest had a peaked point and was called the Empire State Building.

George saw New York coming toward him, a heavy island of concrete that seemed to be reaching for the sky, almost as though it could rise by itself. On the right a long bridge joined it to a stretch of land filled with low buildings, just as George had always seen the land from the sea, before coming upon that silhouette of spires.

For a moment, facing those giant's teeth, so smooth and foreign, he understood the difficulties in starting over again in another world. Of course he had carefully planned every move, and was able to count on the presence of the company even in New York, but he wondered if he would be able to start a new life now that he was over sixty years old.

Behind him was a war that had pushed him relentlessly toward that shore without granting him any alternative; ahead of him lay the slow admission procedure, the forms to fill out, the declarations to be translated before a notary. For the first time he hated, relentlessly and to the bitter end, the stupidity of men, the violence of their gestures, the blindness of actions done senselessly, out of pure instinct.

The sky was high and blue, an American sky, the same that his uncle Benjamin had seen but hadn't been able to describe to anyone in his family. Because he had never returned.

George would not allow those dreadful men who had expelled him from his continent to win. No, he would not die in America, he would have the strength and the good fortune to return home. He would see Ivan again, of that he was certain.

That voyage of theirs had to be only temporary. It lasted, as a matter of fact, for six years.

Amsterdam 1942–1943

Saul's Dream

WHO KNOWS IF the man noticed she was beautiful, if he noted her fine blond hair, her regular features, her blue almond-shaped eyes; or if he understood her suffering, her fear renewed every day, her difficulty in understanding what was happening and why.

She stood in front of him for a few seconds, perhaps a minute; for the time it took the man to open the drawer, remove a packet, and give it to her. For those brief moments he, the man without a name, did not change expression, did not look her in the eye, did not say a word. Perhaps it was his way of reassuring her: *Look, I haven't seen you, wouldn't recognize you, couldn't betray you even if I wanted to.* Or maybe he, too, was afraid and hoped in this way to minimize his fear. *What woman? We didn't see anyone here, we don't know anything.*

It all lasted a few seconds, a minute at the most. Then Betsy took the packet, put it in her purse, and whispered, "Thank you."

Without waiting for a reply from the man without a name, she ran out of the office, a place that represented her salvation, but at the same time filled her with anxiety, as if her persecution might reside there also.

She knew the money from her uncle George had arrived, the money that would pay for their survival, and which had to be picked up at the branch of the Société Générale de Surveillance of Amsterdam. There were words agreed upon, revealing who she was and what she must receive, but no names used, not for the woman who greeted her at the entrance, not for the young man who pointed out the room for her to enter, not for the man who gave her the packet, and not even for herself. Thus a modest bookkeeper had become the man without a name, and in the days that followed she continued to refer to him that way.

The operation had been simple, just as the preparation had been long and complicated, waiting for the message from her uncle to arrive, establishing the amount, finding the best way to receive it. And all those hours of waiting, despairing, and hoping seemed to Betsy to concentrate on the few seconds spent in front of the bookkeeper, as though that man had made an accounting of her life, and in the end had given her the pass to her salvation. Instead he, the man without a name, had not even looked her in the eye, had not formulated a judgment or reached an opinion, confining himself to doing what others had requested: giving her the packet. And then Betsy van Straten went out of his life forever, as quickly as she entered it.

Now the Germans were taking Jews away, even Dutch Jews. They sent them to internment camps, like Westerbork, and then shipped them on to the east, to places where they were never heard from again. Many continued not to believe the rumors, many hoped for a way out that did not exist. But Betsy's husband, a practical man, had made calculations, looking for solutions for the two of them, and for their children, Saul and Bernard, who were only four and three.

She did not understand how they had come to find themselves in that situation. She remembered a normal world, where her eyes were beautiful and boys wanted to take her out; the world of vacations at Scheveningen, of her adolescence, when her cousins looked upon her as a queen. It was a comfortable world, a sweet and familiar world to live in, where a girl had nothing to do but enjoy herself. In that same world she had been married, with the same ineffable, unquestioning ease, won over by Meier's love, which continued to surprise her every day.

Then everything suddenly changed. The war, the invasion, the laws and regulations for Jews. A difficult life that oppressed her, that left its mark on her eyes and the corners of her mouth in an unnatural way, for it was not the years that had wounded her, but the change in her existence. For a long while it had seemed possible to adapt and wait for better times, even as her clothes grew shabby, the music vanished or was reserved for the occupiers, and the country grew dark. But it was always better than ending up on a train heading east, as was happening now.

Betsy had done nothing to deserve that treatment, there was no guilt or reason. To be Jewish had always been a natural and secondary condition for her, a family way of loving or hating, nothing more. For this reason Betsy wondered how all this could be happening and did not understand that such questions were pointless, if not dangerous.

While Meier and Simon, her sister's husband, looked for solutions, Betsy looked on the world without understanding it, and at the same time she refused to disappear, to humble herself by trying not to be noticed, by becoming transparent. She was proud of what she was and how she looked.

Now, however, the money had arrived and she was going home, holding on to her purse with all her might, as if a purse could fall from her arm unawares, as if it were possible to lose it without realizing it. And for a moment when she reached home and closed the door behind her, she felt free and secure.

He was awakened while it was still night. It seemed strange that they would pull him out of bed in all that darkness, because he had forgotten what Mama had told him earlier, what he had understood only in fragments, becoming confused immediately.

He remembered only that Mama spoke sweetly, but her eyes

were bright and close to him, her hands holding him tighter than usual. What was happening? What were they afraid of?

Now Mama was dressing him, putting on his shirt and trousers, combing his hair with her hand, coaxing him awake. Papa, standing near them, spoke to Mama in a low voice, calmly, as if trying to explain something she didn't understand.

Saul heard a phrase repeated, but did not understand its significance, a new and tender phrase: *to immerse ourselves*. Papa said to Mama, "You have to trust them, they have already done a lot, it's our only hope: to immerse ourselves." Saul had a feeling this had something to do with water, like disappearing under the bathwater, like slipping under a down comforter. And he understood it was tied to fear, to a means of defending oneself from fear.

They took him to the entry hall, where there was a little suitcase waiting in a corner, along with his brother, standing next to another small suitcase; there was also Mama, holding a packet tightly in her hand and stroking his hair, but as if she were thinking of something else, as if she didn't recognize him.

Suddenly Saul began to cry.

"Hush, darling, there's nothing to cry about," Mama told him, crouching beside him. "You are going to take a trip with some nice young people, a trip to the country. And before you know it Papa and I will come to get you."

She hugged him and he tried to stop crying, almost succeeding, except for the itch in his nose that he paid as little attention to as possible, but Mama kept holding him, and Saul felt something wet on his ear where he brushed against her, and he thought maybe when there are too many tears they come out of your ears, too.

"We will come soon," Papa repeated, his face close to Saul's.

But Saul did not know what *soon* meant, or how much time would go by before he would feel Mama's soft touch again, her way of holding him in her arms. Saul did not want to go away from their home, from everything familiar. His brother Bernard didn't seem very convinced, either.

Then the doorbell rang and Mama jumped as though a bomb

had exploded, but she did not open the door. Papa went to the door and turned the bolt. A boy and a girl stood there, smiling. Saul wanted to cry again, but this time the tears did not come because he was distracted by the boy, who looked at him with dark and lively eyes.

"Now you must go with them," Mama said. "You must be good and obey them and soon we'll all be together again."

So Saul followed them outside to the street, beyond the canal that ran in front of their house. On the horizon, visible behind the houses, rose a great orange sun, which you could look at without closing your eyes.

Meier had been decisive; they could certainly try to get away with false documents. With a new identity they could hope to slip unobtrusively around the city as long as the Germans remained there, for months or even years. But not the children. It would be impossible for them, too difficult not to be betrayed in some way, too risky to stay in the old house at the mercy of all the neighbors who knew them and knew they were Jews; the Germans paid informers. No, the boys must *immerse themselves*.

There were organizations that helped people in their situation. Money was necessary, of course, to persuade peasant families to take the children and pretend they were theirs. But with money they would keep them as long as necessary, and in the country, where there was more food and better living conditions.

How reasonable Meier was as he said these things, and yet it took Betsy a long time to resign herself. How could they trust strangers? How could they survive without the children, not knowing if they were well, if they were safe, if they were well treated? Could they ever forgive themselves if something bad happened?

No, they had to stay together, united, all of them safe or no one. Betsy shook her head, pleaded with Meier, the money must be used to get them another identity, like any *goy* family in Amsterdam. She couldn't imagine leaving the boys for months, maybe years.

Meier kept talking to her, trying to convince her; even her

sister and Simon had done the same with their son, Maurits; even they had decided to take that risk.

Finally Betsy looked in on the boys late one evening after they were asleep, one beside the other. She sat on the floor and watched them until she understood they had the right to be saved, they before anyone else in the family. They deserved to survive this war and destruction, in order to have a real life at its end. It was their right, truly, the only way to respect the dreams they held. And if Meier's plan was the best solution, then let it be.

Betsy got up, returned to the other room, and embraced her husband, telling him to call the organization and say they were ready; soon they would have the money.

"But can't we at least leave Bernard and Saul together?" was all she asked, hoping the reply would be affirmative.

"I'll request it," Meier said.

Instead the organization separated the boys for security reasons, entrusting them to different families.

As Bernard and Saul were leaving the house, Meier lowered his eyes in order not to see them. He didn't want that image to remain with him, ready to reemerge, to weaken him at every difficult moment he would have to face. For many months, for years, he would have to live as though the boys did not exist. Not out of selfishness, but in hope of survival, of being able to retrieve them when they surfaced again after the end of that war.

And he didn't want Betsy to detect signs of weakness in him, to see his eyes tear up, his hands attempt to wipe his eyelids surreptitiously.

Betsy, meanwhile, ran to the window and wanted to watch her boys leave. Then she threw herself on the bed and began to weep.

"We'll see them again," Meier said, sitting on the bed next to her. "We'll be back together again. Soon."

But he was not able to say that *soon* convincingly, because he didn't believe it himself. And she continued to weep, clinging to the pillow. Then she raised her head suddenly and looked him in the eye.

"How will we find out anything about them? I can't imagine not seeing them again until who knows when; I already miss them too much."

"Betsy, for heaven's sake, don't go on like this. You owe it to them, you owe it to me. Don't think about it, don't focus on the boys. All of us must be saved. All four of us."

She nodded, but her eyes, those eyes that Meier had fallen in love with, looked at him, full of animal terror, mad and uncontrollable. He hoped they weren't right.

Betsy took the tram on no particular day in that hellish year of 1943. With her purse on her arm and her hair gathered in a bun, with her eyes never lowered. She had the protection of those documents. The Germans and the Dutch police had already had occasion to check them, and had indicated with a wave of the hand that she could go, everything was in order.

So she went back to leaving the house, to taking the tram, searching about for something to eat, or paying a visit to a trustworthy friend.

She had received news of the boys and dreamed of the moment she would be allowed to go see them. They had let her know she might even be able to visit them in time. Though it actually seemed to her that everything was getting worse, that the approaching defeat made the Germans even more pitiless, and therefore they had to be more rather than less cautious. In any event the boys were safe, and sooner or later the war would be over. So Betsy envisioned, as if a dream, a street full of people dancing, laughing, and singing, and she was running about among them with Meier and the boys. And sometimes, on the tram, that dream became a smile on Betsy's face. Then the circles under her eyes and the lines at the corners of her mouth seemed to disappear. There was a glimmer of youth beyond that awful war, a scrap Betsy could still hold on to.

Other times it seemed the end to the suffering had slipped beyond the horizon and the condition in which they were living would last forever. Then a feeling of desperation came over her, which Meier detected immediately. So she often went out for the sole purpose of not letting him see her.

In any case, she never lowered her eyes, even when she was sad.

There was an unpaved street, parallel to the canal, that ran from the farm to the nearby town. That was where Saul had been brought, along with a dark-eyed boy. Then the boy left, although he returned occasionally to see Saul and speak with the man and woman who had taken him in. Saul, meanwhile, stayed there among the plants and animals of an unfamiliar world, waiting for Mama and Papa to come for him. He often looked toward the dirt road, convinced they would come from that direction soon, as they had promised.

Saul did not cry, because he knew he shouldn't. Inside him a knot would sometimes press on his chest, but he could forget about it if he didn't mention it to anyone. He had decided it was better just to keep quiet.

The man and woman were not mean, but they never hugged him, never took him into their bed, even when the night was very dark and there was thunder and lightning. When Saul got scared he covered his head with the down comforter and dreamed of immersing himself.

There was no sea where they had brought him; no ships went by, and Saul barely remembered the times Papa took him to the port to watch ships come and go. So he had forgotten the water and its reflections. The only things resembling water in that place were the fields of wheat or grass when the wind blew over them, and then waves ran toward the flat horizon of the countryside. But not even then did ships come up the dirt road from the direction of town.

Betsy never lowered her eyes, and so in the tram on no particular day in that hellish year her eyes met those of a woman sitting a few rows in front of her. She was standing up holding on to the strap. Her almond-shaped blue eyes met those other eyes, and a mouth, and a face. Just enough time to form the impression that it wasn't the first time she had seen her. Seconds, only seconds. She turned away, but the woman sitting a few rows ahead of her, with her light stringy hair, her straight nose and little eyes, had recognized her, too.

There was a policeman on that tram. He was also standing, but a bit ahead of Betsy, almost beside the conductor. The seated woman gave him a look, then she turned again toward Betsy, who continued to look out the window with determination. The streets, the sidewalks, the people walking, the automobiles; she thought it would be wonderful to be able to change into almost any object outside the tram. But she had to remain standing there, in the hands of some woman who could betray her for money or decide to save her life. And she wondered if there was anything she could do, anything at all, to stop that woman, to keep her from calling the policeman and turning her over to the Germans.

The tram was already slowing down in sight of the next stop, and Betsy had moved toward the exit, when the woman stood up, went to the policeman, and touched his arm. She whispered something, looking in Betsy's direction, and the man turned toward her. Betsy moved closer to the door, but the policeman came and stood beside her. With an absurd gentleness, he took her by the arm.

"You have to come with me, ma'am," he said. "A routine check."

An empty space seemed to enlarge around her and no passenger dared breach it.

"She's a Jew," she heard the woman say behind her.

"She's a Jew," someone repeated as the door opened.

For a moment she thought of running, running out of the tram, disappearing in the crowd, but now the policeman's grip on her arm was firm. She knew she couldn't wrench free.

And so she got off with the man. They might have seemed a couple if it weren't for the uniform.

"Where are we going?" she asked.

"To the German command," was the answer.

—૭

They took him from the farm and brought him to Amsterdam, to Papa and his aunt, but much time had gone by and Saul had forgotten many things, even important things. There was another boy whom he didn't recognize at first. Then they told him the boy was his brother Bernard and he hugged him.

The city didn't seem frightening; there were no uniforms and people moved around freely, but Mama was not there. Everyone was waiting for her, but she didn't return from the country far away where they had taken her. Aunty was nice, but it wasn't the same for Saul, she wasn't Mama.

Little by little he understood what had happened, because he was growing older and things were becoming clearer, but at the same time he noticed that the others preferred not to talk about what had happened. Papa was silent, especially after it became obvious Mama would never come back. And that silence was a lot like fear, as if that terror could always return, as if a thousand things and reasons could bring it back to life.

Many years later Saul asked Papa if he would buy him a dog. He would like to have a dog to take care of, to keep him company. The answer let him know there was a period that would never pass from Papa's mind.

"A dog?" Papa said. "A dog is an animal for Germans, not for us."

—◌ XXX ◌—

Castellina in Chianti (Siena) 1943

The Telegram

*T*INA WORKED IN the town post office, and when she received the text of a telegram she copied it in her clear, round
handwriting on a standard yellow form. Then she folded and
sealed it, and instead of calling the postman she delivered it to the
addressee herself. The telegrams were few, and it wasn't an impo-
sition to help speed up their delivery. Tina was proud of her work,
and she felt important because a great deal of the town's commu-
nications with the rest of the world depended on her.

But this time, after preparing the telegram with her usual diligence, she decided to wait a bit before delivering it, giving herself
the time necessary to find a way to mitigate its effect.

The dispatch had arrived from the command of Siena and was
addressed to the carabinieri office in town. It was a short telegram,
without details, written in a bureaucratic and laconic style, but
that neutral, detached style was what made it so odious. In response to a direct request from the highest military German au-
thority, it said, all foreign Jews residing in the commune of
Castellina in Chianti must be arrested and taken to the prison in
Siena. The order was to be executed with the greatest speed and
in any case not beyond midnight of that same day.

It was early afternoon on a sunny October day, with the countryside still seeming to ignore the beginning of autumn, the trees
full of barely yellowed leaves, and the fields as bright as they had
been in summer.

Tina opened the telegram and recopied it onto the other form,
changing only the hour of its arrival. Sixty minutes wasn't much
time, Tina thought, but it would be enough for her to do what she
considered necessary: try to save at least one of those Jewish foreigners residing in the town.

She put a wool shawl over her black work smock, because at six
hundred yards above sea level the October sun did not always
manage to warm the air, and that day seemed chillier than usual.

Tina ran quickly down the main street with her hurried step
resounding on the pavement, warmly greeting the people she
passed because everything must seem the same as usual, and no
one must notice that something distressed her, something that
seemed unjust and should be circumvented.

She reached the old building that stood at the southernmost
edge of town, toward Siena, which housed the winery of Signor
Straccali, or "Sor" Giulio, as everyone called him. She went in
and asked for him.

He was sitting at his office desk in a room situated on the first
floor, just beyond the entrance, with the worn pavement where
carts came to load wine flasks and demijohns.

"What is it, Tina?" he asked, surprised. "Do you have mail
for me?"

She shook her head and closed the door behind her. Sor
Giulio looked at her questioningly as he rose with some difficulty
from his chair and went to her.

He was an imposing man, almost bald, with a wide, sweet face
and blue eyes. He wore a light-colored suit, with a handkerchief
in his jacket pocket, and he had on large brown-and-white two-
toned shoes.

"What's wrong?"

Tina was afraid, and for a moment she thought of not saying

anything, of letting things unfold as if she did not exist, as if she had not seen that telegram or had not understood it. Now not talking had also become a choice, the worst one.

"A telegram arrived for the carabinieri. It says to arrest all foreign Jews who are staying here. And Signor Ivan is on the list."

"How much time do we have?"

"An hour. I can wait an hour before delivering it to them. Only an hour."

"We'll make that do, Tina," Giulio replied. "We'll make it do."

He took her hand. "Thank you," he said.

"If there is anything else I can do . . ."

"Go on. You've already done enough."

Tina ran back to the post office and waited for an hour, as she had promised, and then, without hurrying, she went to the carabinieri office and delivered the telegram.

Giulio put on his hat and went out the back door of the building, which opened directly onto the countryside. At that point the town wall met the building's foundation, which was wide enough to leave room for a terrace. From there steps led to the fields.

The land sloped down into a valley to a stream that remained hidden by vegetation to those looking from the building. It then rose on the other side until it reached some farmhouses. In one of these houses lived Ivan, his son-in-law, the guest of a tenant farmer's family. After the armistice of September 8, it had seemed safer to remove him from town, but now — as with so many other things — even this decision appeared to be wholly inadequate for a war that was spreading to the heart of Italy, growing more ruthless every day.

Giulio had to think quickly, had to find a solution. He looked at his watch: Ten minutes had already passed. Even though it was likely the carabinieri would wait until the curfew, and surely wouldn't begin their rounds at his house, time was short. He couldn't waste a minute, because the foreign Jews in Castellina, aside from Ivan, were only those Germans staying at the Mariani pension.

He saw Bruno, one of his workmen, coming up from the fields below him toward the "farm," as they called the building, considering the use they had made of it for decades.

"Bruno!" Giulio called.

The man looked up and waved, continuing to walk toward him.

"Yes, Sor Giulio!" he shouted from the walls.

"Run to Castagneto and tell my son-in-law to come here right away." When the man nodded yes and was about to turn, he added, "Tell him to come immediately. Bruno, it's important, very important, and time is short."

They went down together toward the valley bottom until they crossed the stream, then they walked along the oak scrub, crossed the vineyard, and began the climb toward town. Bruno led, older and heavier, but more accustomed to walking in the fields than on an asphalt street, while Ivan followed him in shoes unsuitable for the outing, wearing the good suit he had put on without knowing what was happening or where he had to go, a coat over his arm.

What did Babbo know — he and Franca called him Babbo to differentiate him from the other father-in-law, who was Papa — sending for him with such urgency, he who was always so calm and optimistic?

The sun had dropped toward the horizon and the bottom of the valley was already growing dark. The grape harvest had taken place in spite of the war, as though the war could still be thought of as far off, when instead it was on its way. The front was coming closer and the Allied troops were advancing from the south. Still, the farmers had harvested the grapes, as if there had not been an occupying army, as if working with nature allowed one to ignore the activities of men.

Ivan, however, had not been able to sdo it, did not have the right, and perhaps had made a mistake by waiting, with nothing to do but let time pass. But one day was all it took to get killed, even one moment of delay, one moment of hesitation.

They arrived, and as they ascended the stairs, breathing

heavily, Ivan was already looking for Giulio, hoping to make him explain what was happening. But Giulio was not there.

"He said to wait here," said the women who were fixing labels on the flasks. "He said to wait here, he'll be right back."

Impossible even to think of taking him to Florence that same afternoon in the car. They wouldn't make it before the curfew, and then the risk would become even greater. Giulio's house would be searched immediately, and if Ivan were hidden with some friend, anyone who saw him might readily talk, because even in small towns there are evil people, and information circulates more easily than in a city.

Half an hour had passed and Giulio had already spied Bruno and Ivan coming up the valley when he had an idea. It seemed so absurd to think that it was the only solution that might really work. And if it didn't work? If it were refused?

Giulio took the white handkerchief out of his jacket pocket and wiped his head, as if perspiring from the heat. Instead it was turning cold, the sun was falling, the sky was stained pink low on the horizon behind the hills. Giulio clamped his hat on his head, and after telling the women to advise his son-in-law to wait for him there, he would return in a few minutes, he left the farm and set out for the podesta's house.

No one had time to worry, to be afraid, to think of being lost. Not the two Germans, who had not been alerted; when the carabinieri arrived they followed them without reacting, almost with resignation. And not Ivan, who ran to meet Giulio when he saw him returning; he was anxious to learn what had happened, and discovered not only the problem but also the solution.

"The carabinieri have an order to arrest you. But I talked to Falassi. He'll take care of it," Giulio said. "And tomorrow I'll take you to Florence."

Giulio had gone up the street with the energy that had long since earned him the admiration of the town. He had worked, had obtained success and money; he made one of the best wines in Chianti. That town was his life, and life had to be more important than politics and war. What he had to request was only the respect of a principle, proof that friendship could survive the brutality of orders and roles.

"Giovanni," he had said to the podesta, who had a hardware store next to the church piazza. "You are a Fascist and I am not, you are young and I am old. I'll be sixty this year. But we are friends just the same because you know I'm an honest man who gives work to many of the townspeople. Besides, I know you well, and know you wouldn't hurt anyone. That's why I'm asking for your help, and I hope you'll give it to me."

Only Giulio himself knew how close he had come to catastrophe. What had made him think that Giovanni Falassi would feel the same way about friendship as he did, that that move wouldn't end up delivering Ivan into the hands of the carabinieri of Castellina?

Certainly they had known each other for years, even though Falassi was young enough to be his son. But the war, the hate that comes from it, the desperation of those on the losing side, all of this can change men without anyone noticing, especially when they are young, until one move, even a single word, betrays the transformation taken place. And often it is too late.

But Falassi, too, was an honest man. Short, robust, his hair slicked back, he took a certain satisfaction in being named podesta, but he hadn't changed because of it.

He had greeted Giulio in the doorway of his store, speaking to him as on any other day. "What's new?" he had said, without any idea of what was coming.

But there was no time for polite conversation, and Giulio answered his question without stopping to take a breath. Giovanni continued to look at him mutely, motioning to the back of the store where they could talk more freely.

"In less than an hour, the carabinieri will receive an order to arrest Ivan, and I can't get him out of town before tomorrow, there isn't enough time before the curfew."

They stood looking at each other in silence for a few seconds. Time enough for Falassi to realize what Giulio had just said, time to weigh his words.

"You can count on me. I'll find a place for him to spend the night. And tomorrow you will both race to Florence."

There are moments when a man's modesty, his reluctance to give in to sentimentality, is suspended and he makes a sudden, unpremeditated gesture. These are merely moments, and they soon pass; only a light trace remains, but it is indelible.

And so Giulio embraced Falassi, holding him tightly, nearly crushing his face against the pocket of his light-colored jacket.

"I knew it . . ." He said no more than this, and then stopped.

Falassi stepped back, took a breath, and replied, "And I know that you would do the same for me. Go now, so no one sees us. They always talk too much in this town."

They weren't well known. He had arrived after the beginning of the war, had spent most of his time in the house, and had a way of acting that seemed haughty, a frown that held him aloof. A foreigner, in other words.

"What do you mean *foreigner*, what are you saying?" Giovanni replied to his wife. "He is Signora Franca's husband!"

She had made only one comment and certainly didn't want to dispute her husband's decision. In fact, her remarks referred to an earlier time that now seemed far off, not because of the days gone by but because of all that had happened since. Today she had more sympathy for that man, for his strange face, for his large, curved nose like a bird's beak, for his thick hair that always remained wavy in spite of his efforts, for all the packs of cigarettes he smoked.

"And besides, what else could I have done?" Giovanni said, as if needing to justify a decision he had made by himself, even though it also affected his wife.

But Iolanda knew instinctively that alternatives are few when the world is on fire; choices become clear. There are orders to follow or to ignore, there are men who save lives or condemn them. Now the choice was up to them.

"You did what was right, Giovanni. You did what you had to. But now where will they put him?"

He and Giulio had agreed to have him pass through the Voltacce, the passageways through the old city wall, where no one would see him. It was already dark, and the Voltacce were always deserted. His wife asked where they would put him, and Giovanni knew where he already was.

He, too, through the chain of command, had been informed of the order coming from Siena, and had avoided making any comment to the commander of the carabinieri. "That man is a dangerous fanatical Fascist," he had told his wife. "It's better to be silent."

And yet he kept thinking that he had been able to do nothing for those two Germans lodging with the Marianis. His being silent had cost them dearly.

He went to the window, told his wife to put out the light, and then he looked out at the narrow street running between the houses and quickly disappearing in the misty night. It was colder than previous nights, as if something in the world order had changed that day. Giovanni looked toward the piazza; there was no one in the street. Then he heard footsteps echoing off the walls of the houses on the Siena side, and he watched the carabinieri patrol come up the street until it passed beneath his window.

The marshal stopped and waved a greeting.

"Everything all right?" Falassi asked.

"We can't find Straten," the marshal replied.

Falassi spread his arms. The patrol continued its way up the street, passed through the gateway in the city walls, and disappeared.

"Iolanda," Giovanni called. "Iolanda, come here. Do you really want to know where Signor Ivan is?"

She looked at him in surprise.

"Why, do you know?"

"He's in the cellar. And by now he's probably hungry."

"Don't worry about me, I can stay alone."

Iolanda laughed.

"I'm sure you can. But the time will pass faster if we have a little chat. Anyway, no one will be sleeping tonight."

She was right, Ivan was well aware, and he accepted her company gladly. Signor Falassi, as Ivan always addressed him, insisting on the formal "*Lei*" had strolled around town to give the impression that nothing out of the ordinary had happened. Then he had returned to the house, because if the carabinieri came to call it would be better if the podesta were there to open the door. And after her surprise at learning Ivan was already under their protection, Iolanda had offered to stay with him in the cellar.

Now they were sitting there, facing one another in the narrow space left between the casks, surrounded by flasks, bottles, and the clutter that had accumulated over the years.

The familiar objects around them assumed a different character in that silence and emptiness; their form seemed more important than their function, which at that moment, in the night and in the war, was nearly forgotten.

Ivan lit a cigarette. "Does this bother you?"

She thought of all the cigars that had been smoked around her without anyone asking permission, and it confirmed her belief that this was indeed a curious man, truly different, and it was nice to save someone so unlike the other townspeople.

The same thought had occurred to her earlier when she had come down to the cellar and found him in the middle of the room, dressed in silk nightclothes, his suit folded in the corner as if he were spending an ordinary evening at home.

"Smoke as much as you like," she replied.

Iolanda, too, felt a little different from the others. She had more education, she was the daughter of a doctor, and her musical talents kept her busy with the Schola Cantorum, the church choir. She was taller than her husband, and younger, almost a girl still, and she liked the idea of spending the night with a man, for no other reason than to talk about their lives.

Ivan also felt he was in some sort of interlude, a point in time outside the rules of daily relationships, where he could say what he wanted rather than what was expedient. He felt like a survivor, like someone who had been lucky enough to escape a fate too easily imagined. And opening before him was an uncertain period of separation from the only loved ones left to him. He had nothing to hide. His life was reflected in the Falassis' metal tools, it spread over the irregular, dusty dirt floor, was nourished by the odors and the thick walls protecting them from the external cold and dampness.

"Would you like something to eat?" Iolanda asked.

They spoke softly, afraid their words would echo off the cellar ceiling and bounce outside.

"No, thank you. I'd just like a coffee."

She made him a cup of real coffee, using a spoonful of her dwindling supply of ground coffee beans because she was ashamed to give him the brew made from acorns that they had been making for themselves: colored water. Then she returned to him in the cellar.

They sat in two straw-stuffed chairs, facing each other, with hours ahead of them, trying not to show the fear they felt at the slightest sound coming from outside. Iolanda sensed the anger in him, borne of powerlessness, with everything depending on others and nothing left in his own hands. She wanted to soothe that anger, and hoped light conversation would do it.

Ivan, too, was looking for a way to make it through to the morning, and thought it would help to construct a bubble of normality in that night: a conversation about children, work, habits, or music; an uninterrupted conversation, expansive and sincere.

And by turns they each recounted the story of their lives.

At dawn the next morning there was a knock on the cellar door. Iolanda didn't want to find out who it was. She wanted to know as little as possible, to keep from betraying anyone. Ivan took his few things, thanked her, and left.

She went upstairs and found Giovanni asleep on the divan, still dressed. She touched his arm lightly and waited for him to open his eyes. He smiled at her.

"Did I fall asleep?" he asked her.

She nodded.

"And he?"

"He left."

Giovanni sat up and looked at her tenderly.

"I need a real coffee," he told her.

In Florence during the months before the liberation of the city on August 11, 1944, Ivan stayed with Elena Angiolini, a distant relative of the Straccalis; afterward he returned to Castellina, where he was reunited with his family.

While in Florence, he was forced to stay in the apartment during the periods of bombardment because he had no documents, and he risked being caught in a police raid by seeking refuge in a shelter. So he sat in his room and listened to the bombs hitting against each other as they fell. He could only hope they were falling somewhere else.

Signor Falassi, who often went to Florence, brought food from the Straccalis for Signora Angiolini. But on those occasions he never saw Ivan.

PART IV

Epilogue

Europe 1945

These Are the Names

"W̶HAT WE CANNOT speak about we must pass over in silence." Ludwig Wittgenstein wrote these words in 1918, after a war, though a different war from the one ending in 1945.

I presume there are more or less valid objections to this statement by Wittgenstein. I would like to express only one exception, without casting doubt on the rule.

Language has its limits, because there are things that go beyond our capacity for description, so every attempt flounders in its inadequacy. In spite of that, one cannot pass over in silence, indeed one needs to speak, to remember, forcing the thought to return again in order to examine the events.

I don't believe one can talk about a death camp; I don't believe it can be adequately recounted even by one who has seen it, much less by someone like me. I am unable to do it, and I don't want to.

I know I don't have words suitable for describing what happened to many of the van Stratens in central Europe, in the territory between Holland and Poland, in the period from 1942 to 1945.

But I am not allowed to pass over in silence, because what happened must not be canceled by silence.

What I can write is a list. Their names, one after the other, their ages and the dates they died, just as I was able to construct them, thanks to the help of my relatives and to what I found in the library of Yad Vashem, the museum in the hills of Jerusalem dedicated to the extermination.

I write these names so they will be remembered, so they will not become numbers, so their fate will not be silenced.

I must tell about the seven van Straten siblings, apart from my grandfather George. Rachel's family stayed in England and was saved.

The other five I will list.

Oom Emanuel was deported and killed at Auschwitz, November 5, 1943, at the age of seventy-one.

Tante Celine did not move from her own home, as she vowed. She had a heart attack when the Germans came to take her away. So they left her there, in her bed, where she died at sixty-nine.

Mina Fles, who had stayed with her, was deported. She was killed at Auschwitz on September 28, 1942; she was forty-five.

Among Celine's other children still alive during the war, Clara was saved because she had married a Christian and had children. The war ended just as the Germans were on the verge of deporting this category of persons, too: Jewish spouses from mixed-faith marriages, with children.

Barthold was saved because he was in America.

Harry Fles Vorst, who returned from Paris with her husband and children after the war broke out, believing Holland to be safer, was deported and killed upon her arrival at Auschwitz on August 12, 1942; she was forty-two years old. Killed with her were her son, Rudolph Vorst, fourteen, and her daughter, Nicole Vorst, six. The three went together, believing they were taking a shower. They had hung their clothes on a rack, which was numbered to convince the deportees they were only showering, they would find their clothes afterward on the way out, they had only to remember their number. Thus the victims entered the gas chambers without resistance.

Her husband Meijer Vorst died in the same camp on September 30, 1942. I do not know if he knew the fate of his family, but he certainly was able to imagine it.

Rosa and Jacob de Levie died before the war. Only their daughters Rachel and Mina survived them; they had married non-Jews.

I do not know where Henry de Levie and Henriette de Levie died, or how, but I know why. Their dates of birth are also missing, and the place. I could reconstruct nothing of their lives and deaths, yet they existed and were killed.

Marie de Levie, thirty-three years old, was deported and killed at Sobibor, March 26, 1943.

Celine de Levie Leezer, thirty years old, arrived at that same camp on July 16, 1943, along with her husband, Siegfried Leezer, and their three children, Jacob George Leezer, four; Rozaline Claire Leezer, three; and Max Henry Leezer, five months. A child conceived at the beginning of 1942 by two parents who were either ignorant or very courageous.

They were all slaughtered upon arrival.

Who knows if there is a destiny in names, something that marks individuals and their histories. Even thinking about it is a form of superstition, and yet I am struck by the fact that all three Henry van Stratens of this story — the older sons of Bernard, George, and Emanuel — died young.

Bernard's Henry was deported and died in an undetermined place in central Europe on July 31, 1944, at the age of thirty-seven; his wife, Lientje Salomons van Straten, died at Bergen Belsen on March 16, 1944.

Bernard died December 10, 1941, following an operation before the deportations were initiated. His wife, Johanna van Vliet van Straten was killed at Sobibor, April 30, 1943, when she was sixty-four.

The other son of Bernard, Jacob van Straten, was deported and killed at Sobibor on May 28, 1943. He was thirty-two.

Mina van Straten Dessaur was the only one of the family to be saved.

I already related how Betsy van Straten was taken. She was deported and died at Auschwitz on October 14, 1944, when she was thirty-seven.

Louise Mina and her husband Samson van Dijk were deported to Auschwitz. Samson was killed October 15, 1942; she a little later, March 26, 1943, when she was sixty-two years old.

Their son Paul was saved; I will relate how further on. His sister Lineke was married to a non-Jew and was not deported.

Gerrit, less a brother than the others, was arrested for anti-German activities and died in the internment camp at Oranienburg on May 3, 1942. He was fifty-two. Sophie de Jong van Straten, his wife, was deported and killed at Auschwitz on February 26, 1943.

Her daughter Marie van Straten was deported and died at Auschwitz on February 1, 1943, when she was thirty years old. Her son, Eduard van Straten, was deported and died at Auschwitz on April 30, 1943, at nineteen.

Out of eight van Straten siblings two were left at the end of the war. Of their twenty- nine children fourteen were alive; that is, almost exactly half.

None of those who were deported returned home.

In 1939, 140,000 Jews lived in Holland. In 1945 there were only twenty thousand.

Holland 1946

In the Flooded Anthill

ROTTERDAM HAD been razed to the ground. The city where George was born no longer existed. He was told not to go there because he would find nothing of what he had left, no recognizable house or street. He hadn't even thought about going that far; there was no one he could still see, no one he would want to see.

But it wasn't only Rotterdam that had been destroyed. His whole world seemed to have disappeared, as if a wind had blown away every thing, every person, making his country unrecognizable. Yet little by little, as in an anthill swamped with water, someone reemerged, reappeared on the surface, surprised he wasn't drowned.

George went to Holland by car. It was 1946. He had recently come back to Italy from the United States, and had immediately wanted to return to his country, to find out what had happened to his family. His chauffeur, Mario, drove across a land whose poverty showed on the people's faces, in the empty store windows; and for the first time, George thought his wealth might be an insult to others. He thought it as he faced the tragedy of that wounded nation, because money, which had certainly helped some of his relatives to survive, was not enough to save many others. The majority of them.

He met Bernard's only surviving child, Mina. He saw her little boy, and Betsy's children. They had thin faces and big, lost eyes that lit up only on seeing the Studebaker of that uncle who seemed a kind of god.

Maurits, Mina's son, offered to be a guide, and he learned the few Italian words necessary to give the driver directions.

"*Diretto*," he would say, to tell him to go straight, or:

"A *destra*."

"A *sinistra*."

And for Maurits, all the miseries and difficulties of the war that had oppressed his ten years seemed to disappear, beyond those bulging black fenders, that slender hood, that trunk as big as a house.

No one had ever thought such cars could exist. And the fact that they existed was one reason for hoping things might improve, a reason to hope life might become less miserable than it had been.

"*Oom* George," Maurits said, the sound of his words suggesting that worlds did indeed exist where people rode around in such marvelous automobiles. "Studebaker," he repeated as though it were a magic formula.

His uncle George searched for words of encouragement, but he felt the family had broken up, with only individuals remaining, little nuclei of survivors. Yes, some ants had reemerged from the water, but they really were like ants: dry, dark, tough.

Just over a year earlier, George had suffered a very serious heart attack that had softened his proud and confident ways, as if those pounds he lost had actually fleshed out the way he faced life, his new demeanor contrasting with the lean, raw state in which he found the others.

He saw George Fles's sister Clara, and her family. She was the only surviving Fles in Holland. He also saw relatives on the Bloch side, among them the two daughters of Henriette's brother, who had come back alive from the camps.

There was no one else to meet besides Louise's children,

Lineke and Paul. George especially wanted to hear Paul's story, parts of which had already been related to him.

"Right after the occupation I joined a group doing sabotage work. There were six of us, very enthusiastic, but badly organized. The Nazis took four of us. I never heard any more about them. I had to run away to avoid meeting the same fate.

"Just think, Uncle, I went by bicycle from Utrecht to Deventer and then as far as Arnhem! I worked on a farm in the summer, and in the fall I began to work underground. This time the organization was stronger, but the Gestapo was clever. I had to hide again. I found refuge in Clara's house. Shut up in the attic I thought I would go crazy, or make them go crazy for the risks they were taking for me. That was when your money arrived and I decided to leave. False documents and a connection that seemed safe; I paid a man to help me go to Spain. Lineke had married a non-Jew and didn't seem to be in danger. It was November in 1942."

Paul was razor-thin, like the rest of his family, in a worn, tight-fitting suit he wore with elegance. His red hair and freckles evoked the boy he had been, but his eyes weren't as sparkling and the fierce energy that once rumpled his little-boy suits and made his shirttail fly was repressed by the orderliness he imposed on his clothes.

"And what happened to your parents?" George asked.

Paul did not reply immediately. They were sitting at a table in a nearly empty café. Its elegance seemed as passé as Paul's clothes.

"They didn't want to hide," he finally said. "I found them a place to go far from the city, in the Veluwe woods, but they said no. They wanted to stay in their house, they didn't understand what could happen to them. They didn't want to understand. In any case they didn't have the strength to resist. I couldn't get them to change their minds."

George nodded. He knew that sometimes people don't accept advice. The war had taught him this, too.

"Then you left."

There were three of them who fled, and the man leading them

seemed sure they would make it across the borders. Such as they were, for borders between Holland, Belgium, and France were practically nonexistent, all being part of the Reich. They crossed the first one in the car with no problem. They slept in a small hotel and left again the next morning. When they reached Brussels their guide took them to the city center, and while they were wondering why he hadn't avoided that route, he entered the courtyard of a building and stopped the car. The guide had them get out, and he began speaking in German. Before they could make sense of what was happening, the man had already turned them over to the Nazis.

Paul was taken first to an internment camp called Breendonck and then to Malines, where he remained for six months.

"I kept wondering how I could escape. That's all I could think about. It was an old barracks. Several of us tried to escape out of windows on the unused fourth floor, but a spy turned us in. Thirty-six lashes and three days in the dark without food, without even being able to lie down."

Everyone just tried to stay alive, in spite of the hard labor, the small rations, the roll calls that lasted for hours. The Germans made the prisoners clean the paving stones with their fingernails. They made them run barefoot over coals. And then the beatings and desperation. It was a transit camp, but hundreds of people died there.

Paul tried his best, but no one left Malines except feetfirst or on a train. The train that carried him was made up of fourth-class German boxcars, packed with people, on a march toward the east, but proceeding slowly because of the Allied bombings. It was going toward Germany, toward an extermination camp.

During the first night Paul noticed a window in the car that was not sealed. The leather strap that opened the window was missing, but still he managed to lower it.

It was drizzling and dark. Guards were standing on the outside platforms, ready to shoot. But what did he have to lose? What was left for him? Wasn't he already a condemned man? So before anyone knew what was happening, Paul was out the window and had already jumped down from the boxcar.

The train was moving slowly, not more than thirty miles an hour. He stayed by the roadbed in the dark, watching the moving cars. It was raining harder. He heard some rifle shots coming in his direction from the platform, but the train did not stop, perhaps out of fear that others would try to escape.

"And in fact ten people did try it that night, I found out later. Eight were caught and shot on the spot. Only a boy from Amsterdam and I were saved. We are probably the only survivors from that train."

After that, he knew only that he was a fugitive, once again in Belgian territory. Just before he succeeded in opening the window, he remembered, the train had passed through a station. So he walked back along the tracks in the opposite direction from the train. Louvain was the name of the town. He arrived there at three in the morning, hearing a clock strike the hours behind the closed windows of a house. He waited under a portico for the end of the curfew, and then went into the first Catholic church he saw. The priest immediately realized his condition and where he'd come from. He let him wash, gave him something to eat and a place to sleep, as well as some money and clothes. The next night Paul crossed the border from Belgium into Holland and made it to Clara Fles's house at Eindhoven.

Once again there was nothing to do but wait, a situation he couldn't tolerate, hearing a threat in every doorbell ring, growing weaker while he waited, until finally he wanted to give up. He knew they would find him if he remained there; the only way to save himself was to do something.

So once again he obtained false documents and renewed his contacts with the resistance movement, deciding it was the surest way to survive.

"Everyone thought I was mad. My sister couldn't believe I was serious. No one had ever done anything like that."

For an instant he smiled. He looked at the glass full of wine on the table in front of him, brought it to his lips, and slowly began to drink. He hadn't had any good wine for years.

No one had told George how Paul had been saved. He had

heard only that his nephew had disappeared for months, and after his return he had not wanted to talk about what happened. "What is it that no one had ever done?" George asked.

Paul put the glass down. Of course, he was taking his time in order to add to the suspense, but that was only part of the truth. Because the words had seized up deep inside him, cemented by the silence he had maintained in order to save his life. He couldn't utter them.

"What is it that no one had ever done?" George repeated.

He looked into Paul's eyes and realized that they were not life-less, only distant, hollowed out by a life grown rich with stories in those impossible months, yet at the same time as fragile as the shell left behind by the cicada after molting. Apt to crumble at any moment.

"I volunteered as a laborer in Germany and left under a false name with a group going to Cologne. A Jew working for the Reich, who would have suspected it? Who would be looking for a small-nosed, redheaded Jew in the middle of the Germans as they were making their last stand for the Führer? And in fact they didn't find me."

George took a cigar from the inside pocket of his jacket, knowing full well that the doctors had prohibited his smoking. But there were occasions, for a smoker there were always occasions, to light up.

He put the cigar in his mouth, but waited a few more seconds before striking a match. The cane that he carried more out of habit than necessity was slipping from the table edge, and he repositioned it.

"Louise would be very proud of you," he said, turning to Paul. "She was good at organizing games, too. And that one of yours was very clever. Not everyone could trick the Nazis."

But Paul did not smile, did not acknowledge the compliment in any way. There was nothing to be proud of, nothing that was like a game.

He knew from the beginning that his uncle George wouldn't really understand what had happened. He needed to have witnessed it himself, and even that might not be enough. If he had told that story, his entire story, it was only in the hope that it might help him forget it. Because never again did Paul have the desire to talk with anyone about what had happened.

"And now what do you think you will do?" George asked.

"I don't want to stay here, in Holland," Paul said, "where I have to keep seeing things that remind me of what happened; my memory is enough. I don't need other things to oppress me. When I walk through the streets and look at the people around me, I can't help but think that one of them could have reported my father and mother, or had Betsy arrested, and that so many of them turned the other way, pretending not to see all those who were being taken away. And so they are all guilty."

But even that was not the point. What offended him was the fact that people had taken up their lives as they left them before the war, with the meanness and selfishness of before. They might even be right, because maybe there was no other way to start over. Paul did not want to waste away in hate. He knew that he, too, must begin to live again, but he was unable to do it there.

"Lineke doesn't want to stay in Holland, either."

"Where do you want to go?" George asked.

"As far away as possible. What's on the other side of the world?" said Paul, and as he posed the question he thought of George Fles, of Ivan, and of what they had said one evening many years ago in Scheveningen, when they were boys and the sky was full of stars. *I would like to go to Batavia* were Paul's words. And he realized that among those there that evening, inside and outside the house, at least half were dead. Where was the farthest place away?

It was growing dark outside the café. The smoke from George's cigar lay thick over the table like a cloud. Their glasses were empty. George was silent.

"I've heard talk of New Zealand," Paul said. "There are great possibilities. Thousands of sheep and few men. With a reasonable amount you can buy a farm, start over."

～ஓ

He asked Mario to slow down in order to avoid bumping over the holes that pitted the road from Amsterdam to The Hague. It certainly wasn't the shortest way to Paris, but George had decided not to leave Holland before seeing the only thing he was sure had not changed.

The morning light illuminated the flat expanse of fields and canals, the silhouettes of the windmills. Occasionally, George was overcome by a strange drowsiness, some kind of mental fatigue, a weariness of his soul. He was running from an absence of hope that went against all the rules of his existence. He would respond to it when he returned to what he had been accustomed to for decades in Italy, but until then he felt it necessary to let himself go, to observe passively that tortured world to which he did not belong.

To keep from being swept away, however, he had to find something from his past, at least one thing, to remind him of how he had freed himself from the bonds of his homeland, to recall the superiority he felt each time he returned.

So he decided to visit the sea, certain it was the same, certain it could not have changed.

They passed The Hague and turned toward the coast after stopping to eat at a roadside restaurant. The car proceeded even more slowly, with Mario uncertain about the way and George directing him with brief instructions, clipped words, vague hand gestures.

Finally they passed a high embankment with a walkway running along its ridge, and the view opened up onto the sea: the long dark beach, the metallic, flat expanse of water, the straight avenue at Scheveningen.

George got out of the car and started walking, leaning on his cane, toward the steps that led to the beach. He realized then that taking that detour to the sea was not only an attempt to rid himself of his feelings of loss. His journey to the water was also a farewell.

He would never again return to Holland, he knew that now. He had seen the children, the hardened ants who would cautiously build the future; he had helped Paul get as far away as possible. The task entrusted him by his father, to protect his family, was now concluded. Not everything had gone according to expectations, but that had been the world's fault, not his.

He walked along the deserted beach. On the horizon were two merchant ships and a sailboat. The cane was no longer any help because it sank into the sand. George passed a hand over his face and closed his eyes. For a moment he imagined himself on that beach more than twenty years earlier, in a jacket and tie, next to Henriette, Ivan, the little girls, and Enrico.

How much had been lost in those twenty years, how many ambitions vanished. And yet he did not want to become sentimental, did not want to give in to sadness. That was not him, not his way.

Then he turned back, opened his eyes again, shook his cane at Mario, and broke into laughter.

"Come on," he shouted. "Let's go home."

Atlantic Ocean 1948

The Last Voyage

*N*OW THIS LONG story is about to end, but there is still a part that must be told.

Franca became pregnant again after the war, and in February 1947 a daughter was born. *Opa* George, called during the night to be informed, said to his son, "You woke me up to tell me a third girl has been born?"

I'm afraid he wasn't joking.

In the course of that same year Nelly, who had remained in the United States after the war, was diagnosed with cancer. Her condition became rapidly worse, and toward the end of the year it was clear she was dying.

George decided to leave, but his heart condition made air travel inadvisable. The only possibility was to go by ship with Henriette. Ivan, who had always felt close to his sister Nelly, offered to accompany them.

I know what awaited them, and once again I should limit myself to telling what happened from the distance of years. But this time I no longer have the patience or the detachment to do it. I want to dirty myself with paint, to be a painter instead of a restorer. That way I will feel no remorse in changing what has already happened, in infringing on the rules. I want to do what every man has at one time or another dreamed of doing: enter the picture as if the surface of the canvas were only a thin gauze, a light curtain of fog to pass through without fear.

I will board the ship, the transatlantic *Saturnia*, along with Ivan, George, and Henriette: now, in my time and in theirs. I will spy on all of them, but above all I will watch my father, who is almost my same age, to see what part of him, as he was then, I have unconsciously absorbed, dragging it with me through the years; this will be our last journey together.

It is December 27, 1947. The *Saturnia*, having arrived from the United States on December 20, in time for its passengers to be in Genoa for the Christmas holidays, is ready to depart again for New York.

It is a beautiful transatlantic ship, the *Saturnia*. Constructed in 1927, it has already been rebuilt twice, the second time right after the war to restore it to passenger service. It combines traditional characteristics, such as the straight vertical prow and the elliptical stern, with innovations, among them the elimination of the quarterdeck and a single wide, low smokestack. Accommodations for first-class passengers are excellent: Some cabins have an outside veranda, and there are numerous halls of double and triple height, many covered and open passageways, even gyms and two outside swimming pools.

The powerful diesel motors allow a speed of twenty-one knots, so the distance between Genoa and New York can be covered in about fourteen days, including a stop at Naples, where goods will be loaded.

The first few days they stayed in their cabins, as if wanting to ignore the length of the crossing, or even to deny the fact of motion itself, transforming that voyage into a lengthy hotel stay.

They appeared at regular intervals to eat, and sometimes Ivan accompanied his parents on short walks along one of the covered passageways, but the inclemency of the wind and the indistinct grayness of the sky and sea soon drove them back to their rooms.

I cannot manage to get near them, or to overhear any words, however few, exchanged between them. None of the other passengers has said a thing to them.

But tonight, December 30, something different happens. George remains at the table even after the waiters clear it, signaling to Ivan and Henriette to stay as well. He waits until the pianist begins to play, then approaches him at the first pause and requests a song.

The man nods as if he had been waiting for the request. He finishes drinking from a glass that has just been filled, then bends over the keys and plays some chords.

Then George, who has returned to the table, looks out over the dining room and begins to sing. It's a simple song that everyone knows, and it even comes naturally to me to join in the chorus. I turn to Ivan. Unlike the others, he has remained silent, but I see him smiling, gazing at his father with a mixture of envy and admiration that I have learned to recognize.

George continues to sing, and during those moments he is completely happy, as though only the temporal space of that song exists, and what came before and after no longer has any meaning. He is playing his part with natural talent; no one can stop him now.

At the tables, many are participating in that collective ceremony, shouting and laughing, and at the final note everyone applauds, clapping for themselves, for the beauty of the voyage, for the privileges of first class, and for that man who no longer seems old, that man whom they could rely on with the same complete devotion that Ivan does. Even the pianist claps and looks at George as if wanting to ask him to continue.

Now I know the heavy atmosphere accompanying this voyage can be broken, and time can roll toward another crossing, one Ivan did not want to make, because this time the son has followed the father.

At that moment his destiny no longer appears as fixed as it

seemed at the departure; in fact, his life can refashion itself according to a new scheme along the same lines as the past, and his sickness can be defeated like Germany in the war: by delivering himself into George's strong hands, into his bright eyes, his still-alert mind. It is not only a song that has conquered Ivan. Perhaps, for the last time, it is his father's energy and will that lead him to relaunch a challenge to the world, as has not happened in some time.

The ballroom is decorated with paper festoons hung on the walls; the lamps on the tables are covered with light, colorful material in shades of blue, red, and yellow. The tablecloths are gold-colored and even the tableware is splendid.

It is the end of the year 1947. Trunks are opened to bring out the most elegant dresses, carefully chosen before the departure; the men are wearing tuxedos.

As usual I have been given a table at the edge of the room: A person alone does not merit special attention. No one, in fact, seems to notice my presence; but this solitude does not make me anxious, as often happens to me in similar situations. Just the opposite. I feel a sense of freedom.

The van Stratens' table is far from mine, near the center of the room. Henriette seems to be hiding inside a bright jersey dress with many pleats that leaves only her arms uncovered. The two men, on the other hand, are wearing their tuxedos with the ease of familiarity, as if the stiff collars, the black ribbons, the cummerbunds holding up their trousers are part of their everyday dress.

The hall is filling, and waiters are running between tables with trays held high, almost over their heads, offering canapés, or immersing bottles of champagne in ice buckets.

At the table next to me sit a small, fat American man and his wife, a Nordic type, taller than her husband, with a pale face and thin hair. The woman has little to say and her husband often turns in my direction, seeking the intimacy brought on by conversation. I avoid meeting his gaze, but I already know he will find a way to trap me in a discussion before the evening is over.

The waiters have begun to serve the antipasti when I notice

some sort of disturbance at the back of the room, as if a current of air has suddenly made the diners seated in that area turn their heads. Then a young woman with long black hair and dark eyes enters the large room. She walks up the aisle between the diners and pauses when she comes to my father's table.

Ivan rises and makes a slight bow, and the woman smiles at him. I cannot manage to look away from this scene, which surprises me, convincing me there are things aboard that ship that concern me and yet escape me, as if the picture is more clearly seen from the outside than in. And in the midst of this surprise the American inserts himself.

"A beautiful woman," he says to me. "A princess, really. Noble blood from some desert."

Now I turn to him with a certain interest.

"Her name is Agamellah," he adds, with the air of one who knows much more than he is willing to say.

The woman sits at a table a short distance from the van Stratens, and continues to lean in Ivan's direction, smiling as she listens to what he has to say to her. George looks at his son as if feeling a kind of pride, as if seeing his son act according to his own preferred rules. Ivan is on the ship with them, and for a moment it seems his backward behavior over the years might be curable.

It is as if Ivan is singing a song, one he thinks his father has requested, a song about the sea voyage and about freedom, about beautiful women who will soon be forgotten, about wives left at home, about life as it should be lived.

Agamellah. The name seems Arabic to me, but she is dressed Western-fashion, wearing a black, low-necked dress, narrow at the waist, with a large ribbon on her breast and a flared skirt that barely covers her calves. Her shoes are also black, laced at the ankles.

The dinner proceeds with the slowness of all year-end dinners. Bottles are emptied, voices grow louder, and the American invites me to sit at his table. His wife has the quavering stiffness of one who mixes wine, sleepiness, and tranquilizers.

On the stage at one end of the ballroom the master of ceremonies, between show numbers prepared for the occasion, yells out the stock phrases of New Year's Eve until his shouts become a loud collective countdown. It is finally midnight. Bottles of champagne are opened, kisses and hugs exchanged. The American offers me one of his cigars, perhaps hoping to seal our friendship in this way. I refuse it, but with thanks.

The music has taken over. A space cleared in front of the stage is immediately invaded by dancing couples. I watch my father dance with the finesse his small body allows him, a grace far removed from my meager dancing ability. There is the circling of Agamellah's skirt, and Ivan's arm around her waist, his thick, wavy hair barely streaked with gray, the string of pearls around the woman's neck. And from the table George watches and laughs.

It is the beginning of 1948. I do not recognize my father in that man dancing in the center of the ballroom, so sure and elegant. I do not recognize myself inside the glasses of spumante I have drunk. I would like to know what this intimacy with the princess means, what conclusion I should draw about their romantic skirmish.

"Do you know where this Agamellah comes from?" I ask my table companion.

The American answers with a laugh, my head collapses on the table. The couple dancing near me disappears into the darkness of night and my drunkenness.

Sitting at a small table I watch my father a short distance away, a cigarette in hand that is consumed more by time than by his smoking it. I recognize the way he crosses his legs: After passing one leg over the other, he does not let the top foot hang freely, but anchors it to the calf of the other leg, as women usually do.

For years I felt annoyed by this gesture, by what seemed clumsy to me; today I watch it knowing that I, too, without realizing it, have begun to cross my legs in the same manner.

I wonder if I could go over and talk to him about it, but he never looks my way, just keeps looking out the window, as if the leaden color of the sky is of vague interest to him. There is a deep sadness in the bar right now, as if Ivan is using this temporary separation from family members to bare the state of his soul, the slow growth of a realization, now that it is the fourth of January and New York draws closer.

But perhaps it just seems this way. It could even be the lack of distraction, the absence of anyone near the counter, the fact that my presence is transparent and no one can recognize me; all this makes my father a man alone and therefore susceptible to his thoughts. It would take no more than a noise, even a slight one, an object falling, the tinkling of a glass, to shake him.

Besides, just a short while ago he was laughing at Agamellah, who was trying to escape his pleas for a photograph, but in the end smiled at the lens in her narrow-waisted, apricot-colored suit.

Now Ivan is looking at the display of bottles behind the bar. He turns his back to me, and I notice his tight-fitting jacket, perhaps a little too finely tailored. As elegant and well cut as it is, it makes him even more vulnerable in my eyes.

"Pardon me," I say, perhaps in a voice too low.

He ignores my words, gets up, and leaves the room.

I overheard a conversation between Ivan and his father. They were lying on the deck chairs in the covered passageway, wrapped in blankets, trying to fend off the cold, which was only slightly mitigated by a pallid, distant sun.

From his vest pocket George took a round, decorated gold watch — Benjamin's watch. He toyed with it with his fingers, opening and closing the lids, as if asking himself if he should keep it or give it to his son. He did not look at him, but continued to stare at the sea beyond the ship's railing.

"Is Lorenza doing well?" he asked him.

"Very well," Ivan replied. "She is really a beautiful baby. You would be proud of her."

George closed the watch with a snap and put it back in his pocket.

"You are the last one to bear the van Straten name, and all you've been able to produce are three females," he finally said.

"What's the difference?"

George remained silent.

—〇〉

Even the ship has its song, a kind of hymn, which the pianist plays several times each evening until all the passengers have learned the words.

The liner is nearing the coast, on this January 10, 1948, and the hymn has been repeated for the last time; the voyage has ended. Ivan stands next to the piano and joins the choir, almost whispering. After the chords die away, the pianist turns to him and asks why he hasn't sung like the others.

"I can't," my father says. "You should hear my sister. She has an extraordinary voice, she could charm anyone with a song. But music is a family talent that skipped me. Some pieces move me, but for most I might as well be deaf."

The pianist nods because he does not know what is happening to Nelly. I am the only one on the ship who could explain what he is really saying, but I haven't the power to do it.

Agamellah is far off, shut up in some first-class cabin, now more distant than if she had remained on the other side of the ocean. Henriette must have already packed their clothes and other things in the trunk and suitcases and is waiting until it is time to disembark. Perhaps George continues to read a book, sitting in the comfortable chair in the cabin, ignoring the passing of time. Ivan lights a cigarette and I think we would both prefer that this journey be just beginning again.

Now I can reveal what I intend to do: stop my father before he goes down to shore, save him from the slow disintegration awaiting him beyond the port of New York; maybe change his destiny.

So I am waiting for him at the top of the ramp, at the exit on the upper bridge. I have decided to stop him, to keep him from descending, because I know what is waiting for him and I want to prevent, or at least slow down, the moment when the news will reach him.

I try to pick the faces of my grandparents and father out in the crowd. I see Ivan first, moving along with his gangling walk. He is younger than I, but his dark suit and his neck hunched into his shoulders age him.

Now that the suspension of the crossing, the truce granted by the sea voyage, has ended, it is no longer possible to forget why they came.

I shift to occupy just enough space to block him in his descent, but not by too much, otherwise I risk attracting the attention of the seaman who is checking the passengers as they leave the ship. I wonder once again if in this kink in time, in this chronological interval that has been granted me, I can talk to my father.

This question distracts me for a moment, and a moment is enough to catch me off guard. My father has suddenly lengthened his stride: a light brush of his shoulder against mine and he has already gone by. Then he stops, turns, but he does not look toward me. He is waiting to help Henriette down the ramp to the wharf. I look at him without finding the strength to move, to stop him. When his mother arrives he takes her arm gently, trying to protect her from the crowd as though she were fragile and apt to break.

I stand still, unable to effect what I thought I had carefully prepared. I watch them among the passengers until their heads blend with the others and I can no longer distinguish them. They leave in the crush of people in the port of New York, at the beginning of January 1948, and I am no longer there, my place and time there have ended.

Thus I have lost my father, for the second time. I find myself once again with my unasked questions, with the same powerlessness I will feel many years later, or some years ago, looking at his body in the emergency room, with the same feeling of inadequacy.

Then everything vanishes. The ship is empty.

I begin my long return home.

When my grandfather George, my grandmother Henriette, my father Ivan arrived in New York on January 10, 1948, on board the *Saturnia*, Nelly had been dead for a day. My father came just in time to have the cosmetics removed that had been put on her face. As if death could be beautified.

Something broke in my father forever. I cannot say that his life was finished, but from then on he moved to repeated rhythms, constructing the habits of a normal existence, without deviations and breaks. Ivan moved with his family to Florence, where he opened an office of the company, even though the sea was far away and business was scarce. And he never moved from Florence. Yet in some way that life of his had come up against a wall of grief that he could not surmount, and he carried on only out of intrinsic strength, out of the inertia that every life contains, that pushes it onward, one day after the next, but without will or objective.

Florence 1999

All the Stories I Have Told

I AM ALL THE stories I have told: not the sum of every destiny, the necessary result, or the finish line. I am only their frail son, the light breeze at the end of a storm, so feeble the weight of these stories threatens to crush me to the ground, an abnormal force of gravity. But I am willing to risk being broken, in order to carry them on my back, to be their voice; in fact, I am obliged to do it now because I wrote of them.

I am the stories I have told, the slow journey of a name. Men and women I have not known. I am something of their faces or their hands. Small gestures, thoughts. Survival in the furrows of time.

Each of them has come inside me and threatens to stay there, as if telling a story were not a liberation, but a pact signed with each one whose story I told.

Now I know I must not forget, I must keep my name a living memory.

I have recited my genealogy as if it were the prayer of a nonbeliever, as if it were a commitment. I have cheated and lied, but I have stayed to the finish.

I represent, in the sixth generation of van Stratens, one of those who preserves the name chosen almost two centuries ago by Hartog Alexander at Rotterdam; it is fitting that I have narrated its history.

To conclude the genealogy: I was born July 6, 1955, and it was then, as I have already said, that I was given Benjamin's watch. It, too, is a pledge for the name I bear. But perhaps I was born too late for my grandfather George to attribute special significance to my birth; he died on October 5 of the same year. My grandmother Henriette, on September 21, 1956.

On December 10, 1988, around nine in the morning, a sister of mine telephoned to say our father had suffered a heart attack and had been taken by ambulance to the hospital.

I went to the hospital emergency room and found him lying on a stretcher, already dead. I realized how much I would miss him, and thought perhaps I had never truly known him.

This book began to take shape in my mind at that moment.

I once read that in Madagascar families disinter their dead every five years. They take them out of the ground, turn them around, almost as if to change the landscape before their eyes, and afterward they rebury them and have a celebration.

I, too, have disinterred my dead, many of whom are buried I know not where. I have counted them, but the more I counted the greater the number grew. I had to stop at some point. The limits can't be seen, but they can be outlined in the mind, and if we don't delineate them, the world will slip out of our hands.

That is why here, at this precise point, I have drawn a line that I will not cross.

ACKNOWLEDGMENTS

I am indebted to many people who have in some way helped me write this novel. Certainly, first of all, I must thank those who are in the book and were willing to share their memories; I must absolve them of any responsibility for what they say or do in these pages, for often their actions are of my own creation. But they do exist, and here are their names: Franca, Iolanda, Mordechai (Maurits), Paul, and Saul.

To Maarten van Aalteren I owe the translations from the Dutch. Thanks go to Maurizio Bossi and Laura Desideri of the Gabinetto Vieusseux in Florence for maps, tourist guidebooks, and travel books, to Eugenio Costa for information about the *Saturnia*, to Leandro Giribaldi for the information and images of *The Passion of Joan of Arc*, to Linda Giuva of the Archivio Centrale dello Stato for a file about my father, to Elisabeth Salina for information about the history of the Société Générale de Surveillance.

Roberta Back Sole and Peter Berman are relatives who do not appear in the book, but who have given me photographs and facts.

From Luciano Berio I have stolen the idea of applying a system of restoration to a creative act: In his case it is *Rendering*, a composition inspired by some sketches by Schubert for a symphony that was never realized.

Thijs Berman has written an extraordinary book about George Fles after finding the dossier in Georgia about the man who was his grandmother's brother: Without Thijs my novel would have been the poorer.

Finally, I thank all those who read the typescript in its various stages, giving me precious advice, and in particular Enzo who encouraged me to write it, and Giovanni who was the first to read it in its entirety. I am grateful for their many suggestions and most of all for their friendship.